The Boy Chums
Crusing in Florida Waters

Also from Westphalia Press
westphaliapress.org

The Boy Chums Crusing in Florida Waters

or
The Perils and Dangers of the Fishing Fleet

by Wilmer M. Ely

with a new introduction by Robert Rich Jr.

WESTPHALIA PRESS
An imprint of Policy Studies Organization

The Boy Chums Cruising Florida Waters
All Rights Reserved © 2013 by Policy Studies Organization

Westphalia Press
An imprint of Policy Studies Organization
1527 New Hampshire Ave., NW
Washington, D.C. 20036
dgutierrezs@ipsonet.org

ISBN-13: 978-1-941472-94-1
ISBN-10: 194147294X

Cover design by Taillefer Long at Illuminated Stories:
www.illuminatedstories.com

Updated material and comments on this edition
can be found at the Westphalia Press website:
www.westphaliapress.org

Introduction
Confronting the Rum Runners

Wilmer M. Ely introduced a whole generation of American youth to boating adventures. This is perhaps his best book. The fact is that when you get out in a boat, life changes. A reviewer of one of my own books about fishing wrote, "As Charles Fox once said, 'angling is the way to round out a happy life' I think reading *The Fishing Club* is another good way for anyone to enjoy life!" He could have added that books about life on the water have been a source of pleasure to folks for many years.

The young heroes have their boat stolen from them in an earlier novel, and without any money they sign on with a commercial fisherman to pursue catch along the coast of Florida. Not everyone they meet is a sportsman, to put it mildly, and they confront rum runners. The criminals are out to sabotage the Chums but the boys acquire staunch allies in honest fisherman who help them beat back the crooks. The stolen schooner, which is smuggling in the Cuba trade, is won back.

I haven't encountered smugglers but thanks to getting out on the water I have met plenty of characters Another book of mine, *Fish Fights*, was reviewed as "fast, insightful sketches of guides and companions, a wonderful selection of slightly askew personalities that reflect the diversity and twists, the

E

surprises and flavor that flows from the open and closed waters of and around the Everglades. I wished I could have been with them, swapping tales, peeling sunburned skin (me, not them) doling out dreams and plotting how to outsmart those cunning denizens of the not-so-deep." In this story one does encounter the romance and surprise of Florida fishing that fascinated Ely many years ago.

Robert Rich Jr.

The Boy Chums
Cruising in Florida Waters

OR

The Perils and Dangers of the Fishing Fleet

By WILMER M. ELY

Author of

"The Boy Chums on Indian River," "The Boy Chums in
The Forest," "The Boy Chums' Perilous Cruise,"
"The Boy Chums on Haunted Island," "The
Boy Chums in the Gulf of Mexico,"

A. L. BURT COMPANY
NEW YORK

At sight of the hole and freshly upturned earth, Hunter
grew livid with rage.   Page 140.

The Boy Chums Cruising in Florida Waters.

THE BOY CHUMS
CRUISING IN FLORIDA WATERS.

CHAPTER I.

OLD FRIENDS.

" Is this Mr. Daniels? "

The busy man at the paper-littered desk swung around in his chair and treated the speaker and his three companions to a brief but keen appraising glance. Swift as it was, he noted that the questioner was a sturdy, well-built lad with a frank open face deeply tanned by wind and sun. His companions consisted of another boy about the same age but of slighter build, an elderly, stout, heavily-whiskered man with the unmistakable stamp of the sailor in his bearing, and a little negro lad with a grinning, good-humored face. All three bore an appearance of health and cleanliness and their clothes, though old and worn, were neatly patched and as spotless as soap and water could make them.

"Daniels is my name," he replied, briskly, "what can I do for you?"

"We want a chance to fish for you, sir."

"Have you had any experience?"

"My companions have never fished any but I put in a couple of seasons at it. We all know how to handle boats and none of us are afraid of work," declared the spokesman of the little party, eagerly.

"I seldom engage green men," said Mr. Daniels, "but I will talk with you a little further, later," he added, hastily, as he saw the look of disappointment on the four faces. "I am a pretty busy man now. I have got to get some letters off on the morning train. Look around and amuse yourselves for half an hour and I will then be at liberty."

The four strangers needed no second bidding. Even as they had been waiting, they had cast interested glances through the open office door at the busy scene in the immense building adjoining. Now, as Mr. Daniels turned back to his desk, they stepped out into the great barn-like room and gazed around with eager curiosity. Everywhere was bustle and hustle. At the far end of the building, a dozen wagons were unloading their burdens in great glistening heaps upon the clean water-deluged floor, fish, fish, thousands upon thousands of them. In one corner rose a great mound of trout, a simmering mass of white, bronze, and rainbow spots, close to these lay a heap of Spanish mackerel, beautiful in their rich coloring of silver and gold; just beyond the mackerel rose a greenish-blue pile of hundreds of blue fish and close beside these lay a snow-like mountain of ocean mullet, while further on, was heaped up, a miscellaneous collection of finny creatures, sea bass, gorgeous in their rich golden bronze, quaint bird-like sea robins, lacey-winged flying fish, repulsive looking flounders, and a hundred and one humble little dwellers of the sea that had fallen victims to the all-embracing nets. Down the length of the room, groups of men were working frantically to lessen the rapidly growing mounds of fish. It almost seemed a combat between the stream of loaded wagons and the busy workers. One group labored furiously at the heaps, shoveling the fish into big, swinging, scoop-like scales. As soon as the scales showed two hundred pounds, they were swung forward to another group and their contents dumped on the floor. This group, with skillful, flying hands, packed the fish in layers into empty barrels. For every layer of fish, a hurrying line of men dumped in a huge shovelful of chopped ice. As soon as it was filled, the barrel was taken in charge by other waiting hands. The head nailed in, it was rolled out on a platform at the far end where a car lay waiting on a side track to hurry it away to the fish-hungry folks of the northern cities.

The little negro lad gazed at the busy scene with distended eyes.

"Massa Chas, Massa Chas," he exclaimed, at last, "dar ain't no use ob you white chillens trying to catch no fish."

"Why, Chris?" questioned the larger lad.

"'Cause dey's done cotched dem all. Dar can't be many left, Massa Chas."

"Nonsense, Chris, there's as good fish in the sea as ever came out of it."

"Maybe so," said the little negro, doubtfully, "but I reckon dar ain't so many ob dem."

"You can not prove there isn't," laughed Charley.

"May be not," said the little negro, with dignity, "but you-alls had ought to take a cullard gentleman's word widout any proof."

"So I will, Chris," agreed the white lad, with a twinkle in his eye, "but there is Mr. Daniels beckoning to us. Let's see what he has to say."

"Take a chair and I will talk with you, now," said Mr. Daniels as they re-entered the office. "Now, first, I would like to know what has given you and your friends this fishing idea. Fishermen are a pretty rough class as a rule and you all seem fitted for a better class of work. Tell me something about yourselves, please."

"There isn't much to tell, sir," said the boy spokesman, modestly. "We four have been comrades for several years and we hate to separate now. We were sponge fishing out of Tarpon Springs but we lost our schooner through trouble with our crew. We saved only the clothes on our backs. We have to get something to do right off. Fishing seems to be the only thing in this part of the state that we would be able to work at and keep together. We heard of you, sir, in Tarpon Springs. We arrived here at Clearwater this morning. In fact, we came here direct from the station."

There was a curious gleam in Mr. Daniels' eye as he listened to this terse, business-like explanation. "What kind of work have you done besides sponging?" he questioned.

"We have been kind of Jack-Of-All-Trades," smiled the lad. "We have raised truck on the East Coast, fished for pearls in the West Indies, hunted plume birds in the Everglades, and gathered wreckage on the Atlantic beaches."

"Your names?" demanded Mr. Daniels, eagerly.

"My name is Charley West, sir. This is my chum, Walter Hazard; this gentleman is our good friend, Captain Westfield, and this," indicating the little negro with a smiling nod, "is Mr. Christopher Columbus."

"I suspected it," exclaimed Mr. Daniels. "You are the boy chums whose adventures have been told in several books. I have a boy at home who has them all. He has made me read them over to him 'til I know them by heart."

Charley blushed, much embarrassed. "I am afraid the writer has made too much of our little adventures," he said, modestly. "We had no idea he was an author when he got us talking about our trips or we would not have talked so freely."

"Well, he speaks well of the boy-chums," smiled Mr. Daniels, "and I am going to take his recommendation. As I have already said, I do not often engage green men but I am going to give you four a chance. But before you decide to go into it, I want you to understand that this fishing business is no picnic."

"We do not expect it to be any picnic," replied Charley, quietly.

"In the first place, it is dangerous," Mr. Daniels continued. "Besides the risk from storms and accidents, there are dangers from fish and sea reptiles. Then, too, there are often troubles with other fishermen. As a class, fishermen are rough and lawless. In my position, with hundreds of men working for me, it would ruin my business to take sides with any one man or set of men in my employ. They must settle their quarrels among themselves. As the old saying goes, 'Every tub must stand on its own bottom.'"

"We will be careful and keep out of trouble," Walter assured him.

" One can not always avoid it," Mr. Daniels replied. " In addition to the drawbacks I have mentioned, fishing is extremely hard, trying, nasty work, although I will say that it seems a wonderfully healthy occupation. Fishermen are seldom sick."

" Does it pay? " Captain Westfield inquired.

" That depends largely upon the fisherman. Of course, there is an element of luck in fishing. Experience counts for something, too, but in the main, as in everything else, it is the amount of work that decides success or failure. Some of my men make as high as two hundred dollars a week, others hardly make a living."

Charley glanced inquiringly at his comrades who answered with nods.

" We will try it, if you please," he said, quietly.

" All right," replied Mr. Daniels, briskly. " You shall have just the same outfit I furnish the rest of my men. Four nets,—that is, one for each of you,—three skiffs, and a motor boat. I furnish the motor boat and the skiffs free, but you are expected to keep them up in good shape and to buy your own gasoline and oils. As for the nets, I sell them to you at cost, I take out one-third of your fish until they are paid for."

" That seems a very liberal arrangement," Charley observed.

" I have to do it in order to get enough fish to

keep my customers supplied. Now, as to shelter, you will have to have a place to stay. Out on the long wharf that runs out into the bay, you will find a number of little houses which belong to me. You can use any one of them that is not already occupied."

"You are very kind," said Charley.

"Not at all. Now, one thing more. Are you supplied with money?"

"We saved nothing from our schooner but the clothes we had on," Charley admitted.

"Then I will tell Mr. Bacon, the store-keeper, to let you have what groceries and clothing you need until you get to earning. Oh! by the way, I forgot to ask you if you can run a motor boat?"

"We have never run one, but we could soon learn."

"Well, I'll send a man down with your nets this afternoon and have him show you the boats that you will use and also give you a lesson in running the engine. You'll soon catch on to it—it's simple. And now," he concluded, "that, I believe, finishes our business arrangements and now I have a favor to ask of you."

"After your kindness, we would do anything in our power," Charley promised, gratefully but rashly.

"Good! I want all four of you to come up to dinner with me. That boy of mine would give me fits if I let the Boy Chums get away from me without him meeting them."

Our little party of chums were too modest to relish the idea of a dinner under such conditions; but, after Mr. Daniels' kindness to them, they could not do other than accept the proffered invitation much as they would have liked to refuse.

CHAPTER II.

GETTING SETTLED.

THE dinner proved less embarrassing than the little band of adventurers had feared. To be sure Mr. Daniels' son, a sturdy little lad of eight, stared at them constantly with wide-eyed hero worship and plied them with an army of questions about their adventures; but the boys, who detested talking of their exploits, skillfully directed his questions to Chris and the vain little darkey, glad of the chance to brag, entertained the little lad with wonderful yarns of their adventures, in all of which he made himself out the hero. Mrs. Daniels proved to be a nice, motherly, little lady who quickly made them all feel at their ease, while Mr. Daniels exerted himself to make the meal pleasant for them. As soon as they decently could, however, the four took their departure, for they were anxious to see something of the little town and to get settled in their new home.

"Let's go down to the wharf first of all," Walter proposed as soon as they were out on the street. "We want to pick out our house the first thing we do."

There was but one main street to the little town and a question put to a passer-by got the information that it led down to the wharf.

A few minutes' walk brought them past the straggling row of stores that comprised the town's business center.   Just beyond these the four stopped to gaze around in admiration and delight.

" My! It's beautiful! " Charley exclaimed.

" A regular Paradise," Walter agreed.

Before them stretched a wide street of snow white lime rock, overhung by gigantic live oak and magnolia trees.   Back a little ways from the street nestled houses almost lost 'mid trees and flowers. Between them and the sidewalks were gardens blazing with a mad riot of color.   The rich yellow of alamandas mingled , with the deep purple of Chinese paper flowers and the warm blue of Lady Alices.   Here and there stood Royal Poinciana trees and a vivid blaze of scarlet.   Great flowered cacti reared their thorny forms high in the air and delicate lace-like ferns grew all around.   In and out amongst the blaze of color flitted gorgeous-hued tropical birds twittering to each other, while here and there frisked little gray squirrels chattering excitedly over the fallen acorns.

Captain Westfield drew in a long breath of the sweet flower-scented air.   " I am going to like Clearwater," he declared.

" Well, we are going to have lots of time to get

acquainted with it," observed Charley, practically.
" We had better be moving on now, it is going to
be a busy afternoon for us."

But at the end of the gently sloping street they
paused again with murmurs of admiration. Before them a long wharf ran out into a great bay,
its waters blue as indigo save where flecked by
foaming white caps. Across on the other side of
the bay, and about two miles distant, stretched a
chain of white-beached islands between which the
foamy churning breakers showed where the waters
of the bay connected with the Gulf of Mexico. But
our little party spent only a moment admiring the
beautiful scene, they would have long weeks to ad-
mire its loveliness. Just now they were more interested in the wide snowy beach on either side
of the wharf. Here was a living picture of part,
at least, of their new occupation. The shore was
dotted with groups of fishermen engaged in tasks
pertaining to their calling. Some were busy mend-
ing long nets stretched out on racks of poles.
Some were pulling nets into their boats preparatory
to a start for the fishing grounds. Others, just in
from a trip, were pulling their wet nets out to dry.
Still others were busy calking, painting and repair-
ing their skiffs upturned on the beach, while here
and there little groups were engaged over camp-
fires from which rose appetizing odors of frying
fish and steaming coffee. Close in to the beach the

fishing fleet lay bobbing at anchor, a hundred skiffs and at least half as many motor boats.

As our little party stood watching the busy scene, a motor boat with three skiffs in tow came chugging in for the beach. When within a stone's throw of the shore it rounded up and anchored. Almost before the anchor had touched bottom a man had jumped into each skiff, cast it lose from the launch, and was sculling in for the beach. Our little party joined the group that gathered at the water's edge to meet the newcomers. The skiffs lay deep in the water and the reason was apparent when they grounded on the sands. Each was heaped from thwart to thwart with flat silver colored fish.

" Pompano! " exclaimed Charley.

" Pompano," snarled a sallow-faced, tough-looking fisherman near him. " That's just the luck of that Roberts gang. Tarnation stuck up guys. Won't have nothing to do with us fishermen. Think themselves too good. They are greenhorns too. Only started fishing this season. They have regular fools' luck though. Just like their luck to hit a nice bunch like that when better fishermen are coming in without a fish. They had ought to be run out of Clearwater."

The man in the nearest skiff heard the sneer and his good-humored face took on a look of scorn. He surveyed the speaker from head to foot as though he was examining some strange kind of

animal. Then he spoke slowly and delib-
erately.

"Run us out of town, you cowardly cur?"
"Why, there isn't enough of your kind in the state
of Florida to run one Roberts. If you ever ran
anything in your life it was a rabbit. I've heard
enough of your sneers and I give you notice right
now to quit. Yes, the Roberts boys do consider
themselves too good to associate with you and your
kind. Not because you are fishermen but because
you are lazy, lying, thieving, rum-drinking bums.
It's time some one told you the truth about yourself. You and your gang seem to have the rest of
the fishermen bluffed so they will stand for your
sneers. You talk about luck. Well, maybe it is
luck, but let me tell you there's mighty hard work
to back it up. We have hunted over fifty miles of
water, been without sleep for thirty-six hours, and
worked 'til we can hardly stand, for these fish.
Luck! You make me sick! If you worked one
night a week like we work right along your poor
little wife would not have to work her fingers to
the bone over the wash-tub to support you. Hunter,
you are a disgrace to mankind."

The sallow fisherman's face went livid and he
gasped and spluttered with rage. His hands clenched
and he made a movement towards the man in the
skiff but evidently prudence got the better of his
rage.

"I'll pay you for this, Bill Roberts. I'll pay you out. You see if I don't," he cried.

"I know what you are thinking about," returned Roberts in level tones. "I know of the tricks you have played on other men that have crossed you. I know what happened to them, but don't you think for a moment that I'll make the mistake they made in going to law about it when they couldn't prove anything. If any such accidents happen to us, I'll not go to law about it. I'll beat the miserable little soul out of your body. Get away from here or I may do it now."

Hunter slunked away muttering curses and the other fishermen strolled off behind him.

Bill Roberts looked after them with a grin. "That fellow gets my goat," he chuckled. "I'm sorry I lost my temper but I'm about worn out from work and loss of sleep and my nerves are on wire edge. I've no use for that fellow anyway, and I guess I would have told him my opinion of him, sooner or later."

"You seem to have been fairly well paid for your hard work," observed Captain Westfield. "You've got twenty or thirty dollars' worth there, haven't you?"

Charley chuckled and Bill Roberts grinned.

"I see you don't savey pompano," he said. "They are a scarce fish. I reckon we've got one thousand pounds of them and they are worth forty cents a pound. Figger that out, Mister."

"Four hundred dollars," gasped Walter. "Whew! I hope we strike a few bunches like that, Charley."

"You folks going to fish, eh?" enquired Roberts. "Well, it's a good healthy business and it pays well for hard work. We don't often strike a bunch like this, but by keeping steady at it, we always make pretty good money. The worst drawback about fishing is the men in it. Take my advice and avoid them all you can. Don't get mixed up with that Hunter gang anyway if you can help it. Drop into our camp,—it's right over there on Tates Island,—whenever you feel like it, and we will give you all the pointers we can."

Charley thanked the friendly fisherman. "We will be over there soon," he promised. "We are new to the place and we would like to get some pointers right off but we are just getting settled and must hurry off now."

"I like that gang," he said to his companions as they hurried out on the long dock. "They seem of a better class than those other fishermen."

"They would not have to be very good to be that," observed Captain Westfield, gravely. "Those fishermen are a tough looking lot. I hope we will not have any trouble with them."

"We will not have any," said Walter, cheerfully. "If we just tend to our own business I guess they will tend to theirs. Well, I guess these are the houses Mr. Daniels spoke about."

They had reached the end of the long dock. On one side of it stood a row of small shacks. Most of them were occupied but at last they came upon a large one that stood empty.

"Golly," exclaimed Chris, as he peeped inside, "dar poor white trash dat lived in dis was sho' dirty."

The floor was thickly covered with filth and rubbish, the walls were tobacco stained, and the windows were broken and covered with grime.

"We'll soon make it look different," said Captain Westfield, cheerfully. "Let's go to work with some system and we'll soon be comfortably settled. Walter, you make out a list of what we need and go up to the store. Charley, see what you can do with those windows. Chris and I will clean out. Bring a broom, Walt."

When Walter got back with his arms full of bundles he found the shack wet inside but clean, the windows shining brightly, and his comrades nowhere in sight.

CHAPTER III.

THE FIRST ALARM.

THE shack contained a rough board cupboard in one corner and a few shelves along one side and upon these Walter arranged his purchases which made quite an imposing array. He had bought carefully but there had been many things that the four of them absolutely had to have. There was a change of rough, cheap clothing for each, four blankets, the same of oilskins, four lanterns, a belt and sheath-knife apiece, and a stock of groceries; this was small, containing only such staples as rice, coffee, sugar, salt, beans, bacon, and flour, for he figured that they would get most of their living from the sea.

His packages arranged to his satisfaction, Walter sat down to await the appearance of his chums.

Charley was the first to arrive. He came out from the shore, staggering under a great load of clean, silver Spanish moss.

"For our beds," he explained, as he spread the soft hair-like stuff on the floor in one corner. "It will take a little of the hardness off the boards."

Captain Westfield soon appeared bearing a large box partly filled with sand.

"What is that for?" Walter inquired.

"That's our stove," the old sailor explained. "It will have to do us until we are able to buy one. Chris is coming with some wood."

The little darkey soon appeared, bearing a load of driftwood that he had picked up on the beach.

"I reckon you-alls can fix up things widout me," he observed as he deposited his burden just outside the door and produced a bit of string and a fish hook from his pocket. "Dar jis' naturally oughter be lots ob fish around dese old dock posts. A mess of dem, fried nice an' brown, would sho' go powerful good for supper."

Charley grinned, for Chris loved to fish with all the ardor of his race. "Go ahead," he said, "we will get along without you."

The little negro needed no second permission, and baiting his hook with a piece of bacon, and getting astride of a post, he began to fish earnestly.

The others occupied themselves in trying to make their new home as comfortable as they could with the little they had to do with. They spread their four blankets on the pile of moss, filled and trimmed their lanterns, made a rough table and some benches out of a few boards they found on the dock, and covered the broken panes in the windows with some sand-fly netting Walter had bought at the store. When all this was done and their new garments hung up on nails, the rude shack took on quite a comfortable, home-like appearance.

"It's not so bad," Charley observed. "It will do us very well until we can get better quarters."

"We have cause to be thankful," Walter agreed. "Only a few hours ago we had nothing in the world, now, we have got a dry place to stay, clothes, a supply of food, and a prospect of soon making money."

The chums' further conversation was interrupted by a rumble of a wagon and a hail from the dock. It was the man with their nets.

"Better put them inside your house until you are ready to use them," he advised. "The nets all look alike and some one might steal them from you if you left them outside. I'll be out again in about half an hour with your boats, they are anchored up the beach a way."

The boys awaited his return with eagerness for they were anxious to view their new crafts. Soon they heard the quick snapping of an engine and a large launch swung out from the beach with a string of skiffs in tow.

"My, she can move some," Charley cried as she swept towards them with a froth of foam at her bow.

"She's got good lines," announced Captain Westfield, with the certainty born of his sailor life, "she is bound to be a good sea boat with that shape."

When within a hundred feet of where the boys stood on the dock, the man threw off the switch and the graceful craft glided up alongside. Charley caught the line the man threw, took a couple of half hitches around a post, and the three clambered aboard.

"By gum, she's a beauty," exclaimed Captain Westfield with delight as he finished his inspection.

"You're right," agreed the man, pleased with the old sailor's approval, "she's one of the best in the fleet. There's only two or three that can run away from her, and she is a peach in a seaway—just like a duck. She is thirty feet over all and sound as a dollar. You will find that cozy little cabin will come in pretty nice in bad weather. Few fish boats have one. Which one of you is going to run her?"

"Not me," said Captain Westfield, decidedly. "I've dealt with sailing crafts all my life and I'm not hankering to start monkeying with engines at my age."

"Both my chum and I would like to learn how to run the engine," Charley said, "so if anything should happen to one of us the other would know what to do."

"All right," the man agreed. "All I can teach you are the principles, you will have to learn to run it by yourself. A gas engine is a thing you have to learn by experience. No two engines are exactly alike. Each has its own peculiarities which one has to become acquainted with. The principles are quite simple. There are only three elements, oil, gas and the spark. See this little valve here? You turn that and it lets the gasoline into this little tank—called a carburetter. This other little valve lets air into the same tank to mix with the gas. Now your gas is on ready to start. See these wires, they lead from four dry battery cells to the switch and from the switch to this plug in the head of the engine called the spark plug. Shove on your switch,—that's right. Now your gas and spark are ready. To start, now, all you have got to do is to rock this big fly wheel a couple of times then throw it over quickly. To stop, just throw off your switch. As soon as you stop, shut off your gas. Keep that oil cup filled. It lubricates the engine. Be careful with matches and lights when your gas is turned on—you can't be too careful." He clambered up on the dock. "Good-by and good luck to you," he called.

"Hold on," cried Charley, in dismay. "You are not going off and leave us this way, are you?"

"Boss's orders," grinned the man. "I can't be with you always. You have got to learn to run her for yourself sooner or later."

The boys sat down and gazed at each other in

consternation as the man disappeared up the dock, then Charley grinned as the humor of it struck him. "It's up to us," he chuckled, "unless the captain will help us out."

Captain Westfield shook his head, decidedly. "You are the engineers," he said, firmly. "I can't make head or tail of that dinky heap of iron. 'Pears to me though that the man said something about turning one of those things there."

"He did," said Charley, with mild sarcasm. He also mentioned several other things. Well, here goes for a try."

He rolled up his sleeves and started to work. At the end of half an hour, he was still turning the big fly wheel and puffing and perspiring much to the delight of a crowd of fishermen who had quit work for the day and had gathered at the dock's edge offering free comments and suggestions.

"He'll sure wear that fly wheel out," observed one in a perfectly audible voice.

"Put rowlocks in her and get a pair of oars, young fellow," suggested another.

Charley stood the chaffing nobly but at last he was obliged to stop for breath.

"I'm sure I don't know what's the matter with the thing," he declared. "It had ought to go. I've cranked it until I've got blisters on my hands."

"Maybe, if you put on the switch it will go," Walter observed.

Charley glared at him. "And you have been sitting there laughing in your sleeves while I've been working myself to death," he spluttered.

"Mr. Daniels wants us to find out such little things for ourselves," observed Walter, grinning.

Charley forced a smile. "Well, I'll let you find out a few things, yourself, while I rest."

"Is the entertainment over for the day?" queried one of the fishermen.

"No, it's just going to begin," Charley prophesied with a grin.

"Oh, I can start it all right," Walter declared, confidently. "Just watch me and I'll show you how."

He turned on the switch, rocked the fly wheel a couple of times, then threw it over with a quick jerk. The engine started with a sharp snapping like a quick fire gun.

"There, I've started her," he yelled, proudly, above the din.

"That is not the way she was built to run," shouted Charley, while a roar of laughter went up from the assembled fishermen, for, instead of going ahead, the "Dixie" had started astern full speed. Charley who was standing ready to cast off took a quick turn of the line around a cleat and stopped her in her backward career. "Stop!" he cried, "or she'll break the line."

But Walter was thoroughly bewildered and stood gazing helplessly at the popping machinery.

"Pour water on it, that's the way to stop it," jeered a fisherman.

"Throw your switch," Charley advised. Walter, recovering his wits, obeyed and the popping instantly ceased.

"Well, I made the engine go, anyway," he replied to Charley's jeers. "I'll get her going all right yet."

Again he threw the fly wheel only to have her rear back on the line.

"Don't tow the dock away," begged a fisherman. "We all live here. We don't want to lose our home."

"Tell you what to do, young fellow," advised another, "just change your rudder and put it on the other end."

Walter, very red in the face, threw off the switch.

"Throw the fly wheel over the other way and she'll go ahead," Charley said.

"Hump!" Walter grunted, as he realized his error, "why didn't you tell me that before?"

"Mr. Daniels wants us to find out such little things for ourselves," observed Charley, sweetly.

Walter laughed. "You're even with me now," he said. "Well, I guess, between us, we can learn to run her, but I guess we had better call it quits for to-day. It's getting late. Let's anchor her out for the night."

Charley agreed and they poled the launch away from the dock and cast the anchor, returning to the wharf in one of the skiffs. It was nearly dark when they entered the shack to find a most disagreeable surprise awaiting them.

CHAPTER IV.

THE WARNING.

CHRIS had started a brisk fire in the box of sand and was preparing to fry a big mess of fish which had fallen victims to his craft.

"Golly!" he exclaimed when the boys offered their assistance, "I doan want none ob you white chillens foolin' around an' spoilin' dese fish. If you-alls wants to help, jes' light up de lanterns an' sot de table."

Charley groped around, found the matches, and struck a light. "Why didn't you get more than one lantern, Walt?" he complained. "We will need four when we get to fishing."

"I bought four. They are hanging right there on the wall," his chum replied.

"There's only one here," Charley announced. "Are you sure you got four?"

"Of course," Walter replied. "Maybe some of us moved them, when we were fixing up the shack."

But a close search of the shack failed to reveal the missing lights.

"They have been stolen," Charley said, quietly. "We had better look and see if anything else has been taken."

But Walter was already looking over his purchases. "Nearly all our groceries are gone," he cried.

The band of chums gazed at each other in dismay.

"It must have been done while we were working with the launch," Charley said. "Chris, did you see any one go into the shack?"

"No, Massa Chas," the little negro confessed. "De fish was jes' naturally biting so fast dat I doan look around much."

"What shall we do about it?" Walter inquired.

"I don't see as we can do anything," said Charley, thoughtfully. "We will just have to grin and bear it and be more careful in the future. Of course, it was one of those fishermen who did it, there was no one else on the dock,—but we have no clue as to which was the guilty one and we can not accuse all of them."

"Wisely said, my lad," approved Captain Westfield, "all we can do is to keep quiet and watch out in the future. We evidently have some tough characters for neighbors. Let's not mourn and get downhearted, that won't bring the things back. Here Chris has got a good supper ready. Let's get at it and be cheerful."

The boys recognizing the wisdom of the old sailor's advice, and hiding their disappointment, they made merry over the crisp, tasty, fried fish, pancakes, and coffee that the little negro had prepared.

As soon as the supper things were cleared away, Captain Westfield produced his old worn, well-loved Bible and read the story of Christ with the discouraged fishermen, after which he prayed earnestly and with simple faith for the Lord's blessing upon them in the new life upon which they were about to enter.

Just as he concluded, there came the sound of shuffling footsteps outside, and a bit of rustling white paper was shoved in under the door of the shack.

Charley picked 'it up and glanced at the ill-written scrawl it contained. With an angry gleam in his eyes, he flung open the door and peeped outside. The retreating footsteps had died away, and he could distinguish nothing in the inky darkness but the glimmering lights in the other shacks.

He closed and fastened the door carefully.

" What was it? " Walter asked, noting the grim, set look on his chum's face.

" Nothing much," Charley replied with a meaning glance. " I'll tell you about it later."

As soon as Chris, who was always early to bed, was snoring peacefully on his blanket, Charley produced the scrap of paper.

"What do you think of that?" he asked, briefly.

Walter and the captain bent their heads over the almost illegible scrawl.

Walter looked up from the paper, his face flushed with anger. "It's an outrage!" he cried. "Why I'd die first."

"Read it to me, Walt," requested the Captain. "I can't make out that writing."

Walter obeyed.

"Strangers,

"We-alls don't allow no niggers around hyar. Get rid of that little nigger you've got with you or it will be worse for him and worse for you.

The White Caps."

The old sailor fairly exploded with wrath as he listened. "By the keel of the Flying Dutchman," he shouted, "that little darkey is better than a ship-load of thieving fishermen. I just wish I had my hands on the fellow that dared write that thing."

"Poor little Chris," Walter exclaimed. "He is as noble a little fellow as ever lived. His skin may be black but he's white, clean white, inside. Think of the times he's risked his life for us and how good, honest and uncomplaining he has always been. Get rid of Chris, never!"

"Of course not," Charley agreed. "The question is what are we going to do. I wouldn't say anything about it while Chris was awake because I knew how terribly bad it would make him feel,— he is a sensitive little fellow, but what are we going to do? The fellow or fellows, who wrote this are liable to do something to him at the first good opportunity they have, especially if he is not warned and on his guard."

" Give up all idea of fishing and leave this place, before we part with Chris," declared Captain Westfield.

" Not much," cried Walter. " Just tell those fishermen, one and all, that Chris stays with us. And if they do him the slightest injury, we will make them suffer for it."

" I don't like either course you propose," observed thoughtful, clear-headed Charley. " As for the Captain's plan, I don't want to leave here. We have a good prospect of making money here if we can stick it out and we are in poor shape to pick up and leave. Besides I don't like the idea of being forced out of a place by any one. I don't think much better of what Walt proposes either. We are no match for a hundred fishermen, and it is foolish to make threats when one can not carry them out. In the second place, if we quarrel with the fishermen over Chris, it will make them more bitter against him and more certain to do him an injury. Lastly, nothing we could do to them for an injury done Chris would help him any after the injury was done. What we need to do is to protect him from any possible harm."

"Well, let's have your plan," Walter said.

"I have none as yet," Charley confessed. "I propose we wait until morning before we decide on any course. Some plan will occur to us, I am sure. There is always a way out of any difficulty if one only thinks hard enough. I am dead tired and I'm going to bed and try to forget about this trouble until morning. I'd advise you two to do the same."

It had been a very full and eventful day and Walter and the Captain were not loath to follow Charley's example. The three crept into their blankets and turned out the lantern; but, tired as they were, they were not to get the sleep they longed for. From the other shacks came the voices of their occupants gradually increasing in number and volume. At first, it seemed as though a kind of celebration was in progress; for the sound of laughter, songs, and dancing filled the air, but gradually, the uproar took on a rougher note. Voices were raised in anger, curses were bandied back and forth, and now and then came the sound of fighting.

"I believe they are all drunk or fast getting drunk," Charley declared.

"Why, I understood Mr. Daniels to say that this

was a dry town and that no liquor was allowed in the place," said his chum.

"Yes, and he also said that there was more liquor drunk here than in any other town in the state," Charley amended. "He says it's a mystery where it comes from. The town authorities it seems, keep a close watch for blind tigers and also keep an eye on the packages that come by freight and express but none of it seems to come in that way."

"Well, it evidently comes in some way," remarked Captain Westfield as a fresh uproar of fighting arose from the dock.

It was useless to try to sleep as long as the din continued, so the three lay talking in low tones.

"Hark!" cried Charley, suddenly. "I wonder what they have done now."

Loud and clear above the din of fighting rang the sharp crack of a pistol. The report was followed by excited shouting and then silence.

"I'll bet one of them has been shot and it has frightened and sobered up the rest," Walter exclaimed. "Let's go out and see."

"No, you don't, lad," Captain Westfield declared, firmly. "You'll stay here if I have to hold you. It's none of our trouble and we don't any of us want to get mixed up in it."

Whatever had happened, it had effectually quieted the wild revelry. Our little party lay for awhile listening but the silence remained unbroken and one by one, they at last dropped off to sleep.

It was perhaps midnight when Walter raised up on his elbow and whispered softly.

" Are you asleep, Charley? "

" As wide awake as I ever was in my life," his chum grunted. " Why, anything the matter with you? "

" Something is stinging me to death," declared Walter, anxiously, " I smart, burn, and itch all over."

" Me too," chimed in the captain's voice. " I've laid quiet here and took it rather than wake you boys up. Jehosaphat, what is it? "

Charley chuckled. " It's nothing dangerous," he explained, " evidently we are entertaining a few thousand of those fishermen's closest friends—bed-bugs. Light up the lantern, Walt, and let's have a look."

An examination by the light showed their faces and bodies covered with red, angry-looking blotches.

" There's no use trying to sleep here," Charley declared. " Let's go out on board the ' Dixie.' It will be pretty close quarters sleeping in her cabin but anything is better than this."

" But our things will be all stolen," Walter objected.

" They will not bother anything to-night for they will think we are inside, and we will be back before they are up in the morning," said his chum.

Chris was awakened and the four crept softly out of the shack closing the door carefully behind them.

To reach their skiff, they had to pass the other shacks. As they came opposite the first one Charley, who was in the lead, stopped short with a muffled cry of horror.

CHAPTER V.

FRIENDLY ADVICE.

THE moon had arisen while they slept and now shining brightly down clearly revealed the fearsome object stretched on the planks at Charley's feet. It was a man lying flat on his back, his arms outstretched, and his face upturned to the stars.

"Dead, murdered!" Charley cried, softly.

"Perhaps he is only drunk," suggested his chum in a tense whisper.

But Charley silently pointed to a gaping hole in the man's forehead and the dark pool on the wharf at his head.

The captain, stooping, felt of the man's wrist, raised his arm and let it drop. "Yes, he is cold, dead, and stiff," he whispered. "Let us get away from here. We can do him no good."

In a few minutes, the four were huddled in the "Dixie's" cabin, talking over the tragedy with bated breath. They were not strangers to the sight of death. In the course of the adventurous lives they had lived, they had often seen the coming of the gristly monster, but the suddenness of this sight had upset their nerves already overtaxed by the events of the previous day and the night, and it was long before they could compose themselves to sleep.

Just as Walter was dropping off into dreamland, Charley nudged him with his elbow. " I've got it," he whispered, softly.

" What? " inquired Walter, drowsily.

" A plan to avoid trouble with the fishermen and keep Chris from all harm."

" Let's hear it," demanded his chum, rousing up a little.

" Wait until morning. I haven't thought out all the details yet. Get to sleep if you can. We'll need all the rest we can get for to-morrow is going to be a busy day."

It seemed to the weary little party that they had hardly closed their eyes when they were awakened by the sun shining in the cabin windows.

Hastily dressing, they got aboard the skiff and made for the dock.

There was a crowd gathered in front of the shacks and they clambered up on the wharf unobserved.

Beside the fishermen, Mr. Daniels was standing in the group and with him was a stocky, determined-looking man, wearing a revolver, whom the boys took to be a sheriff.

" Good morning, friends," called Mr. Daniels when he caught sight of the little party. " Come here. Perhaps you can tell us something about last night's affair. These fellows here seem to know nothing about it."

Briefly, Captain Westfield told the little they knew of the trouble.

" That don't help us much," observed the sheriff, when he had concluded. " As long as these fishermen will not talk it is going to be hard to locate the murderer. The man who was killed was a pretty bad egg, although that does not excuse the murderer. I wish I could find out where that whiskey comes from. It is that which causes all the trouble."

It was on Walter's tongue to tell Mr. Daniels of their own troubles but he remembered the fish boss's declaration that they must fight their own battles and he checked himself.

The sheriff soon left, taking with him as suspects a couple of fishermen who were known to have quarreled with the dead man the day before. Before he left, however, he addressed the assembled fishermen.

" Now," he said, firmly, " these affairs among you have got to stop and stop right now. Most of you men are not bad at heart. It's the liquor makes you crazy and ready to follow the lead of the reckless ones. I don't know where you get the booze but I am going to find out and the guilty ones are going to suffer. I'll give you a chance to come square with it. I'll give a reward of five hundred dollars to the man who puts me next to this booze business, and promise him that he will not be punished unless he is one of the main offenders. You know where I live. I am ready to talk any time to the man who will come to me and help me put an end to the accursed business."

None of the fishermen spoke but it was evident that the mention of the large reward was not without some effect. Some faces showed eager cupidity while others betrayed great uneasiness.

"That reward offer is a bomb in their midst," whispered the observant Charley to his chum. "Some of those fellows will squeal to the sheriff unless they are too afraid of what the rest would do to them. I guess those that look so uneasy are the guilty ones, they have cause to be scared. Five hundred dollars is a big temptation for some one to turn state's evidence. But come, we have no time to stand around. We have got lots to do to-day. Chris, will you see if you can rustle us up a little breakfast?"

"Now for our own troubles," he continued as soon as the little negro was out of hearing. "We all know now that we can not stay here. If those fellows will kill one of their own comrades, they certainly would not hesitate to do the same to

Chris or one of us if they got a good chance. So we must get away from here at once. As soon as we eat breakfast, let's get all our things on the 'Dixie' and pull out. I've a sort of plan in my head for a new home but first I want to go over to the Roberts camp and have a little talk with them. There are several things I want to find out. Before we go, though, I want to say a few words to these fishermen."

The fishermen were still standing as the sheriff had left them, talking excitedly together and Charley approached the group. "Men," he said in a clear, manly voice, "please give me your attention for a moment." A surprised silence fell upon the group, and the lad was quick to take advantage of it.

"We only landed in this place yesterday. We came here broke, seeking a chance only to work and earn. Mr. Daniels was kind enough to give us that chance. We have started in strangers to all of you and with no malice or ill feeling towards any of you. Last night we received a note signed the White Caps stating that we must get rid of our little colored cook or suffer serious consequences. Now suppose, men, that you had a friend who for years had been faithful, loyal and true to you. Suppose that he had again and again risked his life for you. Would you turn him down at some one else's demand, even if his skin was black? Could you do it and retain an atom of your own self respect? No, you could not. Nor can we. That little darkey has been all of those things to us for many years and we can not and will not turn him adrift. You, or some of you, object to his presence on this dock. Very well, we will leave the dock. He will not bother you even with his presence. All we ask is that if you come across him elsewhere at any time that you do him no harm. We appeal to your sense of fair play. We do not believe any American lacks that sense. We ask this not through fear but because it is right and just."

A murmur ran through the group of fishermen when the lad concluded and turning around walked back to his friends. He had little hopes that his words had done any good but the chance had seemed worth the attempt.

Chris soon called them to breakfast and as soon as it was finished, the boys brought the " Dixie " alongside and stored their belongings in her cabin.

After a few attempts Charley succeeded in starting the engine and with the captain at the wheel and their skiffs in tow behind, they swung away from the dock and headed across the bay for a little island on which stood the Roberts camp. As they approached the place, they were delighted with the looks of the little camp. They landed at a neat little wharf, on either side of which were neat, well-built net racks upon which were neatly hung well-mended nets. The skiffs hauled upon the shore were well-painted and in excellent shape. A trim little path bordered with sea shells led up up to a neat, cozy, white-painted cottage nestling in amongst a group of cocoanut palms.

"These Roberts are tidy as sailors," observed Captain Westfield. "We can bank on their being pretty near all right. I never saw a clean, tidy man that was a bad man."

As Charley had expected, they found the Roberts at home taking a needed day's rest after their hard work.

They greeted the little party cordially. "Glad to see you," said Bill Roberts, heartily. "Hope that you will drop in on us often now that you have found the way."

"We have come to bother you already," Charley said. "I thought perhaps you could tell us if there would be any objection to our making a camp on one of these islands."

"What, tired of life on the dock already?" grinned Bill.

Charley briefly related their experiences with the fishermen. Bill and his brothers, Frank and Robert, were indignant. "It's some of that Hunter gang's doings," Bill declared. "Most of the fishermen are not such bad fellows but they are afraid to oppose the gang for fear of what might be done to them on the sly. You have done just right to leave there, now, you won't be mixed up in any of their troubles. Sure you can make camp on any of these islands. They are owned by the state and no one has got any right to object. You could build a shack right here on our island but I've got a better idea than that. You see that island right over there opposite the Clearwater dock? That's Palm Island. There is a pretty fair abandoned house on it which with only a little fixing up would do you first rate. There's a good spring of cold water on it too. I'll take a run over there with you and show you where the spring is."

The little party gratefully accepted his offer. Just as they were shoving off from the dock, the younger brother came running down with a rifle in his hands. "Better take this," he offered. " We have got an extra one and it may come handy to you. You can return it later on if you find you have no use for it."

Our friends thanked him for his kindness. A weapon was what they had been longing for since their acquaintance with the fishermen. They hoped to never have occasion to use one, but its possession gave them a sense of security.

They were delighted with the little cabin and spring that Bill showed them on Palm Island. The island itself was a small one of about ten acres and densely covered with palms. It was long and narrow. One of its snow-white beaches fronted on the Gulf of Mexico and the other on the bay. The cabin was in a good state of repair, and the spring gushed up clear and cold from under a clump of rock.

Their new friend soon took his departure giving them one last piece of advice before he went.

"Better leave one man in camp all the time," he said. "It needs one to do the cooking and keep nets mended up, and it's best not to take any chances. That Hunter gang may drop in on you any time."

As soon as he was gone, the little party fell to work fixing up their new home with which they were one and all delighted.

CHAPTER VI.

THE MIDNIGHT LIGHT.

" I wish we could get to fishing right off," Charley observed, " but I believe it will pay us best to get everything fixed up right first, then we will have nothing to bother us and we will be able to fish steadily without any interruptions."

" Issue your commands, boss, and they shall be carried out," Walter assured him.

" The cabin is the first thing to be attended to. There isn't much fixing required, as I can see, except to clean it up a little. But we need something for beds, bare planks make pretty hard sleeping. How do you suppose some clean dry sea moss would do for couches? "

" Just the thing," Captain Westfield declared. " I like the sweet salty smell of it. I'll bring some up from the beach, and clean up the house too, that's my job."

" We had ought to have some kind of a fireplace to cook on," Charley continued. " It's a little trouble to build one, but there's lots of rock on the beach and it hadn't ought to take very long."

" Dis nigger's goin' to 'tend to dat," announced Chris. " I'se de cook an' I knows jes' what kind ob oven I wants. I'se goin' to see if I can't find something to eat too. We ain't got but mighty little grub left an' we best save it all we can."

" Well, Walter and I will try to manage the rest of the work, then. Come on, Walt, we have got to build a small dock and racks for our nets."

There was plenty of driftwood on the beach and with proper tools the two boys would have taken but a short time to complete their tasks, but the only implements they possessed were their sheath knives.

" This is a case where necessity has got to be the mother of invention," Charley observed. " Let's pick out our driftwood as near of the same length as we can, that will save some cutting which would be an almost impossible job without saw or axe. We had better tackle the dock job first because it's the hardest. Let's see—we will want six stout pieces for posts, three others for cross pieces, and a lot of planks for the top."

Although the driftwood was plentiful, it took the boys some time to find just what they wanted and carry it all to the place they had decided to have their wharf.

" Now comes the hardest part of the job," Charley announced, as they dumped their last load on the sand. " That is to get our posts set. I don't see any way to do but get overboard and work them down by hand."

" Here goes, then," said Walter, beginning to shed his clothing.

The water was not very deep and the boys stood one of the posts upright and attempted to work the end down into the bottom by swaying the top back and forth.

" It's no go," panted Walter after half an hour of hard labor which only sank the post a few inches in the hard sand. " It would take us ten years to put them all far enough down to hold."

" I expect we will have to give up the dock for the present," Charley agreed, ruefully. " Too bad. Of course one is not absolutely necessary but it would save us a good deal of trouble and also wet feet."

" It is lucky that your assistant is a person of great intelligence," Walter observed, slyly. " Your methods are primitive, clumsy, hand-labor methods. This is an age of machinery and brains. Now, if I were boss of this, job, I would call in the aid of machinery to replace the hand methods which have been tried and found wanting."

" I resign as superintendent in your favor," Charley grinned. " There is more honor than pay attached to the position, anyway. It will be a good opening for you. You will be able to say in future years that you held at least one position where you were not paid more than you were worth."

" Your words are prompted by intellectual jealousy," declared his chum, calmly. " However, it is the misfortune of the truly great not to be appreciated until they are dead. If you will bring the launch in here, I'll explain my plan so simply that a child, or even you, can understand it."

Charley, deciding that he was getting the worst of the good-natured banter, obediently waded out and brought the launch in.

" I don't know whether you are well enough acquainted with engines to realize it," mocked Walter, who had only made the discovery himself that morning, " but the cylinder of this engine, as you will see when I point it out, is inclosed in a hollow iron jacket. This thing down here is a pump, and you will notice that there is one pipe running from it down through the bottom of the boat and also another pipe leading into the jacket. Observe also that there is a short piece of pipe in the jacket to which is fastened a piece of hose that runs out over the side of the boat. Do you take in all that?"

" I do," said Charley, briefly.

" All right, though I am quite surprised. Now, when the engine is running that pump sucks up water through the pipe that goes through the bottom of the boat. The water is forced through the other pipe into the jacket and passes overboard again through the short pipe and hose. The constant circulation of cold water keeps the engine from heating up and exploding."

"You know more about engines than I suspected yesterday," Charley said, dryly.

"I know many things that would surprise you," observed Walter, calmly. "Now, I will show you how simple it is for a brainy person to make practical use of such things. Now, we'll just fasten the end of that hose to the end of the post and start up the engine. The force of the expelled water will wash away the sand from below the post permitting it to sink."

"Yes, and you will start the engine the wrong way and pump the poor post out of the water," Charley jeered.

"The superintendent does not stoop to manual labor," replied Walter, calmly. "I shall simply order my assistant to start the engine."

The joke was on Charley and he owned it by starting up the engine without further parley.

"Now get overboard and hold the post steady," Walter commanded, and his chum meekly obeyed.

The idea was really an excellent one. The post sank rapidly and in an hour all six were sunk to the required depth. Charley labored in the water with suspicious willingness while Walter, barebacked, sat proudly and comfortably in the launch tending the switch and giving orders with sarcastic comments on the worker's ability. From time to time, Charley glanced up with a malicious grin at him sitting in naked state by the engine. That grin made Walter uneasy, for it was not often that he got the best of his chum in a joke and Charley's meekness was suspicious.

"Now for the cross pieces. Put them on next," he ordered. "By jove, how are we going to fasten them though. We have got no nails or hammer."

"This is an age of machinery and brains," quoted Charley. "Surely my brilliant superintendent can overcome such a little difficulty."

Walter puzzled for a few minutes. "I'll have to give up," he admitted. "I resign as superintendent. Give your orders, Mr. Super and I'll execute them." He flopped over the launch's side into the water.

"Ouch!" he yelled. "What's the matter with this water? It smarts me like fire."

"There's nothing the matter with the water," grinned Charley, "it is just nice, cool, clear sea water. I am enjoying it. The salt in it does not agree with a badly sunburned back, however."

"My! I should say it doesn't," agreed his chum, as the reason for the smarting dawned upon him. "Now laugh. Go ahead, don't mind my feelings. I am not sensitive."

And thus with good-natured banter, the two boys

made light work of their heavy, disagreeable task.

Charley solved the lack of nails and hammer, by plaiting some stout ropes of cocoanut fiber with which he securely bound the cross pieces in place. After that it was only a few minutes' task to lay on the planks for the top and their wharf was completed.

The net racks gave them less trouble, as they consisted merely of two poles about four feet apart set up on posts.

By noon, the boys' tasks were completed and they repaired to the cabin where they found that the captain and Chris had not wasted their time. The cabin had been made neat and clean and in each corner was a great heap of dry fragrant sea moss upon which their blankets were already spread.

Just outside the door, Chris had cunningly constructed a kind of rude, flat-topped stove out of rocks, and the fragrant odors coming from it caused the boys to quicken their steps.

" My, Chris, if that dinner tastes as good as it smells, it will be all right," Charley said.

The little negro beamed with delight. " Trust dis nigger to git plenty to eat," he grinned. " Don't make no difference if dat poor white trash steals all the grub, dis nigger can get up a good meal all right. I'se just got up a kind of feast to-day 'cause hit's our first meal on de Island."

And a feast it truly was. First came a thick soup or stew that was delicious. "What's this, Chris?" Charley asked, as he smacked his lips over the first spoonful. "It's a new one on me."

"Dem's stewed scallops. I find lots of dem on the flats," declared the delighted little negro. "Dey are powerful hard to open an' clean, but dey sure beat oysters all hollow for tastiness. Don't eat too much ob dem, Massa Chas, 'cause dar's lots ob other things comin' yet."

The next dish was a large fish baked until the juicy meat was dropping from the bones. With it came the tender, baked bud of a palmetto cabbage, and great red, boiled claws of stone crabs. To top off with, there were golden brown, feather-weight flap-jacks with syrup and white, milky cocoa plums.

The little party ate like cannibals, while Chris urged more upon them, tickled with the success of the feast he had prepared.

"I hate to quit, but I haven't got room for another mouthful," Charley declared, at last. "Come on, Walt, stop it. There is more work to do this afternoon and I don't want to do it all by myself. Besides you are going to get another meal to-night."

"That's right, begrudge me a few mouthfuls of food," grumbled Walter as he rose slowly and painfully from the table.

The afternoon was busily spent in putting their

nets on the racks, overhauling the skiffs, and making themselves more familiar with the launch's engine.   Night found all hands tired and sleepy.   As soon as supper was over, they stretched out on their soft spicy couches ready to get back the sleep they had lost the night before.

At midnight Charley sat up suddenly wide awake. For a moment he sat still and alert.   Everything was quiet.   Yet he knew that something unusual had occurred to rouse him from his sound slumber. This sudden awakening was a habit bred by his adventurous life amid the perils of sea and forest. Silently he waited, every nerve alert, to sense what had happened.   At last it came again, a deep, mellow, horn-like sound.   One, two, three times it vibrated on the still night air, then came silence again.

Softly he crept over and awakened Walter and the captain.   " I don't know what's the matter, but some one is signaling on a conch shell," he explained, " and the sound is not far off."

CHAPTER VII.

THE MYSTERY.

LEAVING Chris still peacefully snoring, the three stole softly outside the cabin. Once outside they paused and listened again for a repetition of the strange signal.

They had not long to wait for in a few minutes, it came again, a long melodious mellow note, three times sounded.

"It comes from the Gulf," Captain Westfield declared. "Let's go down to the point. We can see both bay and gulf from there."

The island terminated in a long sand point that ran out into a passage that connected the bay with the Gulf of Mexico. To it, the three hastened their steps. Just as they stepped out on the sand spit, the mysterious signal sounded again.

"There it is," Charley cried, pointing out to sea. "It's a ship."

Out in the Gulf, about three hundred yards from where they stood, a dim shadowy mass loomed up vaguely in the darkness.

"It's a ship all right," Captain Westfield agreed,

"but thar's something queer about her. No ship ever comes in close to these shores. With all the reefs thar are around hyar it's too dangerous unless one knows the channels mighty well. Then, that ain't no distress signal she's sounding,—four long blasts is the distress signal the world over. Then too she ain't got lights—that ain't proper and shipshape."

Even as he spoke, a bright flash blazed up from the strange vessel's deck. It only lasted a few seconds, but in that brief space it lit up the mysterious stranger, showing a huddled mass of men in her waist and throwing into sharp distinctness every rope and spar.

"A flare," cried Walter, "they are certainly signaling some one."

"There is something familiar about those spars," Charley exclaimed. "Did you notice them, Captain?"

"No. I was looking at the hull. She sits low as a pirate craft. She's schooner rigged and about one hundred tons burden. Hallo! Here comes some one who has heard her signals. We can find out about her all right."

From the bay came the quick chug chug of a motor turning up at full speed. As she swept into the passage, the little party could tell even in the dim light that she was a large launch and traveling at a rapid rate.

"Ahoy!" hailed Charley, as the strange launch came abreast.

The launch's engine was stopped at his call, but no answer came to his hail.

"Ahoy!" he shouted again. "Can you tell us what ship that is and what she wants?"

A string of low-muttered curses came from the launch, and almost at the same minute a single fiery rocket hissed aloft from her deck. Immediately her engine began to throb again.

"Why, she's turned around and going back!" exclaimed Captain Westfield in amazement.

"Look at the schooner!" cried Walter.

From the mysterious ship came muffled orders and the creak of blocks as sails were hoisted and sheeted home.

Slowly the put-put of the launch's engine died away in the distance from which it had come, and the mysterious schooner, under full sail, glided silently away in the darkness.

"I'll be joggered!" exclaimed Captain Westfield. "That's queer. I wonder what they were up to."

"Something that will not bear the light of day, I guess," said Charley, thoughtfully. "I believe it was our hail that frightened the fellows in the launch and their rocket was a signal to the schooner to clear out. Well, I guess the excitement is over for the night and we might as well go back to bed."

Walter and the captain lay awake for some time discussing the strange incident but Charley lay long awake on his couch, silent and thoughtful. He was puzzling to determine where he had seen the strange schooner before. In the second, the flare had revealed her in the darkness, he had sensed something vaguely familiar in the low graceful hull and the set of the raking masts.

" Where have I ever seen a foremast that raked aft like that one," he pondered. Suddenly it flashed vivid and distinct in his groping memory. " No, no," he muttered to himself. " It simply can't be her. It must only be a chance resemblance. That flare only lasted a second. Guess I am getting to imagine things. I'd better forget it and try to go to sleep."

Never-the-less it was long before he rid his alert brain of the tormenting thought and compelled sleep to come.

When he awoke, it was to find his chums up before him. Chris had breakfast cooking and Captain Westfield had just returned from taking a morning plunge in the surf. Walter was not in sight, but he soon appeared bearing a sack full of turtle eggs which he had found on the beach.

" I've been exploring our island," he announced. " Say, some of the fishermen must come over here to hold their celebrations. There are several well-worn paths on the island. I followed two of them and they both led into the same place, a little clearing in a thick bunch of palms. It looks as though there had been several fights there for the ground is all trampled up as though it had been dug, and I found a couple of long, queer-looking clubs and this full bottle. What's in it, Charley? I can't make out the label."

Charley took the big black bottle and examined the label that had puzzled his chum. "It's in Spanish," he announced, then translated rapidly: "Aguardiente, 100 Proof, Manufactured by Sicava & Sons, Santiago, Cuba." He pulled the cork and a pungent reeking odor filled the air.

"Why, it's rum," said Captain Westfield.

"A kind of rum," Charley agreed, "only far stronger and more fiery. No wonder the fishermen fight if this is the kind of stuff they drink. It would make a rabbit spit at an elephant."

"Throw it away," Walter said. "We don't want the vile stuff."

"No, I think I will keep it," said his chum, thoughtfully. "I have a notion that this little bottle is going to be mighty useful some time."

"How's that?" Walter questioned, but the spell of silent thoughtfulness was still upon Charley and he paid no heed to the question.

"I wish you fellows would go down and pull the nets into the skiffs," he said, as soon as breakfast was over. " I will be down as soon as I take a dip in the surf."

" Why, what do you want the nets on so early for?" Walter protested. " We don't fish except at night, do we?"

" We need to have a little drill," Charley explained. " It will be easier for you to learn how to handle the nets in the day time, and we will not have to waste any of our precious night time practicing."

As soon as the three were gone, Charley left the camp himself. He did not pause at the beach to take a swim, however. Instead he turned into one of the well-beaten paths Walter had spoken of. He was following up a vague suspicion that had been growing in his mind and, for good reasons, he wanted to follow it out alone. If he was right in his surmises then would be the time to tell his chums. There was no use of worrying them until he was certain.

His keen eyes noted one peculiar thing that his chum had not observed the significance of. All the paths led inward from the gulf beach and none from the bay.

A few minutes' walk brought him to the cleared place Walter had described. It was only a few feet in extent and was densely surrounded by a thick growth of cocoanut palms. No one a few feet distant would have suspected its existence so well was it hidden from sight.

At the entrance to the little space, Charley picked up two heavy pieces of timber about six feet in length. " These are Walter's clubs," he grinned. " Well, I suppose one could take them for that but clubs don't generally have a nice smooth rounded hand grip at each end and clubs the length of these things would be awkward to handle at close quarters. I have an idea these were used to carry heavy burdens. They would come pretty handy for that. Just lay the thing to be carried across them and one man take hold of the ends in front and another man at the back. Strange, Walter did not notice an odd thing about this clearing too. There is not a root or twig on the ground. Men would hardly fix up a place as clean just to fight in. He is right about one thing, though, this ground does look as though it had been all dug up, and unless all my guess is wrong, it has been dug up. Let's see how near I've hit to the mark with my suspicions."

He got down on his knees and began to dig in the soft earth. In a few minutes he came upon that which he sought. It was not unexpected for all his theories had pointed the one way. As he dug over here and there, however, he grew amazed at the magnitude of his discovery. At last he ceased his digging and carefully filled up the many holes he had made trying to smooth over the face of the ground the same as it was before. This accomplished to his satisfaction, he stood up with a thoughtful frown on his face.

Should he tell his companions of his discovery, he pondered. It was of no use to any of them at present. Would it be wise to tell them yet? Some one might let slip a word in an unguarded moment that would spoil everything. "The more that knows a secret the greater the chance of its leaking out," he reflected. "No," he would not tell them at present.

Having reached this decision, he made his way back to the beach. Stripping, he took a hurried plunge in the surf and hastily dressing hurried across the island to the skiffs.

"We have got the nets all aboard," Walter greeted him with.

One glance at the heaped up nets in the skiffs' stern and Charley's face fell.

"Whew!" he whistled, "you have sure done it now. Well, it's all my fault. I should have explained to you how to boat a net. They don't want to be piled up in a heap like that. You can't run out a net in that shape. It would all tangle up and go out in lumps and bunches. When you boat a net, you want to pile the lead line up carefully on one side of the stern and the cork line on the other letting the loose webbing fall in between, then it will run out smoothly without tangles and snarls."

The nets had to be all tumbled out of the skiffs and hauled in again as Charley had directed.

His chums were quite crestfallen over their mistake, but he only laughed. "Everything is new to you and you are bound to make a lot of mistakes at first," he assured them, "but you will soon catch on. Don't get discouraged over a little mistake like that, you'll make many bigger ones before you get used to the business. Hallo, I guess we are going to have some visitors. That launch out there is heading in here."

CHAPTER VIII.

THE VISITORS.

THE boys glanced up from their work from time to time at the rapidly approaching motor boat.

"My, but she is a fast one!" commented Charley, noting the crest of foam at her bow and the rapid popping of her exhaust. "I believe she is as fast, or faster, than our 'Dixie.'"

Within a few minutes after they had sighted her, she was near enough for the chums to distinguish her passengers or crew.

"Why, the man at the wheel is that fisherman Hunter," Walter exclaimed, "and there are four more with him, some of his gang, I suppose."

"I wonder what they want with us," speculated the captain, uneasily.

"Nothing pleasant, I guess," said Charley, gravely. "I believe those fellows are bent on making trouble for us. Let's not have any words with them, if we can help it. If we have got to have a fuss with 'em at all though, I guess now is as good a time as ever. I'll get Chris out of the way," he added, in an undertone to Walter. "He does not know yet that he is the innocent cause of our trouble, and there is no use letting him if we can help it. It would make the poor little chap feel awfully bad."

As soon as it was apparent beyond all doubt that the launch was coming in to the little dock, he called the little negro to one side.

"I want you to go up to the cabin and stay there until I call you," he directed. "If I give one long whistle, come a running and bring the rifle with you."

The little negro was barely out of sight, when the big launch, its engine shut off, glided in to the dock.

Besides the sallow-faced Hunter, it contained four fellows almost as vicious and mean looking as himself. Hunter made the launch fast to a post and climbed out on the dock followed by his companions.

Our little party greeted the visitors with a pleasant good morning.

"Good morning," grunted Hunter with a snarl, "I didn't come all the way over here just to say good morning though."

"Then what did you come for?" demanded Walter curtly, his quick temper beginning to flare up at the fellow's insolent tones.

"I am going to let you know mighty quick,"

snarled Hunter.   " You brought that little nigger over here with you, didn't you? "

" We did," Charley answered briefly.

" Well, you-all have got to get off this island— and get off of it mighty quick," he declared.

" Why," Captain Westfield demanded, his own anger beginning to rise.

" First place, 'cause you ain't got any right to stay here.   This island belongs to a friend of mine and I've got charge of it."

Charley was keeping his temper well in hand though he was as angry as his chums.   " We have been advised that this island belongs to the state," he said, coolly, " and we believe what we have been told.   We have got as much right on state land as you or any one else."

" Well, I give you notice to get off right away. We don't allow no niggers in the fishing business 'round hyar."

" Now look here, Hunter," Charley said coolly, " you fellows objected to our having the little negro with us on the dock.   Very well, we moved over here to avoid trouble.   Now you come over here and try to order us off this island which we have as many rights to as you.   That's going too far and we are not going to stand for it."

" We ain't going to have no niggers fishing 'round hyar," repeated Hunter doggedly.

"Chris is not going to do any fishing. He is our cook—and a mighty good one too."

"Don't make any difference. You fellows have got to get off this island."

"Which we refuse to do," Charley said defiantly.

"Amen to that," agreed Captain Westfield, hotly.

"You'll have a hard job making us," chimed in Walter.

Hunter's sallow face reddened with anger. "If you smart Alecks ain't off this island before tomorrow night you'll get what's coming to you," he snarled.

"Look here, Hunter," Charley said, quietly, "it strikes me you are a little bit too anxious to get us to leave here and I think I know the reason. Now you fellows had better get in your boat and go. We want nothing to do with you and your gang. We will tend to our own business and you had better tend to yours. If you bother us any more, well, I know of an officer who would be willing to pay a good big sum to know about a strange craft that haunts this coast in the night, and a motor boat that answers her signals."

It was a chance shot on Charley's part but it went home.

"We wasn't out at all last night," denied Hun-

ter. "We were all in bed, didn't even go fishing."

"I never mentioned last night," said Charley,
quickly, and Hunter muttered a curse as he saw the
slip he had made.

"You're only doing a lot of wild guessing, and
guessing ain't proof," he snarled. "Take all the
guesses you want to your officer. He won't do
anything. He's got to have proofs."

Charley realized with regret that his veiled
threat had failed, but he tried not to show his
chagrin.

"Leave here," he ordered. "Get into your boat
and go."

"I'm leaving right now," Hunter snarled.
"But you'll be leaving here for good before two
days are gone. Before I go, I'm going to slap
you around a bit to teach you some manners, you
young whelp. Look out for them other two,
boys, while I give this smart Aleck a dressing
down."

His companions drawing their sheath knives,
crowded threateningly towards Walter and the captain while he lunged forward at Charley who stood
his ground a little pale but unafraid. He came at
the lad with a rush, both fists swinging. "Keep
back," Charley cried, but Hunter aimed a swinging
blow at his head with all his force.

Charley ducked with the quickness he had learned

in a Y. M. C. A. gym and at the same instant drove his right fist forward with all of his weight behind it. It caught the sallow fisherman fair on his chin and sent him reeling backwards. He staggered and almost fell but recovering himself with an oath whipped out his sheath knife and came rushing at the plucky lad.

It was a desperate situation. A lightning glance out of the corner of his eye showed Charley he could expect no help from his chums. They were menaced by the three ruffians with upraised knives. Their own knives lay in their fishing belts up in the cabin. No stick or club was within his reach. It was a case of bare hands against naked steel. Hunter came at him with a savage thrust. The lad leaped lightly to one side to avoid it. His foot slipped on a mossy rock and down he went on the sand.

With a yell of triumph the fishermen leaped for him as he lay half-dazed by his fall.

Crack, crack, crack came three sharp reports and the shrill whine of whistling bullets sang above the prostrate lad.

The effect on the fishermen was startling.

With a cry Hunter turned and ran for the launch and his companions crowding at his heels.

" We'll get you yet," he yelled as he hurriedly cast off. " We'll get you when you ain't got that little nigger behind a tree guarding you with a gun. We "—but his curses were lost in the crackle of the engine as he threw on the switch.

Walter and the captain hurried to Charley and helped him up from the sand.

"I am all right," he declared as soon as he was on his feet. "I came down so hard it knocked the wind out of me for a moment but I am all right now."

"Chris shot just in time," Walter exclaimed. "I thought you were going to be killed before our eyes."

"I don't believe they would have gone that far," said his chum. "Hunter might have beat me up a bit but I think he aimed to frighten us off the island more than anything else."

"I wonder why he is so anxious to drive us away from here," pondered Walter, puzzledly.

"That's easy to tell," Charles declared. "His gang are smuggling aguardiente here from Cuba. That was the meaning of that schooner, the motor boat, and those signals last night. I found a cache of the stuff in that cleared place this morning. There must be five hundred bottles of it."

"Then all we have to do is to tell the sheriff and he'll put the gang where they will not bother us any more," Walter exclaimed in relief.

"That's what I tried to bluff Hunter into thinking," replied his chum, "but it did not work. You see, we have got no proofs and he knows it. We see a schooner at night acting queerly, also a motor boat, and we find a stock of aguardiente buried on the island, but that proves nothing against the Hunter gang or anyone else for that matter. Of course, I feel sure that they are the guilty ones but that isn't proof."

"I reckon we are in something of a mess," said Captain Westfield, worriedly. "We are going to have trouble with those fellows sure. They can't carry on such a game with us here on the island, and it ain't likely they are going to stay quiet and lose all that stuff they've got cached."

"It looks bad," Charley admitted, gravely. "We must talk it over carefully and decide what is best to do. But where's Chris? It's funny he don't show himself. Something must be the matter."

With a sudden alarm, Charley hastened up for the cabin, followed by his chums.

As soon as he came in sight of the hut, he slackened his speed with a sigh of relief for the little negro was seated in the doorway with the rifle in his hands.

"Good work, Chris," he exclaimed. "Your shots came just in the nick of time. I am glad you didn't hit any of them though."

"I ain't shot none, Massa Chas," protested the little negro. "You dun tole me to stay right hyar till you whistle an' you ain't whistled yet."

"Then where did those shots come from?" Charley demanded.

"Hit sounded like dey come from where you-alls was," Chris declared.

"Then they must have come from the fringe of palms close to the beach," Charley decided. "Well, some one on the island has done us a good turn and we better look him up and thank him. Likely he didn't want to be seen and recognized by Hunter."

But at the end of an hour they were back at the cabin, a thoroughly mystified little group. They had been all over their little domain but no sign of a human being had they discovered.

CHAPTER IX.

MORE TROUBLE.

ALL the little party were greatly puzzled but Chris was the one most troubled. The superstitious little negro was quick to attach an uncanny meaning to the strange incident.

"Hit was a ghost," he declared, solemnly. "Dat's jes' de way de ghosts do on Cat Island. Nobody can ebber find 'em when dey look for 'em. Dey jes' melt into de air."

"Bosh, Chris," derided Charley, "there are no such things as ghosts."

"Yes dar is, Massa Chas," persisted the little darkey. "Plenty of people has seed dem a heap ob times. My ole daddy on Cat Island dun seen one once. He come 'cross hit on de road one moonlight night. Hit was all white an' bigger den any man an' dar was blue fire comin' out ob hits eyes, an' nose, an' mouth. Daddy run like de wind an' he dun got away from hit. But he always 'lowed if he hadn't had his conjurer charm tied 'round his neck hit would hab cotched him sho'. Sho' dar is ghosts."

Walter laughed. "Well, if there are bad spirits there must be good spirits also, Chris," he observed, " and this one seems to be a pretty good sort. He certainly done us a good turn. If I ever meet him, I hope he will not do the vanishing act for I want to thank him."

But Chris was not to be reassured and he went about his task of getting dinner muttering darkly to himself.

"Frankly, what do you make of it?" Walter inquired of his chum as they waited the preparation of the meal.

" I? I don't know what to think of it yet," Charley confessed. "As soon as I found out that it was not Chris who did the shooting I thought maybe one of the Roberts boys had landed on the other side of the island and happened to come across just in the nick of time. I can understand that no one would want to be seen by the Hunter gang for the sake of avoiding future trouble with them, but I can not for the life of me understand why the unknown should wish to avoid us, also. That is the puzzling part. Why did he vanish, and where did he go to? He had no time to get away in a boat without our seeing·him. It's a mystery to me."

" I ain't worrying much about that," observed Captain Westfield. "Whoever it was he was friendly to us and that's more than we can say for that Hunter gang. We are bound to have more trouble with them, I fear, and I don't see any way to steer clear of it unless we pick up and leave this part of the country."

"We can't do that," Walter declared. "We are penniless and there is no other work we can do around here. Besides we owe a good big bill at the store and it would not be right to go away and leave it for Mr. Daniels to pay."

"No," agreed the captain, "we can't do that. Well, I don't know what is best to do. What's your opinion, Charley?"

"Of course, we can't leave here," replied the lad, decidedly, "and I for one, don't want to leave. There are four of the Hunter gang and there are four of us. It's true, we have only one gun amongst us while they are probably well armed. In a way, I do not think the question of weapons is so very important. I do not believe that they will provoke a serious open fight. That demonstration this morning was to frighten us away. There is law in this state and officers capable of enforcing it, and, bad as that Hunter gang is reputed to be, I do not believe the members of it are going to run the risk of being hung for any open killing. What evil they will try to do to us will be done secretly and in such a way that we can not have them arrested for it. I judge, that is the way they have always done their meanness from what Bill Roberts said to Hunter that day. If we stay here that is what we will have to always be on our guard against. Of course such a state of things will not be pleasant but I believe we are as bright as they and by being watchful we will give them little chance to do us any injury."

"What about that stuff they've got cached," objected Captain Westfield. "It's worth too much money for them to let it lay where it is and they won't dare take it away as long as we are on the island."

"I've been thinking of that," Charley answered, "and I believe, the best thing to be done is to get the stuff off the island. If we catch any fish to-night, we will have to take them over to Clear-water and just tell Mr. Daniels about our finding the stuff. Likely, he will see that it is removed at once. That will rid the Hunter gang of the necessity of driving us off the island and it will likely scare them so that it will be some time before they attempt to smuggle any more in."

"Wall, I reckon, that is the best course for us to steer," agreed the old sailor. "Of course, they'll have a grudge against us for the loss of the stuff but they've got one against us anyway, so it don't make much difference. We'll have to leave some one in camp all the time so as to protect our grub and things."

"We will leave Chris," Charley decided. "One of us will have to cook and keep the nets mended up anyway and Chris is certainly the boy for the cooking job. We will leave the rifle with him. At night, or when there is any sign of trouble, he can bar himself up in the cabin and be safer than he would be with us. It's strong as a fort, and the palmetto logs it is built of will not catch fire easy if any one should try to smoke him out."

Accordingly when dinner was finished, Charley explained the situation to the little negro, only telling him of the cached liquor and not mentioning the objections made to his presence amongst them so as to spare the little fellow's sensitive feelings. Chris protested vigorously at the plan to leave him behind.

"I ain't scared ob dat poor white trash," he declared, "but hit ain't noways nice to stay hyar alone wid a haunt walking 'round on dis island. I jes' naturally can't do dat, Massa Chas."

In vain his three companions argued with him. All the superstitions of his race were aroused. "A spirit was a haunting de island," he declared, "an' hit warn't noways wise to stay alone whar a haunt was.

"If I only had my ole daddy's conjurin' charm, hit might be all right," he said, doubtfully. "Hit dun saved him from a ghost once."

"I'll tell you what I'll do," said Charley at last. "I'll let you have my one ghost charm. It will ward off any ghost that ever walked this island."

" Has you got one for sho', Massa Chas? Let's see hit," exclaimed the relieved little darkey.

Charley gravely produced from his pocket a tiny stone, Chinese mannikin, which he had once used as a watch charm and which had found its way into his pockets along with a few other worthless odds and ends. It was grotesquely carved and hideously ugly but Chris viewed it with delight.

" Hit sho' looks like a powerful charm," he declared with the longing for possession.

" I'll guarantee it to protect against any ghost I ever saw," declared Charley, truthfully and solemnly.

" If you could dun spare hit to me, I reckon I wouldn't mind being left behind, Massa Chas," offered the little negro.

" All right," Charley agreed, delighted with the success of his ruse. " You want to be careful not to lose it though. I don't know where I could get another like it."

They left the appeased little darkey engaged in fastening the ugly mannikin with a string around his neck, and took their way down to the dock for the practice drill Charley had decided upon.

" Now, I don't want to be bossy," the lad explained as they made their preparations for the trial, " but, as things are, I happen to be the only one of us who has had any experience in fishing. I would much rather that some one else could take

the lead for fishing is one business where the leader
must be obeyed without argument or question. His
followers must give him the same quiet service
that a military company gives its officers. It is
upon such unquestionable following that the suc-
cesses in fishing largely depends. The leader's
position, running head boat it is called, requires
quick judgment and swift action, and these can
not be had if argument or explanations have to pre-
cede them."

"That's all right, I understand what you mean,"
said Captain Westfield, placidly. "All you will
have to do is to give your orders."

"Sure," agreed Walter, "we wouldn't know
what to do unless you did."

"All right," agreed Charley. "I want to say,
though, before we start, that this fishing is a nerve-
trying business, as you will soon find out. Sometimes it wears a person's temper to a wire edge and
he will say things and do things he afterwards regrets. If I should happen to speak shortly or
curtly any time please overlook it if you can and I
will do the same with you. I've seen this fishing
game break up old friendships more than once.
And now," he concluded, "for our practice. We
will suppose now that we are stealing up on a school
of fish. Our positions are this. My skiff goes
ahead. The captain in his skiff keeps ten feet behind me and a trifle to the left. You, Walter, keep

nearly opposite me but about four hundred feet distant. Now, when I give the signal to make a run, I will stop rowing. The captain will back the end of his skiff up to mine and I will tie our two nets together. Then I will shout to you and you will throw the end of your net overboard and we will all start rowing as hard as we can. You will watch my boat, Walter, and keep just opposite me all the time. When our nets are pretty well run out, I will shout again and we will both head directly for each other. When we come together, I go around your stern and cross your net with mine. As soon as you and I start, the captain starts also. He swings away from me and heads for where you dropped the end of your net. He crosses it, and, if he has any net left in his boat, he rows back inside the circle and zigzags back and forth until it is all run out. If we do this all·right and luck holds good, we will have our fish penned up like this." With a stick he drew on the sand this simple diagram.

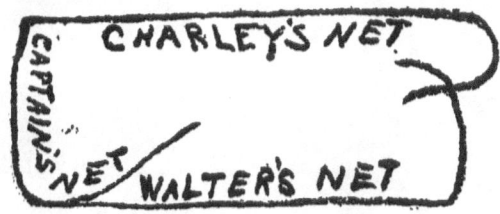

" As soon as our nets run out," he continued, " we row around inside the circle and beat on our skiffs

with the oars and make all the racket we can to
drive the fish into the nets. Then, each man rows
back to the end of his net and takes it up being
careful to pile it right so that it will run out
smoothly and also be careful not to break meshes
taking out fish. I guess that's about all."

"Why, that's simple as can be," Walter exclaimed.

Charley grinned. "Let's try it and see," he
said knowingly.

CHAPTER X.

ONE NIGHT'S SPORT.

"Now just imagine that we are really hunting fish," Charley directed, as he shoved his skiff from shore. "Take up your positions exactly as I directed and make as little noise as possible with your oars."

His companions eagerly obeyed and the three skiffs slowly crept ahead as if stealing up on a school of fish.

But their leader was not yet ready for real fishing and they had proceeded thus but a little ways when he gave the captain the signal for a run. The old sailor deftly backed up his skiff and threw Charley the end of his net. The lad caught it and quickly made it fast to his own. "Give way," he shouted, seizing his oars, and the three boats darted away while the nets ran out smoothly over their sterns.

When he judged that three-fourths of his net was out, Charley shouted to his chums and the two boats swung around for each other. The last of Walter's net ran out just as Charley passed around the stern of his skiff and turning back into the circle rowed out the few remaining yards of his own net.

" That's one important thing to remember," he commented as he rowed up to his chum's boat. " We always want to turn when we have got just enough net left to reach each other with. If our nets don't come together the fish all run out through the gap."

" Whew," Walter panted, " I never dreamed those nets were so long. I thought my arms were going to break from rowing so hard before you gave the signal to turn."

Charley grinned. " They are four hundred yards each—nearly a quarter of a mile long. Wait until you get one full of fish and it will seem forty miles long. The captain's got that other end closed up nicely, and now for the drumming up."

The three rowed around inside the circle while Charley showed them how to frighten the fish into the nets by pounding on the bottoms of the skiffs and beating the water with the blades of their oars.

" Why, the circle is full of fish," Walter suddenly exclaimed. " I can see hundreds of them darting about."

" I saw them before I gave the signal to run," Charlie said coolly, but his words were lost in the din the captain and his chum were making in their excitement. Walter was beating the water frantically with his oar while the old sailor standing up in his skiff was clapping his hands and shouting "Shoo, shoo" much as though he was driving a flock of chickens.

Charley rested on his oars and watched them with a broad grin on his face.

"Don't get excited," he remarked, when at last they stopped from sheer exhaustion. "Captain, it's no use straining your voice yelling at the fish. They can't hear you. The only thing that scares them is a vibration of the water they live in. That beating the water with your oar is the proper caper, Walter, only it happens that these fish are mullet and you can't drive mullet into a gill net in the day time. Fine as the twine is, they see the meshes and back off. And, now, let's row back to the ends of our nets and pick them up."

· His two crestfallen companions meekly obeyed, and after considerable blundering due to their inexperience the nets were once more got aboard the skiffs.

The two novices' arms and backs were beginning to ache but Charley insisted on another trial.

It was well he did so for Walter had not rowed out a third of his net when some leads caught in the webbing and the pile turned over into a tangled heap that took the three a good half hour to straighten out.

"You must be careful how you pile your net in the boat," Charley cautioned, when the mess was at last straightened out. "If that had happened when we were really and truly fishing it might have meant the loss of forty or fifty dollars' worth of fish. You must keep your loose webbing piled clear of your lead and cork lines. I noticed you had piled your net carelessly, that's why I wanted to make another run. There's nothing like experience to make one careful."

"You might have told me about it and saved all this hard extra work," grumbled Walter with a flash of temper. "My arms and back ache like a tooth ache."

"Cheer up. We'll go ashore now, and have a rest and supper before we start out for real work," said Charley, cheerfully, ignoring his chum's remarks.

A long rest under the palm trees and one of Chris' capital suppers put Walter into good humor again. "I guess, I got mad a little too easily," he half apologized to his chum over the meal. "I didn't stop to think that you had been working as hard as I and that you would not have put us all to that extra work if you had not thought it necessary."

"That's all right," answered Charley, heartily. "Just forget it. Every one gets a little riled sometimes, and fishing is mighty hard on the temper."

But the lad knew that the flashes of temper would come many times before his chum became a seasoned fisherman. "Oh, well," he consoled himself, grimly, "it's no use trying to avoid them, the sooner they come and go, why, the better."

Chris had prepared a lunch for the fishermen to carry with them to eat during the night, and just as the sun went down, the three boarded the launch and with the three skiffs in tow set out for their first attempt in their new calling.

The memory of that first night will linger in Walter's and the Captain's memory for years to come. They had run about two miles in the launch when Charley shut off the engine.

"I think we had better anchor here and take to the skiffs," he said. "These are strange waters and we might pile the launch up on a rock in the darkness."

·· A lantern was lit and placed on the launch's bow to guide them back to her, and the other lanterns were also lit, turned down low and placed in the bottom of the skiffs.

"None of you must ever allow your lights to show while we are hunting fish," Charley continued. "A light frightens them worse than anything else. A flash of lightning makes them all scurry for deep water. There's no use taking to the skiffs for a little while, it isn't dark enough to fish yet."

" That's one thing which puzzles me," Walter said. " How are you going to find fish at night. Of course, I understand how you can tell where they are in the day time, for if you can't see the fish themselves, you can tell they are there by the ripples they make in the water."

" They are oftentimes easier to find at night," Charley affirmed. " There is nearly always more or less phosphorescence in the water and a fish can not move without leaving a glowing streak in his wake, that is, if he is within ten feet of the surface. An expert fisherman can tell by the character of the bright streak the kind of fish that makes it. Each species makes a different kind of movement and an expert can read their trails like a hunter reads tracks. Nights when the water does not fire it is harder, for then the fisherman has to go by sound. Each kind of fish makes its own peculiar noise but it is hard to distinguish some of them apart and still harder to tell their size. Our nets are made for mullet and that is the only kind of fish we need be concerned with."

" Why, there is a lot more to fishing than I thought," Walter commented. " I supposed it was simple and easy to learn."

" It takes years of experience to make a skilful fisherman," Charley assured him. " I do not claim to be one. I only just know the rudiments of it."

" I reckon it's that way with most everything,"

Captain Westfield remarked, thoughtfully, " from running a ship up to running a nation. Thar's always a heap more to larn than the man outside thinks thar is."

" But all the knowledge a man can get does not help without plenty of good hard work," Charley amended. " And it's time for us to begin ours now. It's dark enough now, I believe. All aboard for our first attempt."

The three scrambled into their skiffs and casting loose from the launch, took to their oars bringing their crafts into the formation they had practiced.

In a few minutes, the launch was lost to sight and they could not see each other. Only the faint glow of the turned-down lanterns rising above the gunwales of their skiffs enabled them to keep track of each other.

As they crept slowly on into the night, Walter was surprised to see how teeming the waters were with life. On every side of his boat, fiery streaks marked the passage of finny creatures. At times, he passed through spaces fairly aglow with the movements of them. As Charley had said, there was a marked difference in the character of the water trails. Some were close to the surface, while others showed deep below. Some were long and continuous in a straight line. Others twisted and turned, while still others seemed to run only a little ways and then stopped suddenly. But they all marked the passage of fish, and he soon began to wonder why Charley did not give the signal to circle them. At first, he consoled himself with the thought that his chum know what he was doing, but as they rowed steadily on mile after mile through the flashing schools, he began to have doubts. After all, Charley had admitted that he was not an experienced fisherman. Perhaps Charley was not passing through the same schools. Perhaps he was not watching close. Walter's arms and back began to ache from the steady rowing and as his fatigue increased he began to get irritated. Why all this steady rowing on and on when there were plenty of fish all about them. The same thoughts were passing through Captain Westfield's mind but he had been bred in a calling which demands constant patient obedience to the one in command. He had elected to follow Charley's leadership and that was the end of it. He would do it without question.

At last Walter could stand it no longer.

" Say, Charley," he hailed, " there's lots of fish around here."

" I see them," came the cheerful answer. " They don't look right to me, though. Let's go on a bit."

Sullenly, Walter rowed on in silence. After what to his tired muscles seemed ages of weary pulling, a crisp order came floating over the water.

" Get ready—Drop your net weight over "—

A pause, then: "All right—all together—pull hard."

Walter forgot his aching limbs in the excitement of the moment. He bent to his oars and sent his skiff flying through the water while his net rippled swiftly out over the stern.

"Come together," at last came the order and he swung his flying craft around to meet his chum's."

"Gee," panted Charley, as he crossed the end of Walter's net, just as the last of his own ran out. "I pulled myself out of breath trying to get around that school. Most of them outran me, but I guess we have got a few penned up in the circle. Put up your lantern and let's rest a bit before we drum up. Good," he exclaimed as the lights flashed out over the water. They are hitting the nets already—Listen."

From all sides of them came a soft peculiar .smacking sound much like that made by a person opening and closing his mouth rapidly.

"Listen, old chap," Charley cried in glee, "you are hearing your first catch of mullet."

CHAPTER XI.

THE QUARREL.

THE new fishermen could hardly wait to beat up the circle so eager were they to see what their nets contained.

"I guess we have got all there was in the circle," Charley at last announced. "Let's start to take up. Fasten your lantern to the end of an oar and fix it so it will shine down on your net so that you can see what you are doing, look out for cat fish. I put a short club in each of the skiffs to-day. If you get a cat fish, kill it before you try to take it out of your net."

"What kind of looking fish are they?" Walter paused to inquire.

"They are a slimy fish without scales," Charley explained. "They have a flat head and on each side of the gills and on the back are needle-sharp horns about three inches long with fine saw teeth along the edge. When the fish are swimming the horns lay back flat against the body, but when they strike a net or anything else, they stick the horns straight out. They are fierce to take out of a net, they will tangle up dozens of meshes on those horns and the fine twine is hard to work off the saw edges.   It's dangerous to handle them unless they are killed for they are liable to flop and stick those horns in you and make a very poisonous wound. Well, let's get to work, the night is slipping away fast."

With lanterns popped out over the skiff's stern the three set to work.

At first it was exciting to haul in the nets with the struggling fish entangled in their meshes, and to watch the pile in their boats steadily grow, but the novelty soon wore off and only the hard work remained.   And hard work it was, harder than either the captain or Walter had dreamed.   A breeze had arisen since sunset and they had to drag their skiffs up against it as they pulled in their nets. When they came to a fish they had to hold the net with their feet, while they bent over under the dim light and freed it from the entangling meshes. Every now and then they came to a great mass of sea moss caught up in their nets, which required all their strength to dump out, nor did they escape painful accidents, although they met with none of the dreaded cat fish, every fish handled by them seemed armed with sharp fins and their fingers were soon sore with a multitude of tiny punctures.   A flopping fish flipped a bit of jelly into the captain's eye.   It burned like a touch from a red hot iron, and the old sailor half blinded grew faint from the intense pain. At last Walter realized what it meant to handle four hundred yards of net. Before he had got half of his in the boat he was fairly ready to lie down and cry from pain and sheer weariness.

Charley, more expert, soon had his net boated and taking hold of the other end of Walter's helped him with the balance, then rowed over and performed a like service for the captain. "Let's rest a little bit and eat our lunch before we start again," he suggested when the nets were all up. "I'll anchor my boat and you both come alongside and tie up to me so we can all eat together."

He had brought a box partly filled with sand along in his skiff and in it he now proceeded to build a small fire on which he boiled coffee and heated up the lunch Chris had given them. The hot meal and steaming coffee made his two companions almost forget for a time their pains and weariness.

"How many do you think we got that time?" Walter inquired, over a second cup of coffee.

"About twelve hundred pounds of mullet," he judged, "some thirty odd pounds of trout and about two hundred pounds of bottom fish," say twenty-eight dollars' worth altogether. "That's pretty fair for one run. If we can get in four more runs like it before daylight, it will make a good night's work."

" Four more runs," cried Walter in dismay, all his aches and pains returning at the thought, " why I don't believe I can last out one more."

" I know it's tough on you two," said Charley sympathetically, " but we have got to do it.   We cannot hope to make money by just making one or two runs a night.   It will not be quite so bad after you get hardened to it.   I know just how you feel.   I once fished every night steady for six months and we made from six to eight runs each night.   I was new to the business then and I thought the first two or three nights that it would certainly kill me.   Tired.   Why many a time I've gone sound asleep while rowing and fallen over into the bottom of the boat amongst the fish without waking up.   Oh, it's tough all right, but you have got to get used to it."

Walter was silent.   He was doing a sum in mental arithmetic, " eight runs a night.   Four hundred yards of net to run out each time and four hundred yards of net to take in.   Eight hundred yards multiplied eight times was six thousand four hundred yards or over three miles besides all the endless rowing."   Why it was more than flesh and blood could stand.   Was any amount of money worth such nerve and muscle racking labor?   He was still pondering this when his chum gave the order to start again and they once more fell into the old formation and rowed silently on into the darkness.

Mile after mile they rowed steadily on until the launch's lanterns showed only a pin point of light in the distance. The ache in Walter's muscles grew to an acute pain. Every stroke of the oars was an effort that seemed impossible to repeat. All around his boat came and went darting flashes of many fish. Again the old question arose. Why all this aimless, senseless rowing. He felt a hot unreasoning resentment against his chum that grew with his deadly weariness and at last flowed out in speech.

"Charley," he snapped out across the water, "I'm getting sick of this nonsense. There's fish all around us. Let's either try to catch them or go home. I'm tired of this rowing, rowing, rowing for nothing.

Charley was silent a moment before replying. Matters had come to the pass he had feared. He had witnessed the same thing many times with new beginners. One of two things must happen, either Walter must learn to have faith in his leadership until he himself had gained experience or else they must give up fishing. No amount of argument would convince him like a bit of experience, as the result of having his own way in something he knew nothing about. It was bitter medicine but it was the only treatment which would check the disease, however, he decided to give his chum one last chance.

"I am doing the best I know how, Walt," he answered. "I have to follow my best judgment in this fishing so long as I am running head boat."

"Judgment nothing," scoffed Walter angrily, "there's no judgment in rowing our arms off when there are fish all around us."

"All right Old Chap, you can run head boat if you think you can do better. I'll follow you without question," Charley replied wearily.

"All right, I will," agreed Walter, shortly. "I can promise you I will not make you row yourself to death for nothing."

In silence Charley changed positions with his chum. They had not proceeded a hundred yards in the new order when Walter's skiff slid in amongst the biggest school he had yet seen.

"All right, let's run them," he shouted excitedly.

Charley smiled grimly as he cast him the end of his net to make fast but he said nothing, and when his chum gave the signal to start he was off at the word.

"Whew," panted Walter, as they came together at the end of the run, "we've made a killing this time. Just look at the bright streaks. Why, the circle is full of fish. Come on, let's drum them up."

" I wouldn't drum any," Charley advised.

" I'm running head boat now," Walter reminded
him shortly, " kindly do as I say."

" All right," his chum agreed, cheerfully, and fell
to beating the water lustily with his oar.

" I guess they are all in the nets now," Walter
at last announced. " Let's pick them up."

Charley rowed back to the end of his net in
silence. He grinned with grim humor as his quick
ear caught queer grunting sounds from along the
lines of net. He seized the end of his and pulled
it aboard, then he paused, adjusted his lantern
carefully, took a drink of water from his jug, laid
his short club handy on the seat beside him, and
settled himself for a long spell of hard work.

Walter reached for the end of his net, tingling
with anticipation. The first few yards came in
empty, then a score of white bellies showed in the
dripping webbing as he hoisted it into the boat.
Pride gave way to dismay. Instead of the clean,
glistening mullet he had expected, these were slimy,
flat-headed fish, loathsome to look at, emitting repulsive grunts and reeking forth a sickening odor.
Each was hopelessly tangled in a mess of webbing.
For a moment, he wildly debated the notion of
casting the net back overboard and fleeing. Then
he grimly, doggedly, settled down to work. His
thoughts were more unpleasant than the task before him. He had brought this upon himself and

not only upon himself but upon his companions also. Because he had become a little tired, he had given way to a fit of temper and made a fool of himself. Well, Charley and the captain would never want him to fish with them again, and it served him right, but his heart ached at the thought of separating from those kind, true, friendly companions after all the years they had spent together. He paused for a moment and listened. From the captain's skiff came muttered exclamations as the old sailor labored over his unwelcome catch. From Charley's boat came only the sharp, frequent crack of the club as he hauled the detested fish in over the stern.

Slowly the minutes lengthened into hours and the night dragged away, while the humbled lad, suffering in every muscle, his fingers bleeding from a score of scratches, and one hand swelling rapidly where a horn had entered, worked grimly on. Slowly Charley's light drew away from him for the other lad's experience had taught him the knack of taking out fish swiftly.

Once, Walter raised his eyes from his task and looked about. The morning star had risen in the east and Charley's light had disappeared. " Got disgusted and gone home," he decided, bitterly. " Well, I don't blame him."

The day was just breaking when Walter, at last, reached the end of his net. The captain had es-

caped lightly and had been through for some time.
He was stretched out on a seat, resting, and placidly
smoking his pipe. The launch was only a short
distance away. Charley had rowed back and was
bringing her up to save his chums the long row to
her.

"Good morning," Charley hailed, cheerfully, as
he shut off the engine, "all through."

Walter almost shouted with joy. His chum was
not angry with him after all.

Charley ranged alongside and peeped into his
skiff.

"What have you saved them all for," he exclaimed, as his eye lighted on the big pile of fish.

"Why, to sell," Walter faltered.

His chum grinned. "No one buys them. Why
you couldn't give them away. But come, both of
you and make fast. We'll just get home in time
for breakfast."

It was a humble and abashed lad that stepped
aboard the launch.

"Charley, I've been a fool," he blurted out, "but
if you can overlook it this time, it will not happen
again."

"Forget it," said his chum heartily. "I hated it
more for your sake than for my own, but it's all
over now. Cheer up, Old Chap."

"How did you know what kind of fish they
were?" Walter inquired, after a brief silence.

" By the streaks. A catfish fires deep below the surface and he only runs a little ways then stops. A mullet makes a long straight streak close the surface. But those were not all catfish we rowed through to-night. There were sharks in one place, a school of porgies in another, and a lot of sea bass and some fish I could not determine and was afraid to run."

CHAPTER XII.

THE GHOST.

" I WANT you two to lie down in the cabin and catch an hour's nap on the way home," Charley said as soon as he got the engine started. " I'll run the launch in."

Walter and the captain protested feebly, but the lad would hear no refusal. " You both look utterly played out," he declared. " There is no use of all of us staying awake, and I am fresher than either of you. Fishing is not so hard for me because I know all the little tricks of handling a net and taking out fish that helps to make it easier. You will soon learn them and get hardened to the work, and then we will take turns running the launch. Now stretch out, that hour's rest will do you a world of good."

His two chums lost no time in arguing the point, but stretched on the cabin floor and pillowing their heads on their arms were instantly asleep. So worn out were they that Charley could hardly wake them when the dock was reached.

Chris had a hot breakfast and steaming coffee

waiting for them; as soon as it was dispatched Charley ordered the two off to bed. " Get rested up good for to-night's work," he announced. " There is nothing that you need do now. Chris will pull the nets out to dry and I'll row across to Clearwater with the fish. There is no need of more than one going and I want to see the sheriff and have a talk with him."

It was only a few minutes' run across the bay to the little town, and Charley was soon tying up to the fish dock. He hurried up to the fish house and notified Mr. Daniels of his catch and waited while a wagon brought the fish up and they were weighed. The catch totaled thirty dollars in cash.

" Not bad for the first night," said Mr. Daniels, encouragingly. " Several of my old experienced fishermen caught less than that last night."

Leaving the fish house the lad hurried over to the store and ordered some supplies he needed sent down to the launch. By the time his purchases were made he judged it was late enough to find the sheriff in his office and there he accordingly made his way.

But here he met with much disappointment, for he was informed that Sheriff Brown was out of town and would not return for several days.

He headed back to his launch greatly troubled in his mind. He had counted strongly on the sheriff taking charge of the cached liquor. As long as it remained on the island, just so long could they expect trouble from its owners. Now he could not decide what was best to do. He was hurrying on debating the question with himself when turning a corner, engrossed in his own thoughts, he almost collided with Bill Roberts hurrying in the opposite direction.

" Starboard your helm a bit and take in some of that press of sail you're carrying," hailed that worthy, " you came mighty near running me down. How's everything? How's fishing coming on? "

Charley warmed to the sight of Bill's friendly, frank, good-humored face.

" The fishing's all right," he answered, brightly, " but some other things are worrying me. I was thinking of them and not noticing where I was going."

" You look tired and worried," said Bill with a critical scrutiny. " Can we Roberts help you out any with what's worrying you? "

" You might help me out with some advice," said the lad with a sudden impulse. " If you can spare me a few minutes' time I'll tell you what's the matter.

" Got all the time in the world," said Bill cheerfully. " We are not fishing for a few days. Our nets are about all worn out and we are waiting for new ones from the factory. There is a seat over there under the tree, come on and sit down a while and tell me all about it. It helps a man sometimes just to tell his troubles."

He listened with eager interest while Charlie told the story of the strange schooner, the motor boat and the buried liquor and of their quarrel with Hunter's gang.

He pondered a while after the lad had concluded. " Kind of a bad mess," he said at last. " Of course it's the Hunter gang that's doing the smuggling, but you haven't got anything to prove it. They ain't going to lose all that liquor they've got buried either, but they ain't going to dig it up as long as there is a chance of their being seen doing it, consequently their only hope is to get you fellows off the island by fair means or foul."

" Just the conclusion I arrived at," agreed Charley, grimly.

" Your plan to have the sheriff take charge of it was the thing, but of course that cannot be done until he comes back. It isn't likely they will seek an open fight with you, they are too foxy for that. But they will try to get at you by every underhanded means they can think of. You'll have to be on your guard every minute until the sheriff returns and takes charge of that liquor. Those fellows are cunning and treacherous. I am not going to tell you of the things they have done to other fellows who have crossed them. It would do no good and only worry you more. I just want to impress upon you that you cannot watch out too sharp. Now I am going to lend you another rifle to keep in the launch; we have plenty of guns, for we hunt and trap when the fishing is poor. As I have said we are not fishing for a few days, and if you should need help any time just fire three shots close together and we will be over in a hurry. We would be tickled to death to catch those fellows in some devilment so that they could be sent up for a good string of years."

"You are very good," said Charley, gratefully. "It's not right to bother you with our troubles, but it has been a great relief just to unburden myself to you."

"Sorry I cannot be of more help to you," Bill replied, heartily. "I hope we are going to be good friends, for I like the looks of your crowd. Our trouble with Hunter's gang has kept us from making friends amongst the other fishermen. They will not meet us half way for fear of the injuries the Hunter gang might do them, if they got friendly with us. You will find it the same way in your case, and it will be pleasant for us to visit back and forth on stormy days when we have nothing else to do. There is another thing I can do that will help you a bit. Come on down to the dock with me and I'll do it now."

Near the end of the pier they came upon Hunter himself, holding forth to a gang of his cronies.

The fellows made to move away at their approach but Roberts hailed him.

"Look here, Hunter," he said in his straightforward way, "I want to impress one thing on you so you will not forget it. This lad and his companions are friends of ours and anyone that does any of them harm, has not only them to reckon with but with the Roberts boys also, remember that!" Then turning his back to the scowling fisherman, he said good-by to Charley and walked away, indifferent to the lowering glances of Hunter's cronies.

"Fine protector you've got," sneered Hunter, when Roberts was out of hearing. "Just mark one thing, young fellow, your gang are going to wish they had never seen Clearwater before we are through with them, and that goes for that upstart Roberts, too."

"We are not afraid of you or your threats," Charley replied, coolly, as he cast off the launch and started up the engine.

As the throbbing little engine drove the launch through the dancing, sparkling water, Charley lay back in the thwart with his hand on the wheel and rested his aching body. He was tired in muscle and brain. It was nearly noon and his eyes were heavy with sleep. He dozed off for a moment only to wake up with a jerk as something cold touched his foot. He glanced down and was startled to see that several inches of water was sloshing around his feet. Thoroughly awake, he straightened up and looked around. He was in the middle of the bay about a mile from either shore. He had evidently dozed but a few minutes, yet the launch had been dry when he dozed off and now there was several inches of water in her and it was rapidly increasing. She must have sprung a leak and a big one at that. Seizing the bailer with his free hand he began throwing the water out in a steady stream. Swiftly he calculated his chances of making the shore. The engine rested only a few inches above the bottom of the boat. If the water reached it the motor would stop. He had no fear for his own safety for he could easily swim across the bay if necessary. But if the launch filled she would sink, their career as fishermen would be at an end, and Mr. Daniels would be poorer the several hundred dollars the launch had cost.

A few minutes' bailing convinced him that the water was rapidly gaining. It had risen to within a couple of inches of the engine. Five minutes more and it would reach the motor. It was a desperate situation and the keen-witted lad took a desperate chance. Letting go the wheel he frantically tore at the thin sheathing that lined the bottom. Luck was with him for the first piece came up easily revealing a large, smooth, round hole, just below the water line, through which the water was gushing in a steady stream. Tearing up his shirt,

he rolled it up into a tapering plug and thrust it
into the hole.   Holding it in place with one hand,
he steered for the dock with the other.   The water
still came in around the plug, but slowly; and with
a sigh of relief, the lad at last ran the launch upon
the beach beside the dock just as the water rippled
up around the engine's base.   As she grounded, the
launch heeled over on the other side lifting the hole
above the water, and Charley had a chance to examine it more closely.   Its smooth, regular appearance and some chips adhering to the edge showed
that it had been made by an augur, and a ball of
waste floating around on the water showed that it
had been plugged to stay closed until the pressure
of swift moving through the water should force it
out.   There was no doubt in the lad's mind as to
who had made it and he began to feel a certain respect for the resourcefulness of his enemies.   It
was a cunning scheme.   If it had succeeded it
would have accomplished its purpose.   With no
launch, he and his chums would have been forced
to leave the island; for without one they could no
longer have carried on their fishing.

Charley whittled out a smooth plug of soft white
pine and drove it firmly into the hole.   He cut off
the plug flush with the planking, and flattening out
a piece of tin from a can, nailed it over the spot to
hold the plug firmly in place.

Chris brought dinner down to him and he

snatched a few mouthfuls and drank two cups of coffee while he worked.

By the time the job was finished and the launch bailed out, it was well along in the afternoon and the lad groaned as he realized that he must face another hard night's work without sleep.

"Massa Chas," said Chris, as they trudged up to the shack together, "I ain't bothered you-alls 'bout it before 'cause I seed you was all tired an' wore out, but I'ze dun got something to tell you."

Charley glanced sharply at the little negro's serious face.

"What is it?" he said, quietly.

"Massa Chas," said the little fellow, solemnly, "sho' as I is a living nigger, I seed dat ghost last night."

CHAPTER XIII.

CHRIS' STORY.

THE little darkey's face was so serious that Charley could not doubt that he had seen, or imagined he had seen, something out of the common. He was so long familiar with Chris' superstitious fears that, ordinarily, he would have scoffed at them, but now, he remembered the shooting the previous day and the mystery surrounding the disappearance of the unseen marksman.

"Tell me just what you saw, Chris," he said, quietly.

.."Hit was soon arter sundown," began the little negro. "I had dun got de dishes washed up an' was fixin' to go to bed when I 'lowed that a little swim in de gulf would make me sleep a sight better. So I starts down for de beach. I ain't more den thirty feet away when I seed hit atween me an' de water. Hit was walking back an' forth, back an' forth, wid hits face turned all de time to de water. Hit was white, all white, Massa Chas."

"What did you do?" questioned Charley, as the little negro paused, shivering at the recollection.

"I don't know 'zackly, but I reckon I let out a yell an' shut my eyes to hide out dat awful sight. Den I remembers dat charm an' I grabs for hit, saying some conjurer words daddy taught me. Dat sho's am a powerful charm, Massa Chas. Hit sho' am powerful."

"Go on," said Charley, impatiently.

"Dat charm sho' did de work, for when I opened my eyes dat ghost was gone. Jes' dun melted into de air. Soon as my laigs quit shakin' so dat I could walk I makes for de cabin an' bars up de door an' windows tight. Dat's all I guess 'sept dat hit was a powerful long time afore I could get to sleep an' I keeps awishin' for you-alls."

"How long did you keep your eyes closed?" Charley questioned.

"Hit seemed like a year but I reckon hit wasn't no more dan a minute."

Charley arose, wearily. "Show me the spot where you saw it," he directed.

The little negro lad led the way without hesitation. When about twenty feet from the water's edge, he stopped. "Hit was right hyar," he declared.

Charley bent down and examined the sand carefully. A glance assured him that Chris' story had some basis in facts for numerous footprints were impressed upon the firm, white sand. He studied them with eager interest. They were not fisher-

men's tracks, or those of his companions, for the
fishermen all wore big, heavy boots, and he and his
chums were shod in rough, broad-toed, working
shoes, while the tracks indicated a small shoe—
possibly a number seven—and their shape suggested
expensive footwear.

" If I were a story book detective, Chris, I could
tell from these tracks the age, size, and color of the
one who wore them; his height, the color of his
hair, and what he ate for breakfast; but, as I am
only a common, every-day mortal, all I can make
out of them is that your ghost was a man, and a
pretty heavy one, too, judging from the way his
feet sank into this hard sand; see, our shoes hardly
make an impression.   If his clothes matched his
shoes, he must have been well dressed.   I should
say that he wasn't very old either for here is where
he jumped at least five feet.   That must have been
when you worked your charm or rabbit's foot on
him."

" I say hit was a ghost," persisted Chris, stub-
bornly.   " Hit was white, all white, an' hit vanished jes' like that."

" And here's where it vanished," said Charley,
following a line of the footprints to where they
led up into the fringe of palms.   " He might as
well have vanished, though, for we cannot track
him in this hard ground; so we may as well go
back to the cabin.   Hereafter, Chris, just as soon

as it comes dark, go into the cabin and bar the door
and nothing will hurt you. The charm will guard
you from any 'stray ghosts and the bars and rifle
will keep anything else out."

" Dat's all right, Massa Chas," said the little
negro, bravely. " I ain't scared much ob de ghost
now, I'ze seed how dat charm works. An' golly!
I reckon dat ghost is de only thing dis nigger ever
was scared of."

Vain as was this boast, Charley knew it was
true. He had seen the plucky little negro in many
dangers and had never known him to show a sign
of fear except at the unknown which excited all
the superstitious fears of his race.

It still lacked an hour to time to go fishing and
Charley lay down on his couch but he could not
sleep. He lay quiet, puzzling over Chris' experience. Coupled with the mysterious shots of the
day before, it made a problem that defied all his attempts at solution. " Who could the unseen one
be? Certainly not one of the fishermen, the tracks
proved that. Chris' oft-repeated declaration that
the ghost was all in white suggested that it might
be a tourist. Tourists often dressed in white duck
or linen in the tropics, while thinner-blooded natives
always wore warmer clothing at this season of the
year. But what would any tourist want on the island, and above all, why remain hidden. After
all, the mysterious one was friendly to them so why

worry about the matter? But was he friendly? Might not those mysterious shots have been aimed at them as well as the fishermen?" And then a startling thought occurred to the lad. "Might not it be an escaped lunatic?" That would explain the queer actions for which he could find no other logical reason. The thought was most distasteful. A lunatic at large on the island, and armed with a deadly weapon was more to be feared than all the hostile fishermen. With an effort, Charley shook off his gloomy speculations and rising, proceeded to don his fishing clothes. He was dead tired and would gladly have staid in this night but he felt that he must not hold back. They must fish every night while the weather was fine and they could get out. There would be stormy nights when they could not get out and they must work their best to make up for their lack of experience.

.. When he was fully dressed, he aroused his companions. They were still stiff and sore from the unaccustomed labor and their hands were swollen and painful from the many pricks they had received, but their long sleep had refreshed them and they attacked with ravenous appetites the hearty supper Chris had cooked.

"I am going in the opposite direction to-night," Charley announced, as they took their places in the launch and started out. "I got a wireless message to-day telling me that there is a big bunch of fish to the north of us. It's a fact," he replied, in answer to his companion's questioning looks. " All day there has been a big flock of pelicans hovering over the water in that direction. They often follow up large bunches of fish to pick up the ones wounded by sharks."

They had run but a little way when he gave the order to cast anchor. " I think we have gone far enough," he said. " It is easier to find a big school at night than in the day time and I do not wish to run by them in the launch. Somehow, I've got a hunch that we are going to strike a big bunch, from the space those pelicans were spread out over the water."

His suppressed excitement communicated itself to his companions and they fidgeted about, impatient for dark to come.

It came at last and they lost no time in getting away from the launch.

For perhaps a mile they rowed on in silence, then Charley ceased rowing and thrust an oar down deep into the water. He viewed the result with dissatisfaction. "For some reason the water does not fire to-night," he announced. " It happens that way very often. I am sorry for we'll have to fish by sound, and that is much more difficult. Now whenever I stop rowing both of you stop also. That will give me a better chance to listen."

Resuming his oars, he continued his cautious advance, pausing every little while and straining his ears for the faintest sound from the water.

At last, he stopped suddenly. His quick ear had caught the sound for which he had been waiting.

" Listen! " he cried, excitedly.

From far ahead came a faint rippling murmur frequently broken by soft pats upon the water.

" That's the school," he declared, eagerly. " It's a big one and they are working this way. All we have to do is to hold our boats in position and wait. They are coming straight for us."

" If those are mullet, they don't sound as though they amounted to much," said Captain Westfield, doubtfully. " I've heard mullet jump when they made a splash like you'd thrown an anchor overboard."

" Mullet working that fashion, you never want to run," Charley explained. " Fishermen have a saying: ' Never fish jumping mullet.' When mullet are schooled up they do not jump high because of injuring others in their fall. That patting sound you hear is the flipping of their tails above water."

Keyed up to the highest pitch our three fishermen waited the coming of the steadily advancing multitude.

" Pass me the end of your net, Captain," Charley at last directed, in a voice that trembled with excitement.

All ready with oars dipped he waited, waited until even in the darkness Walter could see the advancing school coming, bearing a tiny wave before them. Nearer crept the wave, fifty feet, thirty feet, twenty feet, then—"Go!" Charley shouted, and the boats, driven by the strength of excitement, leaped in amongst the frightened school. Around them the water boiled and foamed with the frightened fish. They struck the sides of the skiffs like hailstones on a tin roof. They battered against the dipped oars making them vibrate like an electric current.

Charley held on his course as long as he dared before giving the signal to close up. When they came together, the end of his net barely crossed over Walter's.

"I came near losing them all by being too greedy," he panted. "A few feet more and my net would not have reached you and they would have poured out of the gap like quicksilver. Well, I guess we've got enough for our breakfast, all right."

"How many do you think we've got?" Walter questioned, eagerly.

"Wait and see," Charley laughed. "Come on and let's get drummed up good and start picking up as quick as we can. I fancy we've got plenty of work ahead of us."

The drumming finished, they rowed back to the ends of their nets. Walter leaned over and dragged his aboard, then gave a shout of delight. "They are sticking in it like pins in a pin cushion," he shouted.

"Same here," agreed Charley, happily, "and I guess, the captain is in the same fix."

In a few minutes their boats had drifted apart and put a bar to further conversation, but Walter grinned as there floated over the water Charley's voice singing all the songs he knew, and the captain's whistle going over and over the one and only tune he knew, "The Sailor's Hornpipe." Evidently things were coming well with them.

For himself, he labored steadily and happily on for every yard of net pulled aboard yielded up at least a dozen silvery captives. Time flew with flying footsteps and when, at last, he straightened up to get a drink of water from his jug, he was surprised to see a gray light stealing over the waters. Day was breaking and the night had passed away. He could see Charley and the captain, plainly. Charley's net was all aboard and he was helping the old sailor with his. Both their skiffs lay dangerously low in the water. He glanced down at his own boat. Her gunwales were nearly level with the water under the weight of the fish in her, and he had still a hundred yards of net to pick up.

CHAPTER XIV.

A CUNNING TRICK.

WALTER had still some seventy-five yards of his net in the water, when Charley, having finished with the captain, ran the launch down alongside of him. "Throw part of your fish in here and then just pull the rest of your net aboard," he directed. "Don't stop to pick out the fish. I'll do that on the way home. We've got to hustle and get those fish over to Clearwater. It is getting late and it will only take a short time longer to spoil them. Some have been out of water nearly all night."

He and Walter changed places, and while Charley picked out the fish with nimble, skilful fingers, his chum started up the engine and headed the launch back for camp. The sun was well up when they reached it, and pausing only to empty the fish from the skiffs into the launch, the launch was headed across for Clearwater, leaving behind the three skiffs, and the captain to help Chris pull out the nets.

"I wish I could let you stay behind and rest up," Charley told his chum, "but I have to have some-one to stay in the launch while I go up to the fish house," and he told his experience of the day before which up to now he had not had the opportunity to relate. Walter was indignant over the underhanded trick and was frankly puzzled by the account of Chris' ghost.

"It is certainly queer how we fall into difficulties in everything we undertake," he said. "Now, we have only been here a few days and already we are involved in a smuggling case, have had trouble with a gang of fishermen, and are tangled up in a ghost mystery. It does beat all how we always seem to get into trouble."

"We have always been lucky in getting out of it," Charley reminded him.

"Yes, but you know the old saying that 'the pitcher that goes often to the well is sure to get broken.'"

"But the pitcher that does not go, gets no water," grinned Charley. "The facts are that we all want to be making big money in a short time and the big money lies in dangerous and unusual pursuits. If we stuck to the slow, well-beaten pursuits, we would have no more troubles than anyone else, I dare say."

"Well, I am beginning to get wearied with too many adventures," Walter confessed. "If we pull out of this fishing business with a good sum to our credit, I'm going to hunt for some quiet pursuit like raising chickens or tending sheep."

" We've got two months of the fishing season yet," remarked his chum, thoughtfully, " then comes the closed season when the law does not permit anyone to fish. Well, if we have good luck, we may make a fair bit in two months. Of course, we cannot expect many catches like last night's but we ought to make something right along if we work hard."

Further conversation was ended by their arrival at the dock. Several fishermen were lounging on the pier and they crawled to the edge looking down with envious eyes at the launch's load. Among them, Charley noted Hunter's sallow, sneering face. He paused only to make the launch fast then hurried up for the fish house.

Walter lay back on a seat and rested while he waited the arrival of the wagons. The fishermen, after a few idle questions as to where the catch had been made, and which way the fish had been working, gradually drifted away to their various duties, most of them heading for shore to work upon their nets and boats, but Hunter and a couple of companions disappeared in one of the shanties on the other side of the dock. " So that's where the rat lives," Walter reflected. " He would have a good chance to take a pot shot at me from there if he dared but he wouldn't try anything so raw as that. I don't believe he would take such a risk in broad daylight with so many around." The lad's meditations were interrupted by the arrival of the first wagon from the fish house. He helped to load it and as soon as it was gone settled back to his resting. As he lay back with every muscle gratefully relaxed, his quick ear caught a peculiar sound. On his guard from Charley's experience of the day before, he raised up and looked carefully around. The sound was easy to locate. It came from the shanty Hunter had entered. He could see something dripping down in large drops from the slat-like floor. "They have got a leaky water pail or something of the kind," he guessed, then, as a peculiar smell was wafted to his nostrils, he lay back again with a grin. "Their gasoline can has sprung a leak," he decided. "The gas is all running out. If it was anyone else but Hunter, I'd call and tell him about it, but as it is his, it can all leak away for all I care," and he lay back and listened with a certain satisfaction to the steady drip of the escaping fluid.

Half dozing he heard footsteps in the shack and a moment later the scratch of a match. The next instant he was on his feet, his heart beating wildly. It had happened like a flash of lightning. All around the launch the water was aflame. Fool that he had been. He had been caught by a trick simple but cunning. That film of oil on the water had only needed a dropped match to set it aflame.

For a moment he stood helpless, bewildered by

the sudden catastrophe. The oil had drifted all around the launch and she was in the center of a sheet of flame. Already he could smell the blistering paint on her hull, and the heat smote him in the face like a fiery blast.

Only for a moment he stood thus paralyzed. Then his wits, accustomed to work quickly in emergencies, swept back. With a leap, he gained the bow and with his sheath-knife severed the rope which held the launch to the dock. Springing back to the engine, he shoved on the switch and flung the fly wheel over. Instantly the motor began to throb and the threatened launch backed slowly out of the sheet of flame. Safe outside the danger zone, Walter shut off the engine and with his cap beat out the patches of flame that clung to the launch's sides. Then he leaned over and grimly inspected his craft. Ten minutes before she had been a dainty thing in her coat of white, now she looked like an ancient wreck with her scorched and smoke-grimed sides on which the melted paint hung in ugly, dropsical blisters. The worst of it was there was no redress for the damages done her. So cunning was the scheme that it bore all the semblance of an accident, though the wrathful lad knew it was anything but that. He could imagine scoundrels chuckling to themselves in the closed shack and his blood boiled in his veins. How we would like to repay them for the fright and damage.

He sat down for a moment and strove to gain control of his temper for he realized that an outburst on his part would do no good and might make more trouble.   As soon as he calmed down a bit, he started up the engine and worked the launch back to the dock.

A wagon was waiting and its driver looked down in amazement at the sadly-altered launch.   " What happened to you? " he questioned.

" Some gasoline and a match," Walter replied, carelessly.   " No damage done beyond some scorched paint.   Please report it to Mr. Daniels and tell him we will repaint her as soon as there comes a spell of bad weather when we cannot fish."

The driver departed with his load satisfied with the explanation for accidents were common amongst the fishing fleet.

In half an hour longer the last of the fish had been carted away and Charley came hustling down with a beaming face, which fell as he caught sight of the launch.   He asked no questions, however, but jumped aboard and shoved off.   Once under way Walter enlightened him.

" Those fellows are clever in their meanness," said Charley, with grudging admiration.   " One would not think from Hunter's looks that he had much brains.   We have certainly got to be on our guard every minute.   That's twice in two days he has nearly put us out of business without exposing himself."

" I wish we could get even with him," declared Walter, wrathfully.

Charley grinned. " In a way we are even with him already. There must be five hundred dollars' worth of liquor in that cache and he dare not touch a bottle of it as long as we are on the island. Seriously though, I would give a good deal to catch him in such a way that we could have the law on him. Until we do, we will have to be watchful and avoid open trouble. He is pretty sure to make a slip sooner or later. The cleverest of rascals do, and then will be our chance if he does not get us first. I am beginning to understand why the rest of the fishermen stand in such fear of incurring his enmity. There is the captain and Chris waiting for us on the dock. I wonder what's the matter. They ought to have been through their work and the captain asleep long ago."

By this time, they had drawn near to the little pier and could plainly see the little negro and the old sailor pacing about in evident excitement. In a few more minutes, the launch glided in alongside the dock and the cause of the excitement became apparent. The two were standing by a heap of broken splintered planks that had once been their extra skiff.

" What does this mean? " demanded Charley, in deepest discouragement.

" I dunno, Massa Chas," replied the grieved little negro, " but I s'pect hit's some ob dat white trash's doings. Late last night I hears a boat acoming. First off I thought hit was you-alls, but pretty soon I 'lowed it wasn't 'cause de engine didn't sound like yourn. Hit stopped at de dock an' I gets to a crack an' peeps out. Pretty soon hyar comes four fellows astealing up de path. I up an' hails 'em an' dey stops short. I guess dey had reckoned dat dar was no one hyar 'cause ob de launch being gone. I shoots off de rifle an' dey took to der heels. Pretty soon I hears a breaking noise down by de dock an' den de put-put ob der boat, as dey puts off. An' dis mornin' I finds de skiff jes' disaway."

" And that ain't all," broke in Captain Westfield, pointing over to where their extra net lay on its rack of poles.

The boys gave a gasp of dismay. The new unused net was a mass of hanging strips. It had been literally cut and hacked to pieces.

" This sort of thing has got to stop," declared Charley, white with rage. " Our catch last night came to a hundred and fifty dollars but it will cost forty-five dollars to replace that skiff, fifty dollars to replace that net, and at least twenty dollars to repair the launch, and all that damage has been

done in a few hours.   Goodness knows what they
will do to us next.   Things cannot go on this way
any longer."

His companions looked at him questioningly but
he shook his head disparagingly.   "I haven't a
ghost of an idea what to do," he admitted, gloomily.
"Maybe a little sleep will clear my head and bring
some plan.   I'm going up and turn in."

He staggered drunkenly as he made his way up
to the cabin.   He was utterly exhausted, nerve and
body.   Once inside, he flung himself upon his
couch and was instantly asleep.

Chris tried to arouse him for dinner but it was
like trying to awaken one, dead.   Nature was
claiming her due.

CHAPTER XV.

THE MYSTERY DEEPENS.

IT was late in the afternoon when Charley at last awoke. The death-like sleep had done him a world of good and, except for stiffness and muscles that still ached, he felt his old self again.

His companions were both up, moving about and he greeted them brightly.

"I am feeling as fit as a fiddle," he declared. "As soon as I get a bite to eat I'll be ready for another night's fishing."

"To-night is Saturday night," observed Captain Westfield, hesitatingly. "I don't want to stand in the way of making money, but I 'low it won't do no hurt for us to lay in to-night. We might get into a school that would keep us working all night, like last night, and it's noways right to work on the Lord's day."

"That's right," agreed Charley, heartily, "I had lost track of the days. We will not go out again until midnight, Sunday night. I don't believe anyone ever really lost anything by obeying the Lord's command to keep his day holy."

"Have you figured out any plan for dealing with the fishermen?" Walter inquired, anxiously.

"Nothing very brilliant," his chum admitted. "One thing I think we had better do at once is to remove all that liquor to another hiding place and let them think we have destroyed it. It may make them feel more bitter toward us but they will no longer have a motive for driving us from the island. I would like to destroy it entirely but we have no right to do that. That is the sheriff's business. One thing, there is nothing like a good sleep to do away with worry and discouragement. I feel quite hopeful, now, but I was almost ready to quit this morning. After all I guess Hunter has done us about all the damage he can. Our other nets and boats we will always have with us and he will not have much chance to injure them if we keep watch of them. With the liquor gone, they will not be likely to bother us on the island, and, if they do, all we have will be in the cabin protected by a good rifle. Let's change the hiding place, now. We have time to do it before dark."

His companions had no better plan to suggest so they readily agreed to his proposal. Taking with them some bits of thin boards for spades they sought the beach and turned into one of the paths that led to the buried liquor.

"This smuggling business must have been going on for a long time judging from the number of these paths and the way they are worn," Charley observed. "Hunter ought to be rich from the enormous profits he makes on the vile stuff. It can be bought for a dollar a gallon in Cuba and on this side, I believe, it retails for five dollars a gallon."

"The man who follows an evil trade, seldom prospers," said Captain Westfield, sagely. "In the end he has to pay for his ill-gotten gains. Generally he has to pay in this life, and he always has to pay in the hereafter."

"I believe you are right," Walter agreed. "I have noticed that saloon-keepers and that class never seem happy. Even those who make money seem to be cursed with drunken children or something equally bad, and if they have a shred of conscience, they must suffer terribly in secret for the misery they cause and the punishment they must expect in the life hereafter."

This conversation had brought them to the cache, and, pulling off their coats, they fell to work with their rude spades.

They worked with a will and sent the loose sand flying for the sun was sinking low and they wished to complete their task before dark. In a few minutes they had made a hole a couple of feet deep, and some ten feet across.

"We ought to be down to it," said Charley,

with a puzzled frown. "It must be covered deeper
than I thought."

They worked on for a few minutes longer, then
Charley threw down the board with which he had
been shoveling. "It has been taken away," he
declared, voicing the conviction which had grown
upon his companions. They got it last night, after
all, Chris."

"I doan see how, Massa Chas,." objected the
little darkey, "I watched dem come up de path an'
I watched dem run away."

"They must have come back after you went to
sleep," Charley said, but Chris shook his head decidedly.

"I doan sleep none arter dat," he persisted. "I
laid awake and watched de balance ob de night."

"Maybe, they had a boat on the gulf beach, also,"
Walter suggested, "and while some of them drew
attention to the dock, the others removed the stuff."

"Well, anyway, it's gone, and I am glad of it,"
Charley said. "Maybe they will not trouble us any
more now. I confess that they were beginning to
get on my nerves. Let's go back to the cabin and
get supper and have a good sleep. Thank goodness we will likely rest one night in peace."

His companions were nothing loath for they had
not yet got entirely over their aches and pains.

The night passed away uneventfully and morning found them entirely their old selves once more.

"We are over the worst part now," Charley assured them. "Of course we will often come in very tired but we will never again feel like we did those first two nights, and the longer we fish the less we will mind the labor."

As soon as breakfast was over, Captain Westfield produced his old, well-worn Bible from which he was never separated and read a couple of chapters of the story of Him he loved with all his big, simple, trusting heart.

The simple service was just over when they heard the throbbing of an engine and they hurried down to the dock just in time to greet the Roberts who had come over in their launch to pay them a friendly call.

It was pleasant to our little party to see friendly faces and hear kindly conversation after all the roughness and suspicion they had met among the unfriendly fishermen. It was good to feel that they were not alone entirely in their new life and that there was someone who took a friendly interest in them and wished them well.

They began to have a strong liking for the three sturdy brothers, they appeared so frank, open and sincere.

Bill had brought over with him the rifle he had mentioned and presented it to them, together with a box of cartridges.

He was deeply interested to learn that the liquor had been removed.

"It is a queer thing," he remarked. "I saw the Hunter gang come in Friday night about midnight. I had got caught over to Clearwater with a loose shaft and I was working on it when their boat came in. I supposed they had been fishing and I glanced into their launch to see what they had caught. It was empty. Of course, they could have hidden a few bottles in the lockers but not any such amount as you say was buried here. They were all mad as the deuce and quarreling amongst themselves. I didn't get the shaft fixed until about two o'clock. Their boat was still at the dock when I left and I could hear them snoring in their shanty. Another thing, I was over again last night to see if our new nets had come and I couldn't help but notice that apparently there was no drinking going on. Saturday night is pay night, and, if Hunter had had that liquor, he would certainly have been handing it out on the quiet and there would have been more or less drunken men about."

"Then who could have taken it, if the fishermen didn't?" demanded Charley, thoroughly puzzled.

"Can't imagine, unless that ghost of Chris' did it," admitted Bill, with a grin. "That was a curious thing to happen, and if I did not know that you fellows are the truthful kind, I would believe you were trying to kid me with that yarn. We have been here some time, and we have never heard of any stranger on this island. Let's take a look over it again and see if there is any cave or other place a man could hang out."

The others readily agreed to his proposal, and all set out together for a closer exploration of the island. They made a thorough search from end to end, and from shore to shore, but could find no place a man could hide out or any trace of human habitation. The shores were sloping sand beaches without rocks or caves and the only growth was the scanty groups of palms.

They returned to the cabin more mystified than ever for they had convinced themselves beyond doubt that they were the only occupants of the island.

" Well, if the fishermen haven't got that liquor, I suppose we must look for more trouble," Charley sighed.

" I expect you may," Bill agreed. " Even if they have got it, I guess, they would not give you a very long rest. As soon as it was gone, they would want to bring in more and this is the only island around with a good gulf beach to land the stuff on. Also it's the handiest and most convenient for their purposes."

" Then it's a case of move or be in trouble all the time," said Walter, dubiously.

" Yes, that's about it," Bill agreed.

" We can't leave yet," said Charley, decidedly, " so we will have to take whatever is coming to us. If we could only catch them in the act of smuggling, we could get rid of them for good and be conferring a blessing on the rest of the fishermen besides."

" That's the very thing I've been thinking of," Bill agreed. " Whether they got the liquor again or not, they are sure to try the game again as soon as they think it's safe. I've been doing considerable thinking about it since I talked to you before and I've got a scheme I think might work."

He proceeded to unfold his plan while the others listened with eager interest.

" It might work," said Charley, thoughtfully, " but, while we are waiting, they may do us all kinds of injuries."

" That's a risk you are running, anyway," Bill reminded him, " and we Roberts will do all in our power to help you. Call on us any time, day or night, if you are in trouble and you will find us ready."

Charley thanked him heartily for his offer and soon after the Roberts took their leave.

The little party were still on the dock watching their launch out of sight when they noticed another launch put out from the Clearwater pier, and it soon became apparent that it was headed for their island.

" It's Hunter's craft," announced Walter, as it drew nearer. " Looks as though he had waited for the Roberts to leave to pay us a visit."

As the launch drew nearer they saw it contained but one person and that one Hunter himself.

CHAPTER XVI.

AN ACCIDENT.

HUNTER greeted the little party with a smile intended to be pleasant but which resembled a grimace on his sallow, evil face.

"Good day, and how are all of you this fine day. Well, I hope," he said.

"We are all right," Charley answered, curtly. "What do you want?"

"Which of you is the leader of this pleasant little party. I want a little business talk with the leader," he said, fawningly. "Just a little business talk. It won't take more than five minutes."

"Wall," observed Captain Westfield, "when we are at sea I'm generally the head man, but hyar on shore an' at this fishing business, I reckon Charley thar does the leading."

"And a good leader he is too, I'll bet," said Hunter, flatteringly.

"Oh, cut out all the soft-soap business," said Charley, shortly, disgusted with the fellow's attempts at flattery. "If you have anything to say to us say it."

"But it's a private business," Hunter protested.

"Just let me talk to you alone for a few minutes."

Charley was about to refuse the request but curiosity as to what Hunter wanted to say prevailed. With a wink at his chums he accompanied the fellow to one side, apart from his companions.

"Now, say what you have to say and be quick about it," he said, curtly.

Hunter hesitated a moment. "Suppose there was something on this island that I was interested in," he began.

"There is," said Charley, with a grin, "but if you want to talk to me, talk plainly. I know you buried that aguardiente on the island."

"All right, say I did," agreed Hunter, defiantly, dropping his friendly pose. "I don't mind saying I did to you. You can't make anything out of that. If you said I told you I did, I'd swear I didn't. That's why I wanted to talk to you alone. I wasn't hankering for any witnesses to our talk.

"Might as well wait and hear what I have to say," he continued, doggedly, "because I won't say a word before the others."

Charley had started to join his companions but he paused in indecision, and Hunter went on eagerly.

"Say, I did put the stuff there. Say, I could make a lot of money off it right now. Say, I ain't going to dig it up with witnesses to see and testify agin me. Say, I'd give you fifty dollars to take your party off the island for one single night, one hundred dollars if you quit the island for good. What would you say to that, eh?"

Charley considered for a moment. "Nothing doing," he replied, slowly. "In the first place, you and your gang have done us more than one hundred dollars' damage. No use denying it," he said, hotly, as Hunter protested his innocence. "You were pretty slick with your tricks but we know who has been responsible for our troubles. In the second place, to smuggle in and to sell liquor in a dry county is a felony. If we connived at we would be guilty also. Third, I wouldn't take your word for anything. Lastly, I don't know where the stuff is, anyway."

"You lie!" snarled Hunter, his little black eyes flashing evilly. "You know where it is buried."

Charley grew white around the lips. "Be careful what you say," he cautioned. "If you will just follow me, I'll show you something."

He led the way in silence to where the liquor had been buried.

At sight of the hole and the freshly upturned earth, Hunter grew livid with rage.

"You've stole it, you've stole it," he gasped.

"We have not touched the stuff," Charley denied. "If you fellows didn't remove it, I don't know who did."

"A likely yarn," Hunter sneered. "Nobody knew it was on the island except you and us." He conquered his rage with an effort. "Say," he said, "let's be partners in this. You can't sell the stuff like we can. You don't know the fellows who will buy and keep their mouths shut like we do. I tell you, even we, have to be mighty careful. Why, you'd get arrested before you got it half sold out. Let's be partners; that's fair. There's good money in it. You fellows could tend to the running of it and we could do the selling. We would split the profits up even."

His earnestness convinced the lad that Bill Roberts was right. The fishermen had not got the liquor.

"I have told you the truth, Hunter," he said. "We have not got the stuff and we do not know who has."

."You're holding out on us," Hunter fairly screamed. "You are trying to hog the whole thing. All right, young fellow, what we will do to you will be a plenty. We haven't started on you good, yet. We'll make you regret the day you were born before we are through with you."

"Get off this island," commanded Charley, his patience at an end. "Try all your tricks you want to. We are on the watch for them now. Sometime you'll make a slip and we'll take a turn. Now go!"

Hunter walked down to his boat sullenly, muttering oaths and threats that Charley ignored.

" That fellow is cunning," the lad said, as he related the conversation to his companions. " He admitted everything, but the admission does us no good. He would swear he had said nothing of the kind and the rest of you could not testify for you did not hear his words."

The incident depressed the spirits of all. They had begun to think the persecutions were over and now they threatened to begin afresh.

" Well, there is no help for it," said Charley. " We will have to endure it until we get our plan to working. We will just have to be on our guard day and night until it is settled. Let's turn in now and forget it while we catch a nap. We will need the rest if we are going out at midnight."

They had no watch amongst them but Charley possessed the not uncommon gift of being able to wake at any hour he desired. When he awoke he satisfied himself by a glance at the stars that he was not mistaken in the hour and then aroused his companions.

As the time was short before daylight, they ran but a little way from the dock before anchoring the launch and taking to the boats.

They had hardly got fairly started with the skiffs when Charley called a halt.

"See anything over where you are, Walt?" he called.

"Yes," shouted back his chum, eagerly, "the water is alive with fish of some kind."

"Same here," Charley stated, "but I can't make out just what they are. They are not catfish, and yet, they don't fire just like mullet. Let's try them with just a little piece of our nets and see what they are before we make a big circle."

They had run out but a few yards of net when he gave the signal to close up. "We will not drum up any," he said, as he halted his boat just inside the little circle. "We will get enough in the nets, without, to tell what they are and will not frighten the rest of the school."

A few minutes sufficed to pick up the few yards of net they had out. Charley scanned his puzzledly as it came inboard. It contained no fish but was filled with great gaping holes here and there.

"Not a scale," he announced, disgustedly. "Did you fellows get anything?"

"Nothing but a lot of holes," said Captain Westfield.

"I've got a lot of the queerest looking fish I ever saw," Walter exclaimed. "Row over and take a look at them. One of them bit me. Gee! but it hurts!"

A few strokes of his oars brought Charley alongside and he peeped over into his chum's skiff.

A score of big, eel-like, repulsive-looking creatures squirmed in the bottom.

One glance and Charley, chucking his anchor
aboard Walter's skiff, sprang into it.

"Quick, show me where it bit you!" he cried.

Walter held out a hand in the palm of which a
tiny puncture oozed out occasional drops of blood.

Charley whipped out a cord from his pocket,
bound it loosely around the wrist of the wounded
hand and thrusting an oarlock in the slack twisted
it around until the cord dented into the flesh.
"Now, stick your hand over into the water and
keep it there," he commanded.

Seizing an oar, he gingerly ladled the repulsive-
looking creature out of the skiff.

"Whew! My arm aches clear up to the shoulder!" Walter exclaimed. "What were those
nasty-looking fish, anyway?"

"Monays, a kind of salt water eel," said his
chum, gravely. "I don't want to frighten you,
dear old chum, but those things are poisonous, almost as poisonous as a snake."

Walter received the startling information coolly.
"I suspected they were poisonous as soon as my
arm began to ache," he said, quietly. "Will I lose
my hand do you think?"

"I guess not," lied Charley, cheerfully. He
could not bear to tell him that he was likely to lose
his life as well as his hand.

Calling the captain to follow, the lad rowed the two skiffs to the launch, made them fast, and helped his chum aboard. As soon as the captain fastened on, he started the engine and headed the launch back for the dock. He was thankful that they had not come far from home, for, short as the distance was, before they reached the little pier, Walter's arm had swollen to twice its natural size and he had fallen into a kind of listless stupor. The captain and Charley helped him tenderly out of the launch and supported him up to the cabin where they laid him out on his couch.

Charley looked about in helpless despair. "If I only had some of that aguardiente, now, there would be a good chance to save him," he said, bitterly. "I don't think there was time for much of that poison to get into his circulation before I got the cord around his wrist and shut it off. Well, it isn't much use, but we will make a fight for it. Chris, heat up some water, quick, and make a big pot of coffee, as strong as you can make it."

The little negro flew to do his bidding and, in a few minutes, Charley had the wounded hand plunged in a bucket of scalding hot water and was forcing cup after cup of strong, steaming coffee down his chum's throat.

CHAPTER XVII.

MORE MYSTERIES.

"WE have got to get a doctor just as quick as we can," Charley declared. "I wish you could go, Captain. I would rather be with him and do what little I can for him. I'm afraid he will not last till you can get a doctor over here."

"But I do not know how to run the launch," the old sailor reminded him.

"That is so, I will have to go," agreed the lad. "Well, I guess, you can do as much for him as I could. Keep his hand in hot water all the time and keep forcing the coffee down him every few minutes. I'll be back as quick as I can."

Seizing his hat Charley started for the dock on a run.

In a few minutes he was back, consternation on his face.

Something's broke about the engine," he cried, "I can't start it up and I can't see to fix it in the dark. You'll have to go over in one of the skiffs, Captain. You will make better time than I could for you row better."

The old sailor was out and gone almost before he finished speaking, and in a minute Charley could hear the quick stroke of oars coming from the water.

" Do you think Massa Walt's goin' to die, Massa Chas?" Chris inquired in an awed whisper as they watched the stupefied lad.

" I am afraid so, Chris," Charley said, sadly. " Some of that awful poison has got into his blood. It checks the heart action. That is what I am giving the coffee for. It stimulates the heart and makes it work faster. But it is not powerful enough to overcome the deadening effect of the poison. It needs a powerful heart stimulant to do that. Whiskey would do fairly well. Oh! how I wish I had a couple of bottles of that aguardiente now!"

He lapsed into silence and sat sorrowfully watching his stricken chum, while Chris crouched at his side, deepest grief on his little ebony face.

Suddenly there came a sharp rap at the door, and Charley sprang to his feet.

" It can't be the doctor so quick," he said. " Come in," he called out.

There was no answer to his invitation and stepping to the door he flung it open.

Nothing but blank darkness greeted his searching eyes.

He stepped outside and looked around but the

darkness was so dense he could not see twenty feet from the cabin.

Puzzled, he was turning back into the cabin when his foot came into contact with something on the step. He picked the object up and bore it to the light."

One glance and he gave a shout of joy. " Aguardiente, Chris," he cried. " May the Lord bless whoever put it there."

He seized a cup and pouring it half full of the fiery liquor forced it down his chum's throat.

He allowed a half hour to pass by, then administered another dose.

At times he fancied he could trace a slight return of color in his chum's pale face but, if any, it was so slight that he could not be certain.

At the end of an hour he gave a third stiff dose of the powerful stimulant.

" I wish the captain would get here with the doctor," he said, anxiously. " I can't see as he is improving any. I fancy most that stuff is doing is to help keep him from slipping away from us."

" Dat's de captain, now," Chris said, joyfully, as there came a brisk rap at the door.

It was not the captain but a young, athletic-looking man bearing a small, black, leather case.

" I am the doctor," he announced. " How is the boy? Still alive? "

" Yes, he is still living," said Charley, in relief,

" but I don't think he will last much longer unless you can help him."

" What have you done for him? " the doctor inquired, as he knelt by the stricken lad and felt his pulse.

Charley told him briefly.

" Very good," the doctor commented. " Probably he would have died before now but for those aids. He is pretty far gone but maybe we can pull him around."

He laid off his coat and went to work. From his case he produced a hypodermic syringe and a box of tablets. " Some warm water and a spoon," he requested.

Chris was instantly at his side with the required articles.

He filled the spoon with warm water and dropped one of the tablets into it. It colored the water a beautiful scarlet.

" Permangate of potash," he explained. " You fishermen ought to keep some always by you. It's invaluable in cases of snake-bites or other poisonous wounds."

He filled his syringe from the spoon and baring Walter's arm injected it into a vein.

" I expect your warm water treatment has drawn most of the poison from the wound, but we had better be on the safe side," he observed. •

He partly filled a basin with warm water and

dissolved another of the tablets in it. Then, with his keen, surgeon's lancet, he cut open the flesh around the puncture, washed it out thoroughly with the solution, and then bound it up in soft, white gauze.

"That is all we can do, now, but watch," he observed, when he had finished.

He sat down with Walter's wrist in his hand and waited the effect of the treatment.

"He is responding to the injection nobly," he said at last. "His pulse is getting quicker and his skin is becoming moist. Evidently there is not as much poison in the blood as I feared. Your prompt action has undoubtedly saved his life."

In half an hour he gave another injection and watched the result with satisfaction.

"Your friend is going to come out all right," he declared, cheerily.

A wave of relief swept over Charley. "We can never fully pay you for what you have done," he said, with a lump in his throat. "Money can never square the debt."

"That's all right," said the young doctor, heartily. "It's a matter of more than mere pay to most of us doctors when we are able to save a valuable life. I can do no more for your friend at present, but I'll leave some tablets with you to give him from time to time. I think the danger is over, although he will be a pretty sick boy for a couple of days from the reaction of the liquor and drugs he has taken, as well as from the poison itself, but with good nursing, he will pull through all right."

Counting out some tiny tablets, he gave them to Charley, seized his hat and case, and with a cheery "good night" opened the door and disappeared in the darkness.

He had been gone a full five minutes before Charley recalled that in his anxiety for his chum he had forgotten to ask his name or the amount of his bill.

"Not very polite, but the captain will find that out," he consoled himself. "I wonder why the captain did not come up with him. I suppose the dear old chap could not bear the sight of Walter's lying so death-like. Chris, make up some more good, strong coffee and cook some breakfast. The captain's going to be all worn out when he gets back."

Daylight was near at hand and with it came the old sailor, looking pale, worn and haggard in the morning light.

"Is Walter dead?" he greeted, in a trembling, anxious voice.

Charley laughed in sheer joyousness. "Dead nothing," he exulted. "He's getting better every minute. Why, didn't the doctor tell you that?"

"I couldn't find the doctor," said the old sailor, in relief. "There was none in Clearwater. I got up the telegraph agent and got him to telegraph to Tarpon Springs for one. He'll come on the noon train. It was the best I could do. I waited to hear from the telegram, that's what's kept me so long."

Charley stared at him. "Do you mean that you did not bring over the doctor that was here?"

"Are you crazy or am I?" demanded the old sailor. "What do you mean?"

"There was a doctor came about an hour after you left," said Charley, slowly. "He staid at least two hours. He gave Walter medicine which has pulled him through. He only left about an hour ago."

It was the captain's turn to stare. "I'll be jiggered," he said in awe, "and I saw no motor boat going or coming. Who was he, and how in the world did he know we needed him?"

Charley shook his head. "I'll give it up," he said. "However, he'll be back again and will solve the mystery."

But the doctor did not reappear. However, the noon train brought a physician from Tarpon Springs. Charley, who, by daylight, had easily found and repaired the engine break, went over in the launch and got him.

The new doctor was visibly annoyed when he examined Walter. "I do not understand why I was called on this case," he said, shortly. "The boy is out of all danger. He has had skilful treatment, most skilful treatment. I would not have come had I known there was already a doctor in charge."

Charley explained the circumstances.

"Your description fits, perfectly, Doctor Thompson of Tarpon Springs," the new doctor observed. "Did he have a finger missing on the left hand?"

"He did, the second finger," said Charley, recalling the circumstance.

The doctor studied the lad's face closely, started to speak, but checked himself.

He was silent during all the trip back to Clearwater but after he got out of the launch he turned and faced Charley.

"Young man," he said, coldly, "I do not know what your object was in telling me that string of lies, but I want to impress upon you that you have not deceived me."

Charley stared at him in hurt astonishment.

"Doctor Thompson dined with me last night," said the physician, icily. "We sat together after and talked in my study until one o'clock. At two o'clock, you say, he was at your camp, an impossible thing for Tarpon Springs is twenty miles away."

With a curt nod he turned and strode up the dock leaving behind him an offended, astonished, mystified boy.

CHAPTER XVIII.

MORE MISCHIEF.

'ALL the way back to the island, Charley pondered over the mystifying occurrence.

"I don't understand it, I don't understand it at all," he said to Captain Westfield whom he found sitting beside Walter who was still sleeping soundly. "There is some mystery about this island that puzzles me. If this sort of thing goes on I'll be converted to Chris' belief in spirits. One unexplainable thing after another happening so frequently is enough to make one lose his wits."

"I wouldn't worry my head about it," said the old sailor, placidly. "The mysterious happenings have all been for our own good. Take this last one. Walter would surely have died but for that liquor and the doctor. I don't fear the kind of people or spirits that do that kind of thing. It's the mean, sly tricks of those fishermen that's bothering me. I cannot help but worry as to what they will do next. Just how do we stand now, do you calculate, lad?"

Charley figured rapidly. "Our two nights' fishing makes one hundred and eighty dollars coming to us. I guess our grocery bills amount to about thirty dollars, it will cost forty-five dollars to replace the skiff, that ruined net means fifty dollars more, and repainting the launch will cost twenty dollars more. Our other three nets are as good as new. That brings our total expenses up to one hundred and forty dollars, leaving a balance of forty dollars to our credit."

"I wish it were a little more," said the captain, wistfully. "If it was twenty dollars apiece, I would vote right now for giving up this fishing business. I've got a feeling that those fishermen are going to do us bad yet. They have pretty near succeeded a couple of times already. Next time we may not be lucky enough to escape. Bill Roberts' scheme might work all right, but it will take time and there's no telling what they may do to us while we are waiting."

"I hate to give up," Charley replied, "but I guess it is the wisest thing to do; so far, they have only injured our property, but there is no telling how soon they will do some one of us bodily injury, they are getting desperate. This accident to Walt has made me see things in a different light. I would never forgive myself if one of you should be badly injured by those scoundrels as a result of my being stubborn and refusing to quit. If it were only myself it would be different, but, I do not want to drag the rest of you into the trouble.

Walt's close shave has taken all the fighting spirit out of me. I agree with you that we had better quit. But we cannot strike out again with only forty dollars between us. It will be several days anyway before Walt is able to travel and we might as well put in as much of the time as we can fishing. We can notify those fishermen that we are going to leave soon and perhaps they will let up on their persecutions."

" Where had we better go from here? " speculated the old sailor.

" Back to the East Coast, I guess," answered Charley, wearily. " It's pineapple season and we will be able to get work in the plantations, I guess. They only pay a dollar and a half per day and the work is very hard. But this is the dull season in Florida now and we can't do better. I don't know as it much matters what we do," he concluded, bitterly. " We seem doomed to fail in all our undertakings."

" Get that idea out of your head, lad," said the old sailor, gently. " If one lacks confidence, he will never succeed. You are tired out and your nerves are all unstrung from worry and loss of sleep. Go take a walk on the beach and a dip in the surf then come back and catch a nap and things will look brighter."

His eyes followed Charley's departing form with pitying fondness.

" Poor lad," he sighed, " he hates to give up, and he is thoroughly discouraged. It isn't often he gets that way though the good Lord knows he has but little to keep him bright and cheerful. No father, no mother, and his whole young life a constant battle against hardships and disappointments."

When Charley returned his gloominess had vanquished. " Nothing like good salt air and a long swim to get the best of the blues, Captain," he announced, cheerfully. " I feel fit to do battle with the world again now. How's the boy coming on ? "

" Fine," the captain declared. " I'm expecting him to wake up hungry."

" I'll be fixed for him, sho'," declared Chris, eagerly. " Dis has been de longest day for dis nigger, he jus' seemed to be in the way an' ob no account, so he's jus' been fixing up to feed you-all, dat does all de work, jus' de best he kin. Golly I got a supper dat will satisfy Massa Walt all right. I got fresh fish fried nice and brown, big fat oysters from off de rocks roasted in dere own juice, scallops chopped up fine and made inter meat balls, nice fresh corn bread an' plenty of coffee."

" It would kill Walt to eat all that," laughed Charley. " Make up a little oyster soup and we will give him that when he wakes up. Your feast will not be wasted," he said hastily, as he saw the little negro's look of disappointment. " You want to remember that the captain and I haven't eaten since yesterday."

"Dat's so," agreed Chris, brightening. "Hit's all ready when you is."

He had little cause for complaint for when the two had finished there was little but crumbs left of the delicious meal.

"Now I am ready to sleep," Charley announced, with a sigh of content.

Walt was resting so easily that both Charley and the captain stretched out on their couches leaving Chris to watch and to call one of them to take his place when he became sleepy.

The captain relaxed his tired muscles with a sigh of relief.

"There's one thing that's been puzzling me a little, Charley," he observed, as he settled into a comfortable position. "How did it happen that Walt caught all those critters while you and I got nothing but holes."

"I hadn't thought of that," admitted Charley, thoughtfully. "It is kind of queer; something jumped up, fish all bore down on one net, but, while that would account for Walt getting them all in his net, it does not explain all the holes in ours."

It was a trifling circumstance but he puzzled over it a long time after his companion had fallen asleep.

The sun was shining brightly when the two awoke for Chris, with unselfish kindness, had watched the night through rather than disturb them.

They found Walter awake and greatly improved, the swelling in his arm and hand was subsiding rapidly. He was very weak and was shaky from the effects of the drugs and liquor but that would soon wear off.

They were hardly dressed when the Roberts arrived in their launch. They had heard of Walter's accident in Clearwater and had come over to inquire after him and offer any assistance they could give.

" Too bad," said Bill, regretfully, when the captain told him of their newly-formed resolve to leave the Island. " We Roberts are sorry to lose you folks. I wish you could stick it out, but, of course, you know your own business best. We will not only miss you but we hate to see that Hunter gang win another underhand victory. With you gone they will take up their old trade of smuggling in booze and making beasts of their fellow fishermen."

" It is too bad," the old sailor agreed, " but it is best for us to go before they do us any more harm. We have more coming to us than we owe now, but if they got to us with many more of their tricks, we would be behind with the fish house and then of course we could not go."

" Well," Bill Roberts offered, as they were leaving, " if you are going out fishing to-night I'll come over and stay with the boy."

Our friends accepted his offer gratefully, for they had been loath to think of leaving their chum alone with Chris, only. It was true he was doing finely but there might come a change for the worse and the little negro would be helpless to get word to them.

True to his promise, Bill appeared before sundown and they were free for another hunt for the finny prizes.

They were not long in coming upon a promising-looking school of fish which Charley decided to run.

Walter's absence made a slight difference in the mode of making the circle, but they got around most of the bunch in good shape.

" I believe we are going to make a good haul," Charley declared, with satisfaction, as they rested after drumming up. " There's a lot of fish in the circle and they seem to be hitting the net good."

But his hopes gave way to dismay as he pulled in yard after yard of his net without getting a fish. Instead the net seemed riddled with a multitude of holes.

" Get anything, Captain," he paused to shout.

" Nothing but holes," said the old sailor, disgustedly. " Got a hundred of them."

" Queer," Charley muttered. He gathered up

some of the loose webbing in either hand and pulled gently. The tested part broke as easily as a spider's web. Every few yards for the entire length of the net he repeated the operation. The result was always the same. He finished picking up and, sitting down, waited dejectedly for the old sailor.

"We might as well go home," he said wearily, as the captain pulled alongside. "My net is rotten from end to end. It would not hold a minnow.".

"Mine is in the same fix," his companion agreed, sadly. "Now, we are in a bad fix. One hundred dollars' worth more nets to be charged up against us, and nothing to fish with."

"We are in a bad fix," Charley agreed. "I don't understand it. Those were both new nets, and of the highest grade of twine. They should have lasted for at least three months and here they are gone after only a few nights' fishing. There is something wrong somewhere. Well, come on, let's go home. There is nothing to be gained trying to fish with these nets, they will not hold anything."

The trip back to camp was made in silence; they were too utterly discouraged for speech.

They found Walter sleeping peacefully and Bill Roberts sitting by his couch reading by the light of a lantern.

The big fishermen listened in wondering sympathy to the recital of their experiences.

" Those nets should have lasted at least three months," he declared, confirming Charley's statement. " They are good nets. Mr. Daniels is a square fish boss and does not give his fishermen anything but the best. Let's see if we can find out what has happened to them. That will not make them strong again, but it will be of some little satisfaction."

CHAPTER XIX.

TELLING MR. DANIELS.

"THERE are several things that can happen to a net to make it rot quickly," Bill said. "Little things that a greenhorn might not think of any consequence. Now, first, have you run into any big bunches of gilly fish?"

"No," Charley answered, "we have been lucky in that respect. I know why you ask the question. The slime from them catches in the knots of the meshes and unless well washed out will hasten their decay."

."Correct," agreed Bill. "Then it is not gilly fish that done that damage. Next, have you been hauling your nets out to dry as soon as you got in, mornings."

"Yes, they have been on the racks drying before the sun got up good. I've fished enough to know that a hot sun on a wet, heaped-up net will cause the twine to heat and rot quickly."

"Well, that does away with another possibility," Bill said. "One of the most frequent causes of net trouble lies with the liming of them."

" Yes, I know," the lad agreed. " Some mix the lime with water in their skiffs and throw it on the nets before it has time to slack thoroughly and it then burns up the twine. But that isn't the trouble. I was careful about that. I fixed up a barrel on the dock before we started in to fish. And every night before we started out I would put in a bucket of lime and fill the barrel up with water. Our nets were limed in the morning from that barrel. At least, I am pretty sure they were. I told Chris to do it. He has tended to the nets."

" Sho', I always used dat water in de barrel," agreed the little darkey. " Only trouble was dat dar wasn't ebber enough ob it to dose all three nets good. By de time I got your's and de captain's fixed good, I'd have to put in more water to hab enough for Massa Walt's net."

" There is your trouble right in that lime barrel," said Bill, with certainty. " It was always weakened down for Walter's net, and you say his net is all right yet."

But Charley protested. " I never made the mixture strong enough to do any harm in the first place."

" I'm going to take a look," announced Bill, picking up the lantern. " Everything points to that lime water and it must be it."

The three followed in his wake as he led the way down to the dock.

He examined the nets first. "Gee," he exclaimed, "I should say they were rotten. Let's have a look at Walter's."

He stepped over to the rack where hung the lad's net and tested several meshes. "It is not as bad as those others," he announced. "Still it is getting pretty weak, I don't believe it would last out if a good school of fish struck it. Now let's look into that lime-water barrel."

He plunged his arm down in the partly-filled barrel and felt the water tentatively.

"Where do you keep your barrel of lime?" he asked, as he straightened up.

"Right there on shore under that palm tree," Charley pointed out. "Want to look at the lime?"

"No," said the big fisherman, absently, "I've seen enough."

He led the way back to the cabin in silence.

"Well, what do you make of it?" Charley asked when they were seated once more inside.

"I'm sure sorry for you, fellows," blurted out the big fisherman, impulsively. "You've been played as mean a low-down trick as was ever played on anyone."

"How?" demanded the captain and Charley together.

"Someone has mixed potash in with the lime in your lime barrel, and it's just eaten the life out of your twine. It has been done to fishermen more

than once around here and by that same gang of
rascals. It never occurred to me that it had been
done to your net, though, till I felt of that water.
Lime water should feel harsh and gritty, but that
felt oily and soapy and I knew then what the trouble
was.

"I wish I could help you out," he said, feelingly,
noting the utter discouragement in the three faces.
"I would gladly lend you nets if we had any but
our old ones are all fished out and we have only
three new ones ordered. It was so near the end of
the season we did not order any extra ones."

"We are mighty grateful to you anyway," Captain Westfield said. "You mustn't mind if we
ain't very pleasant company just now. This last
business has put us in a bad fix and we have got
to study some way out of it."

"I know," agreed Bill, sympathetically, "and as
I can't do any good here now, I'll run over to camp
and turn in. I've got to go over to Clearwater in
the morning to tend to a little pressing business.
Anything I can get you there?"

"No," Charley said, thanking him, "we have got
to go over ourselves to-morrow and tell Mr. Daniels about the nets."

When the kindly-hearted fisherman was gone,
the three sat long debating gloomily what they
should do but arriving at no decision. "We might
as well turn in," said Captain Westfield at last.

" Thar's only one thing I can see clearly.   We must go to Mr. Daniels to-morrow, like men, and tell him about our loss.   If he can give us any work to do, we must take it and work until we have paid him every cent we owe, if it takes a year to do it."

His two companions heartily agreed to this statement.   It was clearly the only honest course to take.

It was late when they at last got to sleep, and consequently late when they awoke.

As soon as they had breakfasted, Charley and the captain started for Clearwater, leaving Chris to look after Walter's wants.

On the Clearwater dock they found Bill Roberts and his two brothers.

" I'll keep an eye on your launch until you come back, if both of you want to go up to the fish house," Bill offered, a proposal they gladly accepted.

For a wonder Mr. Daniels was not busy and Charley poured out the story of their losses in a manly, straightforward manner.

" We don't want you to think that we are asking you to take up our quarrels for us," he concluded, flushing.   " We simply want to make it plain that we have done the very best we knew how.   As we figure it, we owe you now about one hundred and fifty dollars which the prospects do not look very bright for our paying at present.   If you have any work we can do, we will gladly work out the debt. If not, we will have to wait until we can get to earning again. But we will pay you every cent just as soon as we possibly can."

"Don't worry your head about the debt," said Mr. Daniels, heartily. "I am sure you and your companions have done your best and I am truly sorry you have met with so many misfortunes. What you owe the fish house can stand until you are able to pay it. If I owned the business, I would cancel the debt entirely but I am only manager here."

"You are very kind to take it this way," Charley said, gratefully. "I was afraid you might be angry at the failure we have made."

Mr. Daniels smiled. "What you have told me about your troubles is not exactly news to me," he said. "You have good friends in those Roberts boys and they have kept me pretty well posted as to how things were going. I would have got rid of that Hunter gang long ago but they are deeply in debt to the Company and the only chance to get any of it back is to take out a little, each week, from the fish they catch. You see, I have got to consider the Company's interests always above my personal wishes.

"What concerns me most, now," he continued, "is what you and your friends are going to do now that your nets are gone. Bill Roberts was up

to tell me this morning that if I would let you have
another set of nets he would stand good for them.
But I told him that was unnecessary.   I would
gladly refit you again on my own responsibility if
I had nets, but we have not got another one in the
house.   Have you any plan for the future?"

"No very clear one," Charley admitted.   "As
you know it's Florida's dull season now.   There's
very little doing except in the pineapple fields."

Mr. Daniels considered for a few minutes.   "I
do not like to advise you to do it, because it's dangerous work, but there is one thing you might pick
up enough money at to tide you over the dull
season."

"What is it?" Captain Westfield demanded,
eagerly.

"Hook and line fishing for groupers and grunts
out in the gulf.   After all, I do not know as it is
very dangerous if one keeps close watch of the
weather."

"The captain here is a regular weather prophet,"
Charley asserted.   "He can smell bad weather
hours before it comes."

"That's a valuable gift for that kind of work,"
Mr. Daniels replied.   "The grouper banks lay out
in the gulf from eight to eleven miles from shore,
and it wouldn't do for a small boat to be caught
out there in a heavy squall.   The more I think of
it, the more I think it would be a good thing for

you. You can keep right on using the launch, and the hooks and lines you need will cost but little. Of course, there is no big fortune in it but you had ought to make more than wages. Very likely, you could earn enough to pull out of the hole."

" I reckon we'd better try it," said Captain West-field. " I've done a lot of hook and line fishing in my time."

" We can start to-morrow," Charley agreed, promptly, his spirits rising at the possibility of a way out of their difficulties.

" Very well," agreed Mr. Daniels. " I'll give you a note to the storekeeper to let you have the lines and tackles, as well as what more groceries you need."

" I would feel quite hopeful," said Charley, as he thanked the kind-hearted manager, " if I did not fear that Hunter would find some way of still fur-ther injuring us."

" Silas Hunter will not bother you for a couple of weeks, anyway," Mr. Daniels assured him. " They took him and a couple of his cronies to the Tampa hospital on this morning's train."

" Sick? " Captain Westfield inquired, with great relief.

" You might call it that," Mr. Daniels smiled. " Bill Roberts got so mad over what he had done to you boys that he came over this morning and gave him a licking he'll not forget in a hurry.

Some of the gang tried to interfere and Bill's brothers gave them a dose of the same medicine. Those boys are good friends of yours, and they are friends worth having."

"Will not Hunter have them arrested?" inquired Charley, in fear for his zealous friends.

Mr. Daniels' smile broadened. "I think not," he said. "Bill warned him if he did, he would repeat the operation over again."

CHAPTER XX.

THE GROUPER BANKS.

" WE are grateful for what you did in our be-half," said Charley, when they again came upon the Roberts on the dock. "We did not expect you to take up our troubles but we cannot find words to express our gratitude for what you have done for us."

Big Bill blushed like a school girl. "We didn't do much," he said, awkwardly. "I was going to do it anyway, sometime. It just came off a little sooner than I expected. I don't fancy fighting much—it's poor business—but it's the only way to handle fellows like that Hunter gang—a decent man can't stoop to meet them with their own tricks."

"It is a rather primitive way of righting wrongs, but I was not thinking of that," said Charley, earnestly. "I was thinking of the loyal friendship, and the kindly feeling you had for us that prompted the act. It was a big, friendly action, all the more so as we are almost strangers to you."

"That's all right," stammered Bill, embarrassed

by his thanks. "I guess I beat Hunter up more than I intended to. He drew a knife on me so I couldn't handle him very gently. What did the fish boss have to say?" he inquired, eager to change the subject.

The captain told him of the new plan that Mr. Daniels had suggested.

"Mr. Daniels is a mighty square man," said Bill, emphatically. "I am glad you are going to follow his advice. We are thinking some of trying the reef fishing, too, until our nets come, so we will likely see a good deal of each other."

"The more the pleasanter for us at any rate," declared the old sailor. "Well, I guess we must be going. Chris will be wondering what has happened to us. Good-by. Drop in on us when you get the chance."

The trip back to the island was made with lighter hearts than they had brought with them, and they were made still lighter at the sight of Walter's improved condition. He was sitting up in bed arguing warmly with Chris that he was well enough to get up and dress, but the little negro had hidden his clothes and could not be moved by threats or entreaties.

"No, Massa Walt," Chris was saying as they entered. "You got to jis' lay quiet. I'se had a terrible time aworryin' an' anursin' you an' I ain't goin' to risk youah getting sick on my hands again through youah foolishness. Golly, I doan know what you white chilluns would do widout dis nigger to watch out foah you-alls."

So much was Walter improved, that Charley thought it safe to tell him of all that had happened since his accident.

"I am almost glad the nets are gone," he declared, when Charley had finished. "I don't believe I would ever have made a good net fisherman. I could never have grown to like the work."

Chris' joy was almost pathetic to see. "I'se sho' going wid you-alls," he cried. "Dis nigger can sho' catch fish with a hook. An' I sho' is glad I doan hab to stay alone on dis ole creepy island at night, no more."

And, indeed, perhaps, the part the little negro had so far taken had been as hard and unpleasant as any of theirs.

The evening that followed was by far the pleasantest they had spent on the island. Fear of the fishermen was over for the present at least. Walter's recovery was another cause for rejoicing, and they all looked forward to their morrow's work with a pleasurable anticipation that none had felt for the hard, nasty, trying net fishing.

So eager was Chris to begin, that he was up long before daybreak cooking breakfast and putting up a hearty lunch for their dinner.

The sun was just coming up as they steered out

of the inlet into the open gulf. Walter had insisted upon coming with them and lay on one of the seats looking somewhat thin and pale but drawing in increased strength from every breath of the bracing, salt air.

The captain was in full command, for, when it was a matter of sea work, Charley quickly gave way to the old, experienced sailor. While they bounded over the blue sparkling waves for the line of coral reefs he brought out the hooks, lines, and heavy sinkers they had purchased and rigged up the tackle for their fishing. It was simple. Just strong braided lines fifty feet long with a heavy lead on one end. Above the lead, he attached three very short lines a couple of feet apart, tying a hook on each.

As soon as he decided that they were nearing the reef he ordered the engine slowed down and cast a line over the stern.

" It's too deep to see when we get on the reef," he explained, " so we will have to feel for it. That lead on the line pulls along smooth over the sandy bottom but when it strikes the coral lumps on the reef it will begin to jerk." He sat with hand on the line until a series of quick, jumping tremors told him they were over the reef when he ordered the anchor lowered.

With eagerness the little party baited the hooks and cast their lines over. They waited breathless for the tugging which would announce a bite, but as the minutes dragged away without a nibble, their high spirits began to lower.

"Golly, I could do better than this on the island," grumbled Chris, as he pulled up his line and examined his bait for the twentieth time.

The old sailor filled and lit his pipe with a twinkle in his eye. "Wait jist one half hour an' they'll begin to bite," he announced, calmly.

"Have you made special arrangements with them," Walter inquired.

"Not quite, but fish have their habits the same as people," the captain explained. "They only bite at certain tides. Seems like they had their regular mealtime as one might say, only they go by tides instead of a clock. It's the last of the ebb tide now. In a few minutes it will be flood tide and the fish will all be hunting their breakfasts."

"But I have caught fish on both ebb and flood tides, captain," Charley objected.

"Yes, an' there are people, too, who are always eating between meals," the old sailor retorted, "but most of them are contented with their regular mealtime."

"Golly! dis nigger often wonders how you keeps track ob dem tides," Chris remarked. "I can't tell nothin' 'bout dem, 'cept when I'se on de shore an' can watch the rise and fall."

"It's simple, lad," explained the old sailor.

" It's the moon that causes the tides.   All one has
to do is to notice the moon.   When the moon is
coming up the tide is going down.   When the moon
is going down the tide is coming up.   No matter
where you are it is always the same."

" I've got a bite," Charley announced, and moon
and tides were straightway forgotten by the eager
little party.

It seemed as though his announcement had been
the breakfast bell for the finny creatures below, for
before he had got his fish to the surface, his companions were hauling furiously on the lines.

Charley gave a shout of exultation as he swung
his prize aboard.   It was a chunky, reddish fish
with mouth and fins of scarlet, and was about fifteen
pounds in weight.

" That's a red grouper," said the captain, spar-
ing a glance from his own captive.   " This one I've
got is a black grouper.   Those flat, silvery fish Chris
and Walter have caught are red-mouth grunts."
But the old sailor had no time for further speculations for the sport grew fast and furious.   Often
they pulled up to find three fish on their line at once,
one on each hook.

As fast as they unhooked their captives they
threw them into the forward cockpit where they
soon grew into a beautiful, glistening heap of red,
gold and silver hues.

For two hours they pulled the fish aboard as

fast as they could bait and cast their hooks. Then, as suddenly as they had begun, the fish ceased to bite.

"We might as well get up anchor and move to another place," the captain announced.

"Has we done catched dem all?" Chris inquired, innocently.

"Hardly," said the old sailor, with a laugh, "but a shark or some other sea monster is prowling around down below and has scared them all away." They weighed anchor and drifted back a couple of hundred feet upon the reef where they found the fish biting there the same as before.

"I'ze got something queer on my line," announced Chris, as he pulled up hand over hand. "Hit don't jerk none. Hit's jest heavy-like."

"A bit of coral, I expect," Charley suggested.

All stared at the curious-looking object as Chris slung it in over the side.

"Why," said Charley, as he scraped off the clinging moss and barnacles. "It's a doll, just a big, rag doll."

"Put it back in the water, lad," said the captain, with a hint of tears in his voice, "put it back. Likely its little mistress sleeps there below the waves. We must not separate her from her dolly."

It was only a guess, but the idea took such strong hold of them all that anchor was again weighed and they dropped further along to another place.

About four o'clock the captain declared it was time to start for home.

"We have done pretty well for one day," he said, "and we have got to get home in time to carry the fish over to Clearwater."

His companions were willing to stop. Although they had enjoyed the sport greatly, their arms were aching from the constant pulling and their hands were sore from numerous pricks from hooks and fins.

An hour's run brought them back to their island. Here Chris stopped off to get supper, and Walt to lie down and rest a bit, while Charley and the captain carried the fish over.

The two were back by the time Chris had supper ready.

"We had twelve hundred pounds of grouper and six hundred pounds of grunts, twenty dollars' worth in all," Charley announced, proudly. "Not bad for our first day's work."

"Why, that's five dollars apiece," said Walter, delightedly. "If we can keep that up we'll make thirty dollars a week for each one of us."

"We can't figure on steady fishing," objected the captain. "That's the worst drawback about this reef fishing. One can only get out in fine weather. Sometimes it blows for a week at a time so that one cannot wet a line."

"Then it's up to us to discover something to

make money at during stormy weather," Charley declared.

It was Chris who hit upon the idea, but the reader will learn about that later.

CHAPTER XXI.

HAPPY DAYS.

FOR a week the weather held fair and each day found our little party, out on the reef, fishing with might and main to make as much money as possible before Hunter returned to his old haunts and tricks. They were thoroughly agreed that they would leave the island when he came back. They were not so much afraid for themselves but they had suffered heavy losses already from his rascality and they did not care to run the risk of being put still deeper in debt.

Meanwhile, they were contented and happy in their new pursuit. They were long, happy days that they spent on the reef with the sparkling blue water all around them. The bracing salt breezes giving zest to their appetites, and the ever-new, thrilling expectancy with which they pulled in their prizes, speculating always before it came to the surface its kind, and size.

On Saturday night they figured up the credit slips they had been given at the fish house and found that they had made one hundred and twelve dollars during the week. On Saturday night, also, they received a bit of ill news which was good news for them. Bill Roberts heard it from the fishermen at Clearwater, and he hastened over to tell them. It was to the effect that Hunter, discharged from the hospital, was well enough to be about, had proceeded to fill up on bad liquor in celebration of his release, and, as a result, was back in the hospital for a couple of weeks' more treatment.

" It's an ill wind that blows nobody any good," quoted Charley, when he heard the news. " That gives us a couple of weeks more to fish in peace. Now if the weather only holds fair we will be able to pay what we owe and have a little left over to take us to some other place."

But the weather did not hold fair. Sunday morning found the wind blowing half a gale from the north-west and the seas rolling high outside. Monday morning it was still blowing with unabated vigor and the sky looked as though there was more to come.

" It's going to last for several days," Captain Westfield declared, " then, likely, we will get another spell of fair weather."

" Why couldn't it hold off for a couple of weeks longer," Walter grumbled. " Every day lost means a lot to us now."

After breakfast, Chris made ready to start out

to secure a change for their bill of fare.   Having nothing else to do the others went with him.

His first move was to secure a supply of the great stone crabs, whose claws, when roasted, they had found so delicious.

These were to be found in great numbers on the long mud flats, out in the bay, when low tide left the flats exposed.   The boys could see thousands of them as they waded out to the flats.   They were feeding or basking in the sun, but at the hunters approach one and all scurried for their hiding places, deep, slanting holes in the soft mud.   But Chris was prepared for such tactics.   He had fixed for himself a long iron rod with a hook in the end which he would thrust far down into a hole and drag out its squirming, clawing occupant.   Then, he would kill it with a stroke of the rod, break off the great claws, and drop them into the sack he carried. In a few minutes the little darkey had secured as many as they could use before they spoiled.

The crabs were not the only inhabitants of the flats.   Clams were there in plenty and in a short time they dug up all they desired.   Then a trip was made to some partly submerged rocks and a goodly supply of big flat oysters secured.

"Strange we never see any Clearwater boys over here getting these things when they are so plentiful," Walter commented, as they started back to the cabin.

"Golly! I'se been studyin' on dat," Chris said. "'Pears to dis nigger dat we could make right smart ob money getting dese things an' selling dem to de folks ober in de town."

"They would hardly buy anything that is so plentiful right close to their homes," Walter objected.

"Oh, I don't know about that," said Charley, thoughtfully. "It's too hard work getting them for some people, I suppose. Others are too busy to take the time from their work, maybe. Likely, a lot more have no boats, and probably there are many who don't know how to get them. There may be something worth considering in Chris' proposal."

"Let's try it," said Captain Westfield. "We don't stand to lose anything but our work."

All went to work with a will and in a couple of hours they had secured ten dozen crab claws, a couple of bushels of clams, and had opened up a couple of gallons of oysters. Chris and Charley took the lot over to Clearwater right after dinner.

In an hour the two were back.

"They sold like hot cakes," Charley declared. "We didn't get over a quarter of the town before we sold out. We got forty cents a dozen for crab claws, fifty cents a quart for the oysters, and ten cents a dozen for clams."

"You robbers!" Walter gasped, in surprise, "they are not worth that."

"A thing is worth what you can get for it," Charley grinned. "Besides, we had to throw in an extra charge for the service, like they do in an expensive restaurant when they charge you two dollars for a fifty cent steak."

"Well, I reckon we can supply them with all they want at those prices," the captain remarked, dryly. "Let's get to work."

And work they did for the next three days, by which time the weather had cleared up, their market supplied for a time, and they, themselves, richer by about fifty dollars. Then they went back to their fishing again until the next spell of bad weather should come.

Often, as their little launch lay bobbing at her anchor, on the reef, great stately ships swept by in plain sight, traveling north or south to various ports. The captain watched them with the eager interest of a boy. Almost his whole life had been spent on the sea, and he loved its ships like a mother loves her children.

They were watching one of these ships one day wondering idly as to what might be her name, port, and cargo, when Charley's gaze became centered on a smaller craft some two miles astern of the first. Something about the cut and set of her sails caught and held his attention.

"That boat is some traveler, Captain," he observed. " See how she is drawing up on the one ahead."

The old sailor studied the distant craft with the eye of an expert.

" She is going some," he admitted. " Fore and aft topsail schooner, about eighty tons' burden. Funny, there seems something familiar in the cut of those sails and the set of those spars."

" That's what I was thinking," Charley agreed. " I'm almost certain I've seen that rig before."

" See, she's changed her course and is standing in for shore," suddenly cried the observant old sailor.

It soon became evident that he was right. The stranger came sweeping rapidly on carrying a wave of white froth before her bow.

Her changed course would bring her within half a mile of where they lay, and, as she drew nearer, our little party ceased fishing and stood gazing in admiration at the beautiful picture she made.

She was a low-hulled, black-painted schooner, keeling over under a press of snowy canvas, until her lee rail was buried in a smother of foam.

" I believe she is headed right for our island," Charley observed.

" If her captain does not know these waters pretty well he'll be liable to pile that beauty up on a rock," Captain Westfield said, anxiously.

It soon become evident that her pilot knew his ground for the schooner's course was shifted again and again as her commander jockeyed her around hidden rocks and through winding channels.

Soon her crew began to take in sail. One after another the snow-white sheets came in until stripped to mainsail and storm staysail she rounded up a mile from shore and hung motionless in the wind.

A tiny blot of color appeared on her deck and crept slowly up her foremast. At the top it opened up, a fluttering red flag.

" She's signalling," the captain exclaimed.

" I have it," Charley cried. " She's that smuggling craft. Her captain is trying to get in touch with the Hunter gang. No wonder I thought I had seen her before."

" I wasn't as lucky as you in getting a glimpse of her that night," remarked the captain, " but I have seen that craft somewhere before. I wonder where it was."

." That likeness to some boat I know struck me hard the night I saw her by the light of the flare, but I guess it's only a chance resemblance," Charley said. " Well, if they are waiting to hear from Hunter, they have a long wait ahead of them."

" I wonder how Hunter communicated with her before he was hurt," Walter pondered.

" There's no mystery about that," his chum replied. " That's the simplest part of the affair. It only takes a couple of days to get a letter to Cuba. I expect she has more aguardiente aboard now.

Likely he wrote to her captain for a fresh supply as soon as he discovered that the other was gone. He doubtless planned to have us off the island before it arrived but his trip to the hospital has upset all his plans."

"They are bold to try to bring it in in broad day-light," observed the Captain.

"Oh, I daresay, they wouldn't attempt to land it until after dark, and there's nothing in her ap-pearance to excite suspicion. If any boat came near her they could quickly slip out a couple of miles further and defy capture. Uncle Sam's juris-diction does not extend out more than four miles from shore."

The beautiful schooner remained hove to all the afternoon and apparently waiting an answer to her signal, but, at last, her skipper, probably deciding that something was wrong, crowded on all sail and glided swiftly out to sea.

When our little party started home the schooner was a mere, distant speck on the horizon.

"This is the second trip she has made and landed nothing," Walter observed. "After such luck, I should not think they would try again."

"Oh, Hunter will likely write them the reason for his not being on hand and arrange for another meeting," Charley said. "They probably make enough money out of the business to be able to stand a few disappointments."

CHAPTER XXII.

TREASURE TROVE.

THE chums saw but little of their good friends, the Roberts, during these busy days. They were up and off to the reefs every morning at break of dawn and only returned in the evening in time to get their catch of fish over to Clearwater before dark. Once, Charley met Bill on the dock and learned that his nets had come and that he and his brothers were fishing every night with but poor success. The big, young fellows looked weary, worn and worried.

." I don't know what's become of all the fish," he said, " we have been hunting over hundreds of miles of water and haven't found a decent school in a week. We need to make a few good catches, badly, too. All our money was in the bank which failed in Tampa the other day. We are almost broke, now, and the closed season, when we are not allowed to fish, is only a few weeks off. It looks like we are in for a long streak of hard luck."

Charley expressed his sincere sympathy.

" Oh, we'll not starve," Bill replied. " But it

does hurt to have all the money you've worked hard for go like that without getting any good out of it. Well, I don't know why I am complaining to you, you have had worse troubles than ours."

It was a different looking Bill who routed them out of bed before dawn a few mornings later. His eyes were shining with excitement and his simple, frank face was beaming.

" Get on your clothes quick as you can and come with me," he cried. " We've got a chance to make a good pot of money."

As they hurried into their clothing he explained.

" There's a big schooner laden with lumber out about two miles in the gulf. She sprung a bad leak three days ago and her crew have worn themselves out at the pumps but the water is gaining on them all the time. If they can't get her into a dry dock within twenty-four hours, boat and cargo will be a total loss. We were passing her when her captain hailed us and asked for a tow. There is a dry dock at Tarpon Springs and he offers one thousand dollars to be towed up to it."

" Whew," Charley whistled, " that's a nice bunch of money. Do you think we can manage it?"

" Not alone, but I've been over to Clearwater and got three of the best fishermen there to help us with their launches. That makes five of us to divide the thousand dollars; two hundred dollars apiece. With luck, we ought to make the tow up in eight hours."

His story had hastened the little party's movements and by the time he had finished they were all ready and eager for the start.

They found the other three launches waiting impatiently for them at the dock and in a few minutes all five were under way standing out for the schooner which was in plain view from the inlet.

"One thousand dollars seems an awful price to pay for a tow of eighteen miles," Charley observed, as the "Dixie" tore through the water leading the little fleet. "Do you suppose we will have any difficulty in getting the money, Captain? The owners might not back up their captain's agreement."

"They will have to do it if we do our part," declared the old sailor, wise in the laws of the sea. "A captain is king of his ship. He can bind the owners for anything he considers necessary for the best interest of his ship or cargo. The only question is whether the owners are responsible persons. Likely, I can tell who the owners are when we get close enough to see her name. I know most of the ship-owners of these waters."

He uttered an exclamation of satisfaction as they drew near enough to decipher the name "North Wind" on the bow of the unlucky ship. "She is owned by Curry Bros. of Key West," he announced. "They are a rich firm, made most of their money out of wrecking. They own dozens of ships. Our money is all right if we keep our side of the agreement."

The unfortunate schooner lay low in the water, the waves almost breaking over her lumber-laden decks. She was barely moving in the light breeze. From every scupper hole gushed forth a stream of bright, clear, sea water as her crew labored at the clanking pumps.

"Why, they are all negroes, even the captain," Charley exclaimed, as the "Dixie" swept closer.

"Most of these Key West boats are manned by negroes," Captain Westfield said. "They are expert sailors and wreckers, and could give a regular lawyer points on ocean law, but they are mighty lazy. They get a share of what the ship earns instead of wages and one would think they would carry as small a crew as possible so as to get big shares, but instead of that, they carry double the men they need so as to make the work as light as possible. Don't seem to care whether they make anything or not so long as they have plenty to eat and little to do."

The numerous, grinning, ebony faces and kinky, woolly heads on the leaking ship testified to the truth of the old sailor's assertion.

The schooner's captain, a tall, lanky, solemn-visaged, old negro, wearing bone-rimmed spectacles, met them as they came alongside.

He glanced at the five launches with evident satisfaction.

" I reckon you-all white gentlemens can get me into Tarpon afore the ole gal sinks," he observed. " I figure we can keep her afloat ten hours longer if I can keep dem lazy niggers working de pumps."

" She hadn't ought to sink even when she fills," Captain Westfield observed. " The lumber ought to keep her up."

" Dar's a lot ob hardware in her, too," the negro captain declared. " Hit's stowed deep in de hold wid such a raffle ob lumber on top ob hit dat we can't get to hit widout throwing all de lumber overboard. She'll go down like a rock when she fills."

" Then we don't want to waste any time talking," Captain Westfield declared. " Pass us your lines and we will fasten on. First, though, you had better repeat the proposal you made to this gentleman here," indicating Bill Roberts. " If we tow you in, we don't want any misunderstanding about our pay after the job is done."

The old negro spoke slowly, evidently considering his words carefully.

" If you white gentlemens tow me in to de dry dock at Tarpon you is to get one thousand dollars for de job. You-alls can draw on Curry Bros. through de Tarpon bank jes' as soon as we gets to de dry dock."

" All right," Captain Westfield agreed. " Pass us your lines and we'll get busy."

In a few moments, the five launches were fast to the schooner and with engines throbbing were slowly dragging the helpless hulk towards her destination.

The fishing launches were all good boats of their kind, but they had not been intended for such heavy work and the strain on their light engines was terrific.

The two boys watched the " Dixie's " straining engine with the anxious care of a mother for her child as they dragged their big tow slowly ahead.

" I guess it will last out the trip," Charley said, " but I wouldn't like to do much of this kind of work with it. It's like overloading a willing horse."

At the end of the fifth mile, the launch ahead of them dropped out of the struggle with a broken piston ring.

" Go on, don't stop for me! " its owner yelled with more unselfishness than they had expected. " I'll manage to limp her back to Clearwater. So long, and good luck to you. You will have to hit it up for all you are worth now or you won't make it. There's a squall making up in the north-west. If it strikes you before you get in behind Anchote Key, you will have to cut loose from the schooner."

Captain Westfield had, for some time, been

watching the small black cloud making up in the north-west.

" It's going to be a close shave to make Tarpon before that thing hits us," he remarked to Charley. " We pulled slow enough when there were five of us and now with only four we are not making over two miles an hour. It's a wonder the engines stand the additional strain. I keep expecting them to break down."

" It's not only that we are one less in number, which counts, but also the fact that the schooner keeps getting harder and harder to pull," Charley observed. " I'll bet she is six inches deeper in the water than when we fastened on. Her captain is doing his best to keep her up—just listen to him," he grinned.

The lanky, solemn, old negro was dancing around the schooner's deck heaping abuse, threats, prayers, and supplications on the kinky-headed toilers at the pumps. He also had noted the gathering squall and was driving his exhausted crew to the limit of their endurance.

The minutes dragged slowly away while the launches with their heavy burden labored gallantly on. They were slowly nearing the island, Anchote Key, which lay in front of the port of Tarpon Springs. But, although they were close to their destination, the squall was close to them. The tiny, black cloud had spread rapidly until it blanketed the entire northern horizon with an inky mass.

"Do you think we will make it, Captain?" Charley inquired, anxiously, as they watched the gathering storm.

"I doubt if we will reach Tarpon before it hits us," answered the old sailor, "but I guess we will be able to get in behind Anchote Key and escape the worst of the seas."

As the squall neared them the wind dropped away and the sea took on an oily smoothness. The air hung heavy, still and oppressive. The sun had long since disappeared behind the wall of black but so motionless was the air that they breathed with difficulty and the perspiration stood out on their hands and faces.

"There she comes," cried Captain Westfield, suddenly.

Away to the north under the low-hanging cloud appeared a wall of foaming white.

Charley steered with one eye on the moving comb of water and the other on the rock-shored island close aboard.

He gave a sigh of relief as the launches and schooner slipped slowly in behind the protecting island just as the squall broke in a roar of wind and driving sheets of rain.

His relief was short-lived, however. They had escaped the fury of the billows outside but it was rough enough behind the key and high seas tumbled and rolled around the boats.

He glanced back to see how it fared with the schooner. What he saw made him leap for the straining tow line, whipping out his sheath-knife as he sprang. One stroke severed the taut rope, and, relieved of the drag, the "Dixie" leaped ahead like a frightened deer.

CHAPTER XXIII.

SALVAGE HUNTERS.

On board the schooner all was excitement and confusion. Nearly awash as she already was the first big wave had swept her from stem to stern. Her frightened negro crew had quickly sprung into the rigging yelling at the top of their voices. Only the solemn, lanky, old captain remained impassive. He still stood at his post, by the wheel, peering over his big, horn-rimmed spectacles, sizing up the situation with shrewd, calculating eyes.

A second wave struck and swept over, and then a third.

" She's sinking," Walter shouted.

Slowly the doomed craft settled down, down until her bulwarks lay even with the water, then stopped.

" She is not going to sink," Charley exclaimed, as he saw her stop in her downward course.

Captain Westfield quickly grasped the strange situation. " She's gone as far as she can," he declared. " She is resting on a shoal. Steer down on the leeward side of her, Charley, and we will take off the crew."

The other launch captains had been on the watch and had cut loose at the same time as Charley. Following the "Dixie's" example, they flocked around to the lee side of the wreck and assisted to take off the crew. The rescued negroes came aboard, wet to the skin, and fright had given their ebony faces a peculiar, ashen hue.

The solemn lanky captain was the last to leave the schooner. Before getting aboard the "Dixie," he made his way up to the vessel's bow and knocking out the shackle pin let the anchor drop to the bottom; a move which Captain Westfield watched with a twinkle in his eyes.

"That darkey sure knows his business," he remarked in an undertone to Charley.

The other launches crowded around the "Dixie," their captains wanting a consultation.

"The schooner's not in bad shape here," Bill Roberts observed. "There isn't sea enough to break her up. The owners can get a sea tug and a steam pump from Tampa, and get her up and keep her afloat long enough to tow her into the dry dock."

"We might as well all run on into Tarpon now and draw on Curry Bros. for that thousand dollars," one of the other captains proposed.

"You-alls can't collect dat money now," observed the darkey skipper, calmly. "You-alls wasn't to get it 'less you got de schooner into de dry dock."

"Didn't we do our best?" demanded Bill Roberts. "Haven't we got you nearly there? Haven't we got your vessel into a place where she will not be lost? Where would your old ship be outside in the gulf in this gale? She wouldn't have lasted out there as long as a snowball in the warm place."

"Dat's all true," agreed the darkey captain, "but you ain't carried out youah part ob de contract. If you white gentlemens had got de schooner into de dry dock all right hit would hab been worth dat thousand dollars to mah owners, but now, dey will have to go to de expense ob a tug an' steam pump, an' dat's going to be a heap ob money. I'se got to watch out for my owners' interests."

"But we have done our best," Captain Westfield protested. "We have spent our time and strained our engines, and we ought to be paid for what we've done."

"Dat's all right," agreed the sable skipper. "I reckon Curry Bros. pay you for dat all right, but not dat thousand dollars. Dat's too much, under de circumstances."

For a few minutes it looked as though the wily, ebony skipper would receive rough treatment from the infuriated launch captains, but the cooler arguments of the Roberts and Captain Westfield prevailed.

"He has got the law on his side," Captain Westfield said. "We can't force the payment of that thousand dollars, although what we have done for the owners is worth many times the amount.   I guess the best thing we can do is to trust to Curry Bros. to do the right thing by us."

" Not for me," declared the captain of one launch. " If we can't collect that bill, I'll collect a bigger one.   That schooner is abandoned.   Her captain and crew have deserted her.   I am going to put a man on her and put in a claim for salvage.   The rest of you can join me, or not, just as you please."

" I am with you," the other fish captains agreed. Bill Roberts wavered and glanced at Captain West-field for advice.

" I don't believe such a course would get us any-thing," the old sailor said.   " These Key West captains are wise to all the salvage laws and Curry Bros. made their money in wrecking.   They would fight any claim for salvage and they have got too much money for us to fight against."

·" Dis white gentleman is telling you-alls the truth," affirmed the darkey skipper.   " Dat ship ain't abandoned.   I'se jes' going ashore to com-municate wid de owners.   I'se dun dropped de an-chor over.   An' she ain't floating helpless at sea."

" All right, you fellows can listen to that nigger if you want to," said the salvage hunter.   " I'm go-ing to take possession of the schooner.   If you are going back, you can take these darkeys I've got in my launch."

His fellow fishermen elected to stay with him

but the Roberts boys decided to return with our party. The negroes in the other two boats were transferred to the "Dixie," and Bill Roberts' boat, and the two launches remaining made fast to the sunken schooner.

As soon as the transfer was made the two return-ing boats headed back for Clearwater with their car-goes of ebony passengers.

It was nearly dark when hungry, weary, and dis-appointed, our party and the Roberts arrived at the Clearwater dock. The rescued negroes at once scattered to seek food and shelter in the colored quarter of the town. Their captain, lanky and solemn as ever, departed to the telegraph office to communicate with his owners.

"You white gentlemen ain't going to lose noth-ing for de way you-alls have done," he assured Cap-tain Westfield, earnestly, before he left. "I'se only a captain an' I'se done got to do what I thinks is foah mah owners' interests. I allows, though, dat Curry Bros. going to treat you all right. I'se sorry dose other two white gentlemens is going to try to make trouble. I'se dun been wrecking foah Mr. Curry foah foaty years an' I knows all about de salvage laws. Dey ain't a ghost ob a show to get salvage out ob dat schooner."

It was not until several days after that, however, that our friends verified the truth of the ebony skip-per's statements.

The first proof came with the return of the two launches which had fastened to the schooner. Their captains were weary and wrathful. They had hung by the schooner for two days. Then a tug and steam pump arrived from Tampa and on board the tug was a United States marshal who curtly ordered them away from the schooner. The schooner had then been raised and towed into the dry dock. The two captains had at once entered suit for salvage claims but what the outcome would be even their lawyers could, or would not, say.

The second proof came in the form of a letter from Curry Bros., thanking them for what they had done and inclosing a check for two hundred dollars. Much to their pleasure they found that the Roberts boys had received a similar letter and check.

The night the check came Charley got out his note book and pencil and figured up their accounts and the result brought satisfaction to them all.

The reef fishing had proved more profitable than they had dared hope, and for it they had credit slips on the fish house for two hundred and seventy-five dollars.

The sale of crabs, claws, and oysters—the work of stormy days—had brought them in another hundred dollars in cash.

Adding to this the two-hundred dollar check they had just received brought the total up to five hundred and seventy-five dollars.

Deducting the two hundred dollars they owed for groceries and nets, left them the comfortable balance of three hundred and seventy-five dollars.

"That's not half bad," Charley observed, "but I think now is the time for us to quit. It will not be long now before Hunter returns and I want to be away from here before he gets back. If he succeeded in working a few more of his sly tricks on us he might put us in the hole again."

His companions were loath to leave such profitable work but they could clearly see the wisdom of his plan. So, after some discussion, they decided that the next day should see their last trip to the reef. Then they would take their departure for the East Coast and seek whatever work they could find.

This settled, they retired to dream happily of new scenes and new adventures.

Their sleep would have been less sound, perhaps, had they known that Hunter had already returned. Their dreams would have been less pleasant, if they had seen the silently propelled row boat creep into their little dock, a slinking figure groping around in the "Dixie," and, after a few minutes, the ghostly row boat departed as silently as it had come.

But they were happily unconscious of these things and slept soundly on to waken only at their accustomed hour at break of day.

Sunrise found them on the reef fishing busily. But for some reason or other they did not meet with their accustomed success.   Bites came only at long and irregular intervals.   They shifted frequently to fresh places but with no better result.

" I shouldn't wonder if there was a storm brewing," Captain Westfield said.   " Creatures in the sea, as well as on the land, seem to have a weather instinct which tells them when a serious change of weather is coming.   It looks bright all around, but it seems to me I can feel a kind of heaviness in the air that only comes before a storm."

Noon came but the sky remained clear and uncloudy.

" I guess you missed the weather, for once, Captain," Charley observed, " but I think we might as well start for home, anyway.   It's our last day and we are not catching enough to pay us to stay out any longer."

His companions were willing so the anchor was hauled aboard and the engine started up.

CHAPTER XXIV.

THE ACCIDENT.

Both Charley and Walter had by this time become quite familiar with their little engine and when trouble with it occurred, as it sometimes did, it generally took them but a short time to locate what was wrong and fix it.

They had covered perhaps half the distance back to the inlet when the steady throb, throb of the engine changed suddenly to a whirling roar. Charley hastily threw the switch, shutting off the spark, and the big fly wheel instantly ceased its wild revolutions.

"Something has come loose," he announced. "Hand me that wrench, Walt. The shaft must have come loose to make the engine turn up at that speed."

His chum handed him the desired tool and the lad raised up the false flooring in the launch's bottom which hid the shaft from view.

What he expected to find was that one of the screws which fastened the propeller shaft had come loose and needed tightening, but what he saw filled his face with dismay. Rising, he stepped back to the stern and peered over under the launch's counter.

"Our propeller's gone," he announced, straightening up. "That leaves us in a pretty fix—five miles from shore. We'll have to take some of these bottom boards and paddle in, and it's going to be slow, hard work."

"I wonder how it happened," said Walter, as he fell to work with a heavy board for a paddle.

"It didn't happen. It was just done," his chum said, grimly. "Evidently our friend Hunter got home before we expected him. He must have done it last night when we were all asleep."

"Are you sure?" inquired Captain Westfield.

"As sure as a person can be who did not actually see it done. The shaft was sawn three-fourths in two. The cut part is bright, showing that it was done recently. It was a clever trick all right. You see, it would not give way immediately but would wear in two, gradually, where it was cut. I guess he was in hopes it would break with us out in a seaway where we couldn't do anything. Luckily, it's happened when it is calm and we are not such a great ways from shore."

But although the distance to shore was not so very great, it did not take them long to realize that it was going to take them a long time to cover it.

The launch was deep and heavy in the water and with their rude, heavy, ungainly paddles they could only force her forward very slowly.

" It's going to be after dark when we reach the inlet," the captain said, anxiously. " I do not believe we are making over half a mile an hour."

Indeed, they were not making as good progress as that, for when dark settled down upon the water, they were a full three miles from shore and their arms and backs were beginning aching with the steady strain of wielding the heavy boards. Soon after the sun set, the wind commenced to freshen and the launch began to bob and drift about in a way to discourage further effort.

" It's no use trying any longer," Charley declared, at last. " We are not getting ahead any and are just wearing ourselves out for nothing."

" We might as well put over the anchor and make up our minds to stay here all night," the captain agreed.

Walter dropped over the anchor and let out all the cable. " There isn't any too much rope," he announced, doubtfully. " The water's deep here. I guess, though, it will hold all right if it does not blow any harder."

So far there was nothing very alarming in the situation. The launch rode easily and high, shipping no water, and they knew that if it were not at their dock in the morning the Roberts boys would notice their absence and be out looking for them. They had a couple of jugs of fresh water aboard, and there was enough of their dinner remaining to make a substantial lunch. This Chris now brought out and all ate heartily, their appetites whetted by the hard work they had done.

As soon as they had finished, Charley brought out a lot of old sacks they had in a locker and spread them out in the little cabin. "Early to bed, early to rise," he quoted cheerfully. "I guess we might as well turn in. There is nothing to sit up for."

They were all tired enough to agree to this and they all laid down, side by side. The launch's high sides and little cabin protected them from the wind and they were quite comfortable. Walter and Chris were almost instantly asleep, and Charley was just on the verge of dropping off when a movement of the captain roused him. He raised up and looked around.

The old sailor had arisen and was standing out in the cockpit gazing at the sky.

The lad crept out softly and joined him.

"What's the matter, Captain?" he inquired, anxiously.

"I don't just like the feel of this weather," said the old sailor, uneasily. "The wind is freshening all the time although it's doing it so slowly one hardly notices it. I am afraid we are in for more than a cap full of wind."

" I don't think so," Charley disagreed. " Why, the sky is as clear as a bell all around. There's not a sign of a cloud."

" I hope you are right. It don't always take clouds to make a wind, though, lad. Some of the worst gales I ever saw came out of a clear sky."

" If it comes on to blow hard we will not be able to hang at anchor," Charley said, thoughtfully, impressed by the old sailor's uneasiness.

" No, the anchor won't hold in this deep water," agreed the sailor. " Even if it did catch on a ledge of rock and keep from dragging, we would have to cut loose if the sea ran high. With one short cable it would help to pull our bows under."

" What direction do you think will the gale come from, if it comes at all? " the lad inquired.

" From the same quarter the wind's blowing now," the captain replied, promptly. " That's the only good feature about a clear gale, the wind never shifts or varies but blows steady from one point."

" Let's see," said Charley, considering. " It's blowing from the north-west now. That would neither drive us ashore nor out to sea, but straight down the coast."

" We might hit some of the capes or cays way down the coast if the launch lasted to drift that far," said the old sailor.

" Well," said Charley, philosophically, " if it comes, it comes. If it doesn't, it doesn't. We can't do any good by sitting up worrying and watching for it, so I am going to turn in."

He crept softly in and laid down by Walter and was soon fast asleep.

He was suddenly wakened out of a sound slumber by being thrown against the launch's side with a force which knocked the breath from his body. He tried to rise to his feet but was flung violently to the other side. Then on hands and knees, like an infant, he crawled out of the little cabin.

Once in the open, it took him but a second to grasp what had happened.

The launch had parted her cable and was now rolling helplessly in the trough of the seas which were now running high. In the darkness, he could just distinguish the captain in the bow. With difficulty, owing to the violent lurching and plunging, he crept forward to his side.

The old sailor was working frantically to rig up a sea anchor with which to bring the launch's bow up in the wind.

"Get me some of those bottom boards, and tear up some of the lockers, too, if you can break them loose," he commanded. "We will need every stick we can get to hold her bows to the seas."

The lad crept aft and soon returned with an armful of boards he had torn loose. Returning again for more, he met Walter and Chris, who, also rudely awakened from their slumber, had made their way out of the cabin. With their assistance, all the loose boards they could get were soon carried up to the captain who, as fast as they were brought, bound them firmly with rope into one solid bundle.

" There ought to be more, but perhaps these will do," said the old sailor, as he fastened the last plank to its fellows.

He pulled in the trailing end of the severed cable, and, making it fast to the bundle of planks, shoved them over the bow. Then all three crept back aft and anxiously awaited results.

For some minutes, they feared that their labors had been in vain, then, slowly, the launch's bow swung around to meet the seas and she rose and fell easily without the sickening lurching from side to side.

" All's well, so far," the captain announced, " but this is only the beginning. It has hardly commenced to blow yet. She can ride out these seas all right, but if this wind keeps on increasing, by morning there will be seas that are seas."

The boys glanced around at the watery mountains tumbling about them and decided that they cared not to see any bigger.

The wild plunging of the launch made sleep impossible and the four huddled together in the little cockpit wondering if day would find them alive or swallowed up by the hungry waters.

As the hours crept slowly by, they could not doubt

that the wind was steadily rising. The seas grew steadily in size and the launch's pitching became wilder and wilder. Accustomed as they all were to the sea, the violent plunging gave them a feeling of nausea closely akin to seasickness. To add to their discomfort, the madly plunging launch sent up showers of spray which the wind drove in upon them soaking them to the skin and stinging their faces like hail.

" She would not float a minute if we were out in the open gulf," the captain observed. " As it is, we are drifting down the coast in between the reef and the shore and the reef breaks some of the force of the seas. A little shift of the wind and we would either be driven out over the reef or upon a rock shore."

" Cheery prospect either way we look at it," Charley said, grimly. " Heads we win, tails we lose."

No one was in any mood for further conversation. Wet, miserable, wretched and anxious, they huddled close together in the little cockpit and waited longingly for the coming of day.

At last, a gray light spread over the rolling waters and grew brighter and brighter till finally the sun peeped slowly into view.

It came up grandly in a blue sky unflecked by clouds, revealing a scene wilder than they had imagined in the blackness of the night.

CHAPTER XXV.

THE STORM.

As they gazed around them, our little party could not help but realize the peril of their situation. To the west, about a mile from the drifting launch, was the reef over which the mountainous waves were breaking in heaps of swirling foam. To the east of them some three miles distant was the shore. All they could see of it was its swaying palms for its beach was hidden by the foaming breakers. All around them rose mighty seas upon which the drifting launch reared and plunged.

So far, they were drifting straight down the lane between the reef and shore, but a slight shift of wind, either way, would send them ashore to be beaten to death in the pounding surf or out on the reef to be smothered in the mighty seas.

Even without a shift of wind, they were in a perilous position. The launch was doing nobly, but she had never been built for such work. A craft so small could not reasonably be expected to live in such a seaway. She rose gallantly to the sweeping combers, but even a novice could see her sea-riding limit had almost been reached. Should the waves continue to increase much in size, the little craft was doomed.

"Oh, well," said Charley, with an attempt at cheerfulness, "we are not as bad off as we might be. While there's life there's hope. The wind may begin to go down any minute, and if it does we will soon be picked up. There are boats traveling this passage all the time. There's a sail, now."

He pointed to where a tiny fleck of white showed in the distance as they rose on the summit of a wave.

All gazed eagerly at the distant fleck of white. They knew that no boat could rescue them in such a sea, but it gave them a spark of comfort to know that they were not alone on the watery deep.

The white speck grew with amazing rapidity. In a few minutes, they were able to see that it was a small schooner scudding before the gale under a close reefed foresail.

It swept by them not two hundred yards away, so close that they could see the pipe in the mouth of the man at the wheel.

They gazed longingly after it until lost to view. When it had disappeared in the distance they felt an intensified loneliness and helplessness steal over them.

The only consolation in their wretched plight was the sun. It shone brightly down with a warmth grateful to their wet, chilled bodies.

"How fast do you think we are drifting, Captain?" inquired Charley, breaking the silence that had fallen upon them.

"Impossible to tell, exactly," returned the old sailor. "As a guess, I would say about five miles an hour."

"And we have been drifting about six hours, that would make thirty miles," the lad calculated. "If I remember the charts right that brings us about off of Tampa. Do you recall how the coast lies below there, Captain?"

"Not exactly," admitted the old sailor, "but I think it holds about the same direction. Of course, there are a good many capes running out into the gulf, but I don't think there is any of them long enough for us to pile up on, short of Cape Sable, and that's a couple of hundred miles away."

"So far so good, then," Charley commented. "We are in no immediate danger of piling up on shore at any rate. Whew, but the salt spray has made me thirsty as a fish. Here goes to get a drink of water." He crawled cautiously forward to the locker where the jugs were stowed.

"Both broken," he announced, after a glance inside. "I might have known it would happen with all the rolling and pitching about. Well, I guess we can manage to do without until the wind goes down."

But before noon, they realized that the loss of

their water was a serious blow.   The salt spray and hot sun gave them a painful thirst.   Their throats grew parched and dry, and they could barely swallow the remnants of food left from their supper. All attempt at conversation was given up and they sat huddled and silent in the little cockpit.

And so the long, dreary day dragged away.   Time and again boats drove past them, scudding before the gale, and once a large steamer passed them almost within hailing distance.   But no attempt at rescue could be made in such a sea.

Night found them still drifting almost too weak and weary to care what happened next.

"I believe the wind is going down a little," Charley said, shortly after the sun had set.

"It is," the old sailor agreed, "but I'm afraid it isn't going down fast enough to help us much. I noticed before dark that our sea anchor is going to pieces.   If it once goes and we swing into the trough of the seas, we are goners."

But the old sailor had done his work well and the sea anchor did not give way as he feared, instead, it held stoutly together while they drifted on into the night.

As the hours crept slowly away it became evident, beyond a doubt, that the wind was steadily going down, and with it the sea, although the waves still ran dangerously high.

They were beginning to gain fresh hope and

courage even in their suffering condition when the unexpected happened.

It was Walter that saw it first,—a dark wall rising high up in the darkness directly in their path. They could do nothing to avert the danger, only sit and stare dully at the looming mass. As they drove down upon it they saw that it was a forest of great trees rising, apparently, right out of the water.

Swiftly the doomed launch drifted down on the submerged forest.

When a hundred feet away the captain roused to action. "Here's a rope," he cried. "Each of you grab hold of it and cling on for life."

The words were barely out of his mouth, when the launch, rising on a big wave, came down with a crash and the next wave sweeping over her carried them off into the sea.

Like drowning men catching at a straw, the four clung to the rope as the rushing comber swept them on with it. Bruised, battered, and breathless, it hurled them upon something hard.

"Quick!" Charley cried, as he realized that they had been safely cast up into shoal water. "Quick! Up for the beach before the next comber!"

His companions had not waited for the command, but were already scrambling ahead. A few strides carried them out of danger—but there was no beach. Everywhere great trees rose up out of water nearly to their knees. Even in the darkness, they could see that the towering giants were almost bare of limb, and from high up above the water great crooked roots grasped down for a hold on the bottom.

Charley grasped one of the elbow-like roots and pulled himself up out of water. "Come on," he cried, "it's high and dry up here. These roots grow so close together one can almost lie down upon them."

His companions climbed weakly up beside him, where they rested, panting to gain their breath.

"Come on, we can make ourselves more comfortable than this," Charley said, when he had regained some of the wind that had been battered out of him.

They followed him as he crept cautiously from root to root. When they got about fifty feet from shore, he stopped.

"We had not better try to go any further," he said. "We're shut off from the wind all right. Now, for a good, long drink."

He slipped off into the water and, stooping, lapped greedily.

"Come on," he said, as he straightened up for breath, "drink all you want, it's sweet and fresh."

Much to their delight, his companions found it true and they drank long and greedily of the sweet, cool fluid.

"Now, for beds," Charley announced, cheerfully, when their thirst was at last satisfied. "Just reach up and break off branches and lay them across the roots, that will have to do for to-night."

By standing on their tip-toes, they were able to reach some of the small boughs and by pulling down—broke them off without difficulty. In a short time they had gathered and placed enough to make a platform big enough to accommodate them all. Upon this they were glad to lie down and stretch their tired, aching limbs and bodies.

" This beats the launch, anyway," Charley observed, cheerfully. " The trees shield us from the wind, our thirst is satisfied, and there is no spray to wet us. The air is so warm we ought to be able to get a little sleep without catching cold. I guess, we could all eat a pretty hearty meal right now but we will have to wait until morning to get that."

" What is this strange floating forest," his chum inquired. " I never saw trees like these before."

" They are quite common," Charley answered. " They are cypresses, and grow only on low, over-flooded ground."

" Have you any idea where we are, lad? " asked the captain.

" I fancy we are on the north-western edge of the great Everglade swamp," Charley replied. " It meets the gulf somewhere below Marco, about one hundred and twenty miles from Clearwater. But we can talk over these things in the morning. Now we had better get a little sleep if we can. We will need all the rest we can get, for to-morrow is going to be a hard day."

Hard and uncomfortable as was the uneven platform, his companions were so exhausted that they were instantly asleep and their snores soon mingled with the hooting of multitudes of owls and the croaking of thousands of frogs.

Charley lay awake a few minutes longer, his mind too full of worry and discouragement for instant sleep.

Their plight was enough to daunt the stoutest heart. Their launch was gone, pounded to pieces on the hard sand, and all the money they had worked so hard to earn and save would have to go to make good the loss. They would, after all their labor, be left just as they had landed in Clearwater with nothing but the clothing on their backs. That is, if they lived to reach Clearwater again.

His mind filled with these gloomy reflections, the lad at last dopped off to sleep.

CHAPTER XXVI.

CASTAWAYS.

THE sun was high in the sky when Charley awoke and aroused his companions who were still sleeping.

" Too much to do to-day to sleep longer," he declared. " We have got to find something to eat, and then try to get out of this place. Let's try the water for food first, and see what we can find.

" We don't want to stray away from each other or get out of hearing of the surf," he said, as they picked their way over the knee-like roots. " Out of sound of the sea, a man would lose himself in five minutes in this uncanny forest. It is too dense to tell directions by the sun and one would stand a good chance of wandering around until death overtook him. Only the Seminole Indians can find their way through this horrible jungle and they have known it for ages."

This little talk had brought them down to the water and they were surprised at the change a few hours had made. The sea was beautifully calm. Only a few smooth, gentle rollers remained to tell of the past storm.

Of the launch nothing remained but a few, broken, splintered planks drifted up against the trees.

Our little party were too hungry, however, to waste time in idle regrets.   They waded at once out into the water looking for crabs, oysters, clams, or anything to fill their aching stomachs.

But their search was fruitless.   Except for a few bits of water-logged limbs, the bottom was bare.

"I was afraid we would find nothing," Charley said, when they at last gave up the search.   "The water is too fresh here from the overflow from the Glades for shell-fish to grow.   We will have to depend on the land for our food until we can get out of this place."

They were turning to retrace their steps to the platform, when Charley spied a small box wedged in between two cypress knees.   He pulled it out and with hands that trembled with excitement lifted up the close-fitting cover and gave an exclamation of delight.   It was the little box which had contained the batteries used to run the launch.   Its contents were perfectly dry.   Constructed purposely to protect the cells from spray, it had floated safely in undamaged.   Besides the four dry cells, it contained a few little odds and ends they had placed there at different times to keep safe and dry.   There was a package of tobacco belonging to the captain, several fish-hooks, some salt and pepper mixed together in a little paper package, and a few other trifles of no particular value.

Hugging the box to him like a precious treasure, the lad followed his companions back to the platform. There, he carefully wedged it in between a couple of roots so that it could not be overturned. He had just done this when a startled cry from Walter sent him hurrying to his side.

He found his chum in the act of killing a huge snake upon which he had nearly stepped. It was a repulsive-looking creature, stumpy and bloated in appearance and nearly as big around as a man's leg.

" It's a moccasin," Charley said. " We will have to watch out for them. I expect there are lots of them around here. There's enough poison in that fellow's sac to kill a full-grown elephant."

" I don't know as it would be much worse to die of snake-bite than to die of hunger," Walter remarked, gloomily, " and there seems to be nothing fit to eat in this awful place."

" There are few places in this world where man cannot find food to eat, if he uses his wits," his chum replied. " God has provided food, everywhere, but has left it to man's intelligence to discover and make use of it."

" We have a hook and line, perhaps we could catch a fish," Captain Westfield suggested, hopefully.

" No bait," Charley said, briefly.

He sat plunged in thought while his companions looked around for something with which to bait the hook.

"Here's plenty of bait," Walter called. "Here's a whole colony of frogs—big ones, too."

Charley hurried to his side. His chum was peering under a great root where were sprawled several, big, long-legged frogs.

"What idiots we are," Charley grinned, as he dispatched one with a stick. "These are more than bait. They are the finest kind of food. Why, their legs are worth a dollar a pound in the New York market. Here was plenty of food right to our hand and we did not have sense enough to know it. Why, they were advertizing themselves all night long by their croaking."

The captain and Chris joined in the slaughter and in a short time forty frogs had fallen victims to the sticks.

"We are not likely to starve right away," Charley remarked, as they cut off and removed the skin from the legs. "There are certainly plenty more where these came from."

"But how is we goin' to cook 'em widout no fire?" Massa Chas?" demanded Chris.

Walter and the captain gazed at him in dismay. In their pleasure at the prospect of food they had never thought of the lack of fire. Their matches were spoiled and useless. They had no steel and flint. They did not even have a bit of glass with which to focus the rays of the sun.

Charley viewed their dismayed faces with a twinkle in his eyes.

" If you will take a couple of those frogs legs and see if you can catch some fish, Chris, I will see to the fire," he said.

Selecting a great root that was slightly hollowed on top, he built up a little heap of dry twigs, moss, and bits of bark, of which the trees around them offered an unlimited supply. Then he brought out from its resting place the box of batteries. Holding the ends of the wires down in the little heap of tinder, he rubbed them together. Sparks flew out on the bark and moss as the wires contracted and in a few seconds the heap was aflame. It only remained to put a few dry sticks on the blaze and the fire was ready for the cooking. Small branches sharpened at the end served for spits and in a few minutes a score of frogs legs were roasting over the coals.

The odor wafted on the air brought Chris hurrying from his fishing. His hunger had overcome his patience. He did not come quite empty-handed, however, but dragged along with him two slender-bodied, long-snouted fish fully four feet in length, covered with armor-like scales.

" Dem things is all I could catch, Massa Chas,"

he said, ruefully.   " I don't reckon dey's **any** good?"

" Those are gars," Charley announced.   " There are better-flavored fish, still, they are not to be despised.   They will go well with the frogs legs for dinner."

His method of cooking them was simple.   He removed the entrails, washed them out carefully, and buried them amongst the coals.   While the legs and gars were cooking, he dispatched Chris down to the shore again to find some bits of the yacht's planking to serve as plates.   By the time the little darkey returned laden with bits of boards, the repast was ready.   The gars were raked out on a plank, and their scale-armored skin stripped off, leaving the flesh white as snow, juicy and tender.

The four attacked the savory fish and delicious frogs legs with the appetites of wolves for they had eaten nothing for a day and night.

When they had finished, the world did not seem so dark and gloomy.   Things had taken on a rosier tinge.

" It is past noon already, I believe," Charley said, as they rested a bit on the little platform after their hearty meal.   " I don't believe it will pay us to start out to-day.   I think we had better wait until to-morrow and get back our strength a bit, for we have got a tough journey ahead of us."

His companions quickly agreed, for they still felt

weak from exposure, thirst, worry, and lack of food. This being settled, all busied themselves in making things more comfortable for the night, and in making what simple preparations they could for to-morrow's journey.

More branches were gathered and their little platform enlarged. There was plenty of long, soft, Spanish moss growing on the branches above their heads. It was far out of their reach and they could only look at it longingly until Walter hit upon the expedient of throwing their rope up over a limb and shinning up it like a monkey. He flung down great bunches of the soft, hair-like stuff which the captain spread out on their platform, transposing it into a soft springy couch.

While Walter and the captain were thus occupied, the other two busied themselves in securing and preparing a store of food for the journey. Fully fifty more frogs and three more gars were caught and roasted.

Each of the little party wore a large bandanna handkerchief around their necks and these Charley collected, washed thoroughly, and spread out on a root to dry. They were the only things he could think of in which to carry the food they had prepared.

It was dark when these preparations were completed, and they heaped fresh wood upon the fire and stretched out on their platform for a good night's rest once more.

"I expect they think at Clearwater that we are all dead," said Charley, as they lay gazing into the glowing embers of their fire.

"And Hunter is doubtless hugging himself with joy over the success of his trick," Walter added, grimly. "He didn't cause our death but he came very near it. I seldom wish any one ill, but he is one man I would like to see punished for the evil he has done."

"He will be," the captain said, with certainty. "The Lord will attend to that. If not in this world, then in the world to come."

"Well, he has succeeded in putting us back where we started," Charley remarked, "and he is left free to carry on his smuggling and liquor selling as he pleases."

"Unless Chris' ghost scares him off," Walter said. "Have you ever formed any theory about it and about the doctor's mysterious visit, Charley?"

"Not a theory," his chum replied. "They are just mysteries I cannot account for in any way. Of course the explanation is simple—if we only knew it—it always is in these mysteries."

The soft couch and the cozy warmth of the fire soon caused conversation to lag and yawns take the place of speech.

Before they composed themselves for slumber,

however, the captain offered up a heartfelt prayer, thanking the Lord for their deliverance from danger, and asking for His watchful care to attend them ever.

This simple act of devotion over, all sought the slumber their tired bodies craved.

CHAPTER XXVII.

HOMEWARD BOUND.

WALTER awoke just as dawn was lighting up the floating forest, and he immediately awakened his companions.

Breakfast was made off the frog legs and gar fish and as soon as it was finished, they took up their journey for Clearwater.

Charley took the lead, bearing the box with its precious batteries, and the others followed carrying the handkerchiefs of food.

They soon found that it was going to be hard, slow traveling. They could only make slow progress picking their way between the dense-growing trees and over the slippery roots. Every few paces they would have to stop and listen to make sure from the sound of the sea, that they were traveling in the right direction. At noon when they stopped to eat lunch, they estimated that they had covered but three miles. But the slowness was not the worst feature of their march, every step had to be made with watchful care. Never in all their Florida experiences had they seen so many snakes. Many were harmless, brightly-colored, water snakes, which riggled at their approach, but besides these, there were dozens of moccasins sunning themselves on the roots,—great, sullen, sluggish reptiles they were, many being as big around as a man's leg. They would not move from the places where they lay and our little party had to pick their way carefully around each, for to be bitten by one would mean a horrible, agonizing death. To add to their troubles, they were constantly slipping and falling on the slippery roots, bruising and hurting themselves.

" I hope it isn't much further till we come to the end of these cypresses," Charley said, as they nibbled at their lunch. " This kind of going is dangerous. We are liable to break an arm or leg before we get out of here."

" Massa Chas," Chris observed, " why don't we-alls take to de water? Hit would sho' be a heap easier an' we wouldn't be runnin' on dem pesky snakes all de time."

" Somebody kick me," Charley cried, sheepishly. " Of all the big fools in this state, we are the biggest. Here we have been wearing ourselves out over these pesky roots when we might have been wading comfortably along in the edge of the surf."

Until Chris had spoken, they had none of them thought of so simple a solution of their difficulty.

Being on shore, it had been the natural thing for them to try to make their way on shore.

No time was lost in following the little negro's suggestion. As already stated, there was no beach, the gulf meeting the forest, but the water along the edge of trees was not much over a foot in depth and the bottom was of hard sand. Their progress was now more rapid and free from the danger of snakes, but, much to their surprise, they found it much more tiring than the route over the roots. Only those who have tried walking in water for a distance, can realize the strain on the leg muscles.

By the middle of the afternoon, they were thoroughly tired out and Charley called a halt.

" We had better make camp," he said. " We don't want to wear ourselves out the first day, and besides, it will take us some time to build a platform and get ready for the night."

. Accordingly, they made their way back among the cypress and fell to work. A platform was built and well bedded with moss and a good fire started for the night.

For their supper, they only swallowed a few mouthfuls of their provisions. Truth to tell, the fish and frogs legs were beginning to pall on their appetites.

" I wish there was some game in this uncanny forest," Walter observed. " This stuff does not taste as good as it did. I believe, there is truth in that old statement that a man cannot eat a quail a day for thirty days."

" This forest is alive with game," Charley declared. " It's here even if we don't see it. Of course, there are no deer or bear for they avoid these watery places, but there are plenty of coons, wild cats, panthers, possums, and such things. I'll bet, there are at least a dozen animals watching our camp-fire right now and puzzling over it. Oh, there's plenty of game. The difficulty is to get it without guns or traps. I have been studying how to get some of it, and I think I have got an idea that may work."

It still lacked some time before dark, and Charley immediately began to carry out his idea. It was absurdly simple. Returning to the gulf's edge, a short search discovered several short, heavy pieces of timber drifted up among the trees. These they lugged back a ways from shore. Each timber was laid upon as flat a surface of roots as they could find. One end was then raised up a couple of feet and supported on a stick. To the stick they tied a couple of frogs legs and some of the bones from the gars.

" It's rather a primitive method of trapping but it may work," Charley observed. " The idea is that the animal pulling away at the bait will dislodge the stick and be crushed by the falling timber. Many animals, though, are too cunning to be tempted under such a dangerous-looking log, and others are quick enough to dodge its fall.

It was now nearly dark and our little party hurried back to their platform and fire for they had no desire to move about amongst the roots and snakes after night.

They were sleeping soundly when a succession of ear-splitting shrieks roused them into frightened wakefulness. It sounded like a woman crying out in mortal agony, but they had heard the sound before in their travels and knew it for a panther's screams. The animal was evidently close to them and they hastened to throw fresh fuel upon the dwindling fire. As the flames shot up the screaming ceased and the crashing of boughs told them of the hurried departure of the midnight prowler. As soon as the sounds died away, they stretched out to sleep once more knowing that they were in no danger so close to the fire.

Their first act on awakening in the morning was to look at the traps. They had set five altogether and every one had been sprung. The first two had caught, nothing in their fall. Pinioned under the third, they found a large, fat possum, the fourth held a snarling coon by one leg, while the fifth and last, was empty but splattered with blood and hair.

"Here's where Mr. Panther got himself a feed," Charley observed. "There was a coon, or possum under this log until he came along and made his supper. I'll bet, he's chuckling to himself right now over the easy meat."

The coon and possum were skinned at once and roasted on sticks over the coals. None of them ate much of the coon—its meat tasted somewhat like young pork but was rather too fat and strong, in flavor. The possum, however, they found delicious, the meat being white, tender and sweet.

As soon as they had eaten and tied up what remained in their handkerchiefs, they once more took up their journey.

They traveled steadily all the morning but with no signs apparent of reaching the edge of the belt of cypress. As far as they could see ahead of them along the shore the forest continued in an unbroken line.

Noon brought them to a serious obstacle, a broad, slow-flowing river of black, muddy water. They were all good swimmers and could have easily swam the half mile which separated them from the other shore, but the sight of several large, floating, log-like objects made them hesitate to attempt it.

" Those are either alligators or crocodiles," Charley said. " We had better make sure which they are before we venture in. Alligators are cowardly creatures, and will seldom attack a man, but crocodiles are not to be trifled with."

It was some time before one of the floating monsters came near enough to reveal its character but when it did they were glad they had waited. It was a vicious, scaly-looking crocodile, fully fifteen feet in length.

"Hard luck," commented Charley in disgust. "That means we will have to follow this bank up until we can find a place we can cross and then follow the other bank back to the gulf again. It may be only a few miles or it may be a hundred. It may take us a day or it may take us a week."

"I wonder what river this is?" Walter said. "If we only knew, we could tell where we are."

"It's impossible to say for certain," his chum replied. "There are a lot of big rivers emptying into the gulf. I am inclined to think, however, that this is the Snake River. It fits the description I've heard of the Snake. Well, let's have dinner and then we'll start to follow it up."

A fire was lit and while it was getting under way, Walter succeeded in catching a leather-back turtle of which there were numbers basking on logs. This they cooked by the simple expedient of burying it in the coals and letting it roast in its own shell.

Ordinarily they would have relished its delicate flavor, but they were beginning to tire of an all-meat diet. They were beginning to crave vegetables, bread, coffee, and the other varieties of food that make up civilized meals.

They were munching the last of their frugal repast when they sprang to their feet in amazed surprise.

"Good morning," said a voice right behind them.

Standing but a few feet away was a splendid-looking Indian lad, leaning gracefully upon a long-barreled rifle. "Good morning," said the young Seminole again, smiling at their surprise.

"Good morning," stammered Charley, in reply. "Who are you? Where did you come from? Where are we?"

The Seminole's smile widened at the volley of questions.

"My name is Willie John," he said in perfect English. "I come from the Big Cypress Swamp. Some of my people are camped there, hunting. You now are at the Snake River. It is about fifty miles from Tampa. Are you lost?"

"Yes," replied Walter, recovering from his surprise. "We are, or rather were, both shipwrecked and lost. We had begun to think that we were the only people in the world. That's why your voice surprised us so."

"I see," said the Indian lad, with his pleasant smile. "Perhaps it will be very pleasant to help you a little."

CHAPTER XXVIII.

THE CHUMS HAVE TWO CALLERS.

" PERHAPS you can tell us how far we will have to go up this river before we find a place where we can cross?" Charley said.

" I can do better than that. I can take you across. I have a canoe but a little ways from here," replied the Indian lad.

" Good," exclaimed Walter, with pleasure. " That will help us out a lot. We were dreading the trip around."

" We can cross as soon as you wish," offered the young Seminole.

" Let's sit a while and rest," suggested Charley, whose curiosity was aroused by the manner and speech of the splendid young savage. " Are there many of your people camped at the Big Cypress?"

" About one hundred. The Seminoles are becoming as the leaves in autumn," said the lad, sadly. " There are only four tribes of us left. One is camped at Fort Lauderdale, one at Indiantown, another tribe is hunting in the Glades, and we are at the Big Cypress. Only four hundred left of a once powerful race." His voice and face took on a deeper tinge of melancholy as he said, " Soon we will all be gone and only be a memory growing dim with the passing years."

" Oh, I guess, it's not as bad as that," said Charley, cheerfully. " The Seminoles will gradually adjust themselves to civilization and begin to increase once more."

" We are a homeless people," declared the lad. " Your race took all, except this swamp. Here we have lived at peace where no white man would live and now even it is being taken from us. Every week from the East Coast, great canals, like rivers, creep further and further into the swamp. And as fast as they creep in follow the whites with ploughs and teams. Houses spring up over night. The forest and deer vanish, and green fields take their place. Soon the great swamp will be no more."

" But surely that is good," Charley argued. " It is the onward march of civilization."

" Civilization," echoed the Indian, bitterly. " Will civilization make my people better? They are truthful, they are honest, they are cleanly in mind and body. Will civilization make them better? "

Charley was silenced. Apart from education, he knew the Seminoles were the superior of his own race in morals.

" No, civilization will not improve us, but it is

coming to us. Nothing can stop it. The white man rejoices at its advance, the red man is sad and troubled. The great writer Kipling says,—

> ' The toad beneath the harrow knows
>   Exactly where each tooth point goes,
>   The butterfly beside the road,
>   Preaches contentment to the toad.' "

Our little party marveled at this strange youth, a savage, yet educated, gentle mannered, and of a wisdom far beyond his years.

In reply to their questions, they learned that a noble white man, Dr. Fish, was spending his life in the heart of the Everglades, striving with all his might to do something for its unfortunate and deserving people. Amongst other things, he was educating the younger members of the tribe and trying to fit them for the inevitable struggle under the new order of things. They learned that their new friend was one of his pupils. That the lad was hunting for skins that he might earn the money necessary to go to college and fit himself to help his race in their distress.

Our little party were filled with admiration for the noble youth's lofty ambition. They reflected sadly that there were woefully few white boys fired by the same high ideals.

They would have liked to have tarried and talked

longer with the interesting lad, but the slanting sun warned them that they must be on their way.

The young Seminole led the way to his canoe which proved to be a cranky, clumsy craft dug out of a big cypress tree. Used as they were to water crafts, they entered it with considerable doubt and care. As soon as they were safely aboard, the lad shoved off and with a long pole propelled the ungainly craft to the other side of the river.

"Follow the gulf," he directed, as they bade him good-by. "You ought to be out of the forest by to-morrow night. You will meet more rivers, but they contain no crocodiles so you will be able to cross them without danger."

He shook hands gravely with each at parting, repeating quaintly the words of a hymn the good missionary had doubtless taught him. As our little party once more took up their weary march, the familiar words so quaintly quoted by the solitary lad in the gloomy swamp kept thrumming through their thoughts.

"God be with you till we meet again,
By His counsel guide uphold you,
With His sheep securely fold you,
God be with you till we meet again."

They tramped steadily the balance of the afternoon and at night made camp on the edge of an-

other large river. Here they were fortunate
enough in finding a large bed of big mussels or
fesh-water oysters, upon which they made a delicious supper.

Sunrise found them again on their way, eager to
be out of the somber, gloomy forest. They had
already spent three days in its gloomy depths and
they were heartily sick of it and its crawling ser-
pents. They paused but a few minutes at noon to
rest a bit, and to eat a few of the mussels they had
brought with them, then pushed on again.

" I believe we are nearly out of this hateful forest," Charley said, as they waded along its edge.
" It seems to me that the cypress are not quite so
dense, and, I fancy, I can get a glimpse of some
trees of a darker green ahead.

An hour's more wading proved his guess correct.
Palmettoes, satinwoods, bays, and even pines, began to be mingled with the cypress. The color of
the water changed gradually from its fresh blackness to the salt tinge of greenish-blue, and, at last,
they came to a stretch of sandy beach which they
hailed with joy for their feet were getting tender
and sore from the constant wading.

Long before dark, they were clear of the dismal,
floating forest and made camp on a high, sandy
bluff by the side of a clear, purling little brook.
Their supper was a feast; roasted buds of the cabbage palmettoes, black bass fresh from the creek,

oysters, clams, crab claws, and for dessert, huckle-berries which grew in profusion around them.

When it was finished, they stretched out on the beds they had made of dry, fragrant sea moss be-fore the glowing fire in more hopeful spirits than they had been in many days. They were lying thus chattering contentedly when they received an unex-pected visitor. He came as silently as an Indian. They neither saw nor heard him until he stepped into the fire's glow. He was a man of about forty years of age, dressed in buckskin and was of rather engaging appearance. His name, he said, was Watson, and he was a hunter and trapper.

From him they learned they were but a day's journey from Tampa, and that a good beach ex-tended the whole distance.

The stranger stayed for at least two hours. He seemed to take an almost childish interest in their account of their misadventures and took an inter-est, that was pathetic, in all they could tell him of the news of the world outside. Events which had occurred two and three years before seemed to be news to him. Yet he appeared an educated, brainy man.

He stayed until the little party's yawns could not longer be suppressed, then departed as silently as he had come.

"Whew," sighed Charley, when at last he was

gone, " I would as soon entertain a rattlesnake as that man."

" Why? " Walter said, in surprise. " I thought he seemed bright and pleasant."

" Is it possible you have never heard of that man, Watson? I thought everyone in Florida knew of him."

" I have never heard of him, either," said Captain Westfield. " Who is he? Tell us about him."

" It's a horrible tale, yet pathetic, too, in a way," said the lad, thoughtfully. " From what I have often heard, we are now in what is sometimes called ' Murderer's Belt.' I have heard it referred to many, many times, but I had forgotten all about it until I heard that man's name. In this fringe of country bordering on the Everglades, it seems that there are some forty or fifty men hiding out. They are men wanted for serious crimes, murder in most cases, for nothing but the dread of being hung would induce men to lead the lives they are forced to live. They live solitary lives. The Indians will have nothing to do with them and they fear or mistrust each other too much to associate amongst themselves. Each one is as alone in the world as though he were in solitary confinement. They get their living with their traps and rifles. That's all they get out of life, just a living and freedom. An army could not capture one of them, except by surprise, for at the first alarm they plunge into the

swamp where none but an Indian could follow them.
I don't suppose that man Watson has even spoken
to a human being in years until to-night. Only our
apparent harmlessness induced him to seek speech
with us, I believe. For Watson is the king murderer
of the lot. He came to Florida some years ago
from Georgia, with the law officers in close pursuit.
It had been discovered up there that he was the
author of a string of mysterious murders. Brutal,
cold-blooded murders that had been going on for
years. Some forty or forty-five years in all, I believe. The officers caught up with him at Tampa,
but he killed two, wounded the third, and escaped
into 'Murderer's belt.' With him was a young
brother, who, so far as could be learned, had taken
no part in his crimes, but the two seemed to stick
together from mutual affection.

"Contrary to the usual custom in 'Murderer's
Belt,' the two did not play it alone together as they
should have done, but met and made friends with a
man by the name of Cox who was about as hardened a character as Watson. The three hung together for a while, but one day there was a little
quarrel and Cox shot the boy through the heart.
He intended to kill Watson also and thought he had
done so but the bullet glanced off on a button and
Watson recovered his senses after a while to find his
brother dead and Cox gone. They are both now
seeking each other in the 'Belt.' Watson will try

to kill Cox at sight to avenge his brother, and Cox will try to kill Watson the first chance he gets to keep from being killed.   Neither can appeal to the law for they are both outside the law.   It's a case of man against man or rather murderer against murderer.   Think of what their lives must be. Every hour, day and night, trying to kill or keep from being killed.   Not seeing each other, but knowing every minute that the other is seeking him with murder in his heart, expecting death from behind every tree and bush."

"Massa Chas," said Chris, with a shudder, "youse gibbin' me de creep.   Please not dat kind ob talk an' let's go to sleep."

CHAPTER XXIX.

AN IDLE DAY.

Much to their disappointment, our little party were forced to remain where they were the next day. The long, continuous soaking in the brackish water had made their feet so tender that walking on the sand was very painful. They prepared as usual for the start but they had not gone more than a hundred yards when they gave up the attempt and returned to where they had camped.

"It is just as well for us to lay by, a day, anyway," Charley observed in an attempt to force cheerfulness from their enforced detention. "Tampa is only a day away and we couldn't go into the city like we are. We would be arrested as tramps as soon as the police caught sight of us. Gee! but we are a tough-looking gang. Captain, you look like a typical 'Weary Willie.' All you need is a stick, a tomato can, and a handkerchief full of hand-outs to be a complete 'knight of the road.'"

"You haven't got any room to make fun of my appearance," grinned the old sailor. "You look like a cross between a coal heaver and a chimney sweep and Walter looks just as bad.   It don't show up quite as bad on Chris."

"Dat's de advantage ob bein' a nigger," agreed Chris, composedly.   "A nigger can't show de dirt much.   If I was one ob you white chillens I'd be plum ashamed ob myself—I sho' would."

And indeed, the little party was a sight to behold. Their clothes were stiff from mud, slime, and brine, and their skins were grimed from the smoke of their camp-fires.   They had washed thoroughly, and often, but the mud and slime of the swamp had made useless all efforts to keep clean.

"First, we had better take a good wash ourselves and scrub good and clean with this white sand. Then wash out our clothes as good as we can. This warm sun will soon dry them out and keep us from catching cold.   While they are drying, we can be getting something to eat for the day and fix up our feet.   When that's all done we want to lay quiet the balance of the day and give our feet a chance to get into shape," said Charlie.

Without soap, the washing of their clothes was a slow, laborious job.   Luckily their clothing was comparatively new and strong or it would never have stood the rubbing and pounding it received. At last, however, the operation was completed and their pants and shirts were spread on the bushes to dry.   This done, they turned their attention to the laying in of a supply of food for the day. While Chris, with the fish-line, sought a likely looking pool near the creek's mouth, Walter and Charley hunted for oysters and clams, and the captain busied himself in picking a generous supply of huckleberries. In a short time, the two boys had collected enough shell-fish for a couple of days, and joined the old sailor in picking the black, glossy berries. By the time they had gathered all that were wanted, Chris had succeeded in landing three big sea bass and a small shark about four feet in length.

"Hold on, don't do that," Charley exclaimed, as the little darkey was casting the shark back into the water. "That shark is the very thing we want. I would not take a dollar for it."

"Hit ain't no good to eat," protested Chris. "Hit tastes so strong you'd have hard work to swallow one bit of hit."

"I'll show you what I want it for," Charley said. "Just start up a little fire while the rest of us open up some clams and oysters for dinner."

When the fire was going briskly, the lad attacked the shark with his sheath-knife. Splitting it open, he cut out the fat and the liver from inside. These he placed in a big shell obtained from the beach and set the shell on the coals.

"Now get some nice, clean, Spanish moss," he directed, "and unravel a yard or so of that rope we brought with us. There's nothing better than shark oil for a liniment. It is going to do our feet a world of good."

As soon as the oil was tried out in the shell, they rubbed it on to their swollen feet. The result was immediate and gratifying. The burning ceased at once and the aching visibly decreased. When they had rubbed the oil well in, they wrapped their feet up in Spanish moss which they bound in place with bits of the raveled rope.

"Now if we lay quiet and don't use them, they will be all right by to-morrow," declared Charley, with satisfaction. "I guess our clothes are dry by now. We had better put them on or this sun will have our backs blistered as sore as our feet."

The boys hobbled over to where they had spread out their clothes and to their satisfaction found them perfectly dry.

They were just slipping on their shirts when the captain descended upon them, wrath on his usually good-natured face.

"What have you done with my clothes?" he demanded, angrily. "This is no time for joking. Stop it right now."

"We haven't touched your clothes," Charley protested, indignantly. "They are just where you left them."

"They ain't," gasped the old sailor, paling, for he knew the lad always told the truth. "They're gone. Someone has stolen them."

"Whew," whistled Charley. "Some one of those murderers must have taken a fancy to them."

"I'd murder him, if I could get my hands on him," cried the captain, wrathfully. "How am I going to go into town in this fix."

Charley grinned as he caught the humor of the situation. "You could go into town all right," he said, "there wouldn't be any trouble about that. It's what they would do to you after you got into town. I don't really believe the police would stand for your present costume, Captain."

The old sailor glared at him in helpless wrath. "What am I to do?" he mourned. "My back is burning already."

"Sit down in the shade of that tree," Walter suggested, "the sun won't hit you there. We'll have to think up something for you. We would hardly care to enter the city with you in your present condition."

Charley had quickly seized upon a plan to clothe the old sailor but he could not resist the temptation to tease him a little.

"If we only had a barrel we could fix you out all right," he said, reflectively. "We could knock out the head and hang it from your neck by ropes."

"But we haven't got the barrel," said Walter, regretfully, catching his chum's wink.

The captain eyed them suspiciously but the two lads' faces were serious.

Walter appealed to his chum, gravely.   "He might pretend he is a work of art," he suggested, " he's got a ship tattooed on his back, a mermaid on his chest, and a flying fish on each leg.   Maybe Tampa is an art-loving city and will receive him with open arms."

"I am afraid not," Charley replied, gravely.   "I expect it's just a big, rough, unartistic city.   I think it would be better for him to enter as a nature-lover who had adopted the simple life."

"Good," exclaimed his chum, enthusiastically. "Just the thing.   What a sensation it will make. I can just see the papers with his picture on the front page and the black head lines.

"Noted sea captain adopts the simple life and discards clothing.   Says, 'go naked and you'll live to be a hundred.'"

"What's the name of that widow lady who was so interested in the captain, Mrs. Wick?   I believe I'll send her one of the papers," said Charley, reflectively.

This was more than the old sailor could stand. "If you young idiots can't suggest anything sensible, for the Lord Harry's sake shut up," he spluttered.

"I don't see much we can suggest," Charley said seriously.   "Our clothes are all too small for you or we would each give something to help dress you. There's no hope of getting your clothes back.   The only thing I can think of, is to do you up in Spanish moss like they do roses and tender plants they send North."

"I guess Spanish moss is the only thing," admitted the captain. "It ain't much, but it's better than nothing."

So, with difficulty, restraining their laughter, the two lads proceeded to cover the old sailor with great bunches of the strong, long, Spanish moss, tying it securely to him with pieces of the raveled-out rope.

When they had finished, he was a queer and wonderful creature.

The sight was too much for Chris. The little darkey lay on the grass and rolled with laughter.

"Massa Cap, Massa Cap," he gasped, "you look jes' like a great big Teddy Bear."

The old sailor grinned feebly at the three, mirth-convulsed boys.

"I reckon I do look some funny," he admitted, "but I don't care. It's comfortable, and a heap sight decenter than nothing."

A look of anxiety came to his face and he winced visibly.

"What's the matter?" asked Charley. "No pins sticking in you?"

The captain scratched vigorously. "Thar's ants in that pesky moss," he declared, at which announcement the three boys let out a roar of laughter that made the woods ring.

It was verily a day of rest for the four wanderers. The balance of it was spent lying on their soft moss couches in the warm sunshine talking over past events and planning for the future.

With the night came Watson again to sit in the shadows by their camp and listen greedily to what they could tell him of the world outside. In spite of the man's bloody record of crime, they could not help a touch of pity for his loneliness. And the truth was more indelibly stamped on their minds that evil brings its own punishment.

They told him about the theft of the captain's clothes, and he listened attentively.

"I guess it was Black Sam took them," he commented. "He was in rags the last glimpse I got of him. He certainly needs clothes but I guess you need them worse. I'll get them back for you."

"Strangers," he said, as he rose to go, "I want you to do me a big favor. When you get outside send me a copy of the Atlanta Constitution. I ain't heard a thing of Georgia in years. Send it to Marco, care of Indian Charley, and I'll get it all right."

Charley promised him they would do so.

In the morning when they awoke, the captain's clothes were lying beside the fire.

They never knew exactly how Watson made Black Sam relinquish his prize but there was a large blood-stain on the shoulder of the cleanly-washed shirt and they formed their own opinion.

CHAPTER XXX.

THE DISCOVERY.

THE day and night of rest, together with the shark oil, had worked wonders with the sore feet and, much to their delight, the little party found that they could travel once more without pain.

After the weary days in the dismal swamp, they rejoiced in the new country they had entered. A broad, white sand beach made walking easy and their eyes were delighted with the ever-changing landscape. Soon they began to come upon signs of human habitation. Now a herd of cows grazing in placid contentment, and later, a little shack perched upon the beach and tenanted by a lone hermit of a fisherman. From him, they learned that they were within fifteen miles of the city of Tampa.

The captain purchased a package of tobacco from the hermit and was soon enjoying the first smoke he had had in many days.

The boys looked longingly at the fisherman's little sloop bobbing at anchor in the cove. They would have liked to have bargained for a passage to Tampa but they had too little money in their pockets to afford such a luxury.

It was nearly noon and the fisherman, with the ready hospitality of his calling, invited them to dinner, an invitation they were not slow to accept.

The meal was simple, but the vegetables tasted delicious after their steady meat diet, and they reveled in the strong, hot, fragrant coffee.

They did not linger long after eating, for they were anxious to reach their journey's end.

When about five miles from the friendly fisherman's, Charley called a halt.

"Listen, and see if you hear anything," he said. "I've been hearing a queer noise for the last ten minutes but maybe it's only my imaginations."

His companions stopped and listened.

"No, it isn't your imagination," the captain declared. "I can hear it, too—a kind of peculiar noise I can't describe."

"It sounds like the soft smacking of a thousand lips," Walter said. "I wonder what it is."

"We will soon find out," Charley replied. "It seems to come from somewhere ahead."

As they advanced, the peculiar noise became more distinct. It grew steadily in volume until at last they stood at what had once been the mouth of a creek, but which was now closed up, at the entrance, by a small mound of drifted sand, thus changing the former creek into a small lake.

"My goodness! Look at it!" gasped Charley, weakly, pointing at the land-locked pond.

" Jumping Moses," swore the captain, the nearest approach to an oath he ever permitted himself to use.

The peculiar noise came from the lake's surface. It was literally covered with tiny, open, gaping mouths.

" Mullet," Charley said, in a hushed voice, " mullet, thousands of them, tens of thousands of them, penned up in there like rats in a trap."

" And we without a net or boat," lamented Walter, bitterly. " Just our luck."

" Golly! " exclaimed Chris. " If we only had dese fish in Clearwater we wouldn't hab to worry 'bout money no more for awhile."

" They must have got caught in here during that gale," Charley pondered. " The heavy sea drifted up the sand and closed up the entrance so they could not get out into the gulf again. They can't live a great while longer in that small body of water. That great number must have about all the oxygen in the water exhausted by now. Their coming to the surface to breathe proves that. They seldom do that surface breathing. Let's have a look at that pond and see what it's like."

A hasty examination showed them that the lagoon was shallow, not more than three feet in the deepest places.

" Just an ideal place to catch them," Charley declared.

"Yes," agreed Walter, excitedly. "If we only had two or three nets we could tie them together and drag them across the pond like a seine."

Charley shook his head, decidedly. "That bunch would tear your nets to shreds if you tried that plan. Why, boy, you don't comprehend how many fish there are in that school."

"Well, I guess it's no use standing here looking at them any longer," said Walter, morosely. "We can't do anything with them, so we might as well be moving on."

"Yes, and moving fast too," Charley agreed, "but I have a hope that we can do something with those fish. They are worth trying for, anyway. It all depends on whether we can get to Clearwater and back again before they die, as they surely will as soon as all the air is gone from the water. Come on, let's hurry."

As they hastened along at top speed, he explained his plan.

"The first thing is to get to Clearwater," he declared. "Get the Roberts boys and their launch and nets, and all the other boats and nets we can get together, then come back here as quick as we can get back. Of course, we will have to divide up with the Roberts but they have been good friends of ours and deserve it. There's enough fish to pay all of us for the trouble if we find them still alive."

"Go your fastest, lad," said the old sailor, briefly, "you'll find us right at your heels."

And go fast Charley did. It called forth all the wind and strength of his three companions to keep up with him.

Just as night was falling, four tired, draggled-looking persons entered the ticket office of the Atlantic Coast Line in Tampa.

"When's the next train for Clearwater?" demanded one of the youths of the party, crisply.

"Just gone," answered the agent, briefly. "No more until morning."

"But we have got to get to Clearwater to-night," said the lad, desperately.

The agent noted the look of dismay on the four faces. "The Northern flier is due here in half an hour," he said, slowly. "She slows down a bit for the curve. If it's a matter of life or death you might be able to board her. I would not advise it, though. She does not slack down much at Clearwater and it would be pretty risky jumping off."

"Where's the best place to get on her?" asked the lad, briefly.

"Right down by the water tank. It's risky, though."

The lad thanked him, and the four hurried off for the water tank.

They boarded the train safely and stood on the platform hanging on to the rails as the fast limited

tore on in the darkness.   They would have liked
to have entered one of the coaches and rested on
the cushioned seats but they were afraid the con-
ductor would insist upon carrying them on to the
next regular stop, a hundred miles beyond their
destination.

It was but an hour's ride to the little town and
the flyer barely slackened speed as she thundered
into it.   As the lights of the station flashed into
view, they stepped down to the lowest step and
jumped.

It was a fearful chance to take, but luck was
with them.   They landed in a bank of soft sand,
and, although the breath was knocked out of them
for a minute, they escaped unhurt except for Walter.   He gained his feet, wincing with pain.

" I've twisted my ankle," he said.   " Don't stop
for me.   I would only be a hindrance to you with
this game foot.   Go on.   I'll hunt up a doctor and
have it tended to."

Charley hesitated.   " I don't like to leave you
this way, old fellow," he said.

" I don't like to be left, either," said his chum,
grimly, " but you can't do me any good by staying.
Go on.   Don't waste precious time."

Charley reluctantly obeyed.

Walter stood gamely watching them with a smile
on his face until the three were out of sight, then
he hobbled for the main street, his face contorted

with pain. His injury was far more serious than he had pretended. He was convinced that some bones in his foot were broken but he had concealed his plight from his chums for he knew they would not leave him if they thought his injury at all serious.

Followed by the captain and Chris, Charley headed for the little station not far away. There were a few loungers on the platform and amongst them he was pleased to see one of the fish-boat captains who had helped in the towing of the " North Wind."

" Is it you or your ghost? " he exclaimed, when Charley approached him. " Everyone thought you and your friends were lost in that gale."

" If we are ghosts, we don't know it," Charley laughed. " Say, can we hire you and your launch for a couple of hours? "

" You can," said the fish captain, promptly. " Fishing is so poor now I have quit it for a while. Where do you want to go? "

" First over to the island where we used to stay, and then across to the Roberts camp, if they are at home."

" Oh, you'll find them there all right. Fishing is so poor, now, it does not pay to go out."

Charley pulled out a five-dollar bill, the only money he had in his pocket.

" Here's your pay in advance," he said. " We

may want to hire you for two or three days, but I'll let you know about that a little later. Just now, we are in a hurry. Can you take us right off?"

"Right away," said the fisherman, pocketing the bill with satisfaction. "My launch is tied up to the dock. Come on if you are ready."

In five minutes our little party was aboard the launch and headed for the island.

"Reckon there ain't much use going there," the fisherman remarked, as they sped along. "Someone has torn the cabin down and broken the dock you built all to pieces.

Charley smiled. Evidently Hunter had been doing all he could to discourage anyone else from occupying the island.

"We don't intend to live there, any more," he said. "I just want to go ashore there for a minute."

As the launch drew in close to the shore, he had him stop the engine and as soon as the keel touched bottom, he jumped overboard and waded ashore, carrying the launch's lantern.

"Wait here for me. I'll be back in a minute," he directed.

Once up near the cabin, he was not long in finding what he was after. He and his companions had taken in over a hundred dollars in cash from their sales of oysters and clams. It was too large a sum for them to risk carrying around in their pockets and they had not cared to leave it unguarded in the cabin while they were away fishing, so they had wisely put it in a glass jar and buried the jar in a safe place, keeping out only enough for pocket money.

The lad found their little treasure undisturbed and stuffing it into his pockets he hurried back to the launch.

" Now head over for the Roberts camp," he commanded, as soon as he climbed aboard.

CHAPTER XXXI.

THE FISH.

"I HAVE rather a personal question to ask you, Captain Brown," Charley said, as the launch ploughed her way through the glowing water.

" Let's hear it," said the fisherman.

The lad hesitated. " It sounds rather impudent, but J want to know just how good a friend you are to Hunter and his gang? "

" Can't say that I am a friend of his at all," answered the man, frankly. " There are quite a few of us fishermen who have no particular love for him, but we all try to avoid trouble with him because he can make things pretty costly for a man in a secret, underhand way which leaves one nothing to grasp upon. I suspect you have found that out for yourselves."

" We have," admitted Charley, candidly. " It's a wonder to me, you fishermen, who do not like him, haven't got together and run him off before now."

" I expect it does look kind of queer to an outsider," replied the man, reflectively. " But it's natural enough when one gets to understand fishermen.

You seldom find a fisherman but who has been more
or less of a roamer and adventurer. Their lives
have made them self-reliant and taught them the
rather hard lesson that it don't pay to take up
others' quarrels. Unconsciously, perhaps, their
motto is 'leave me alone and I'll leave you alone.'
They may really be in sympathy with a man, but
they seldom will assist him in his disputes. That
trait in them explains why Hunter lasts so long.
They simply will not combine against him."

"I see," said Charley, thoughtfully, "that puts
the matter in a new light to me. I had supposed
they stood for Hunter and his ways because they
approved of him and them."

"Not at all," said the other, warmly. "Most of
the fishermen are pretty good fellows at heart, but
'hands off' is their policy."

"I am glad to learn that," Charley said, frankly.
"I want to hire a few fishermen and their launches
for a couple of days, but the work is rather important, and I want only men who will work for
the interest of the man who pays them and not play
into the hands of someone like Hunter."

"The fishermen will be true to their employer's
interests," declared the other, emphatically.

"Good," said the lad. "I am going to trust to
your judgment. As soon as you land us at Roberts'
dock, I want you to go back to Clearwater and get
four more launches with their skiffs and captains.

Get the best and most trustworthy men you can pick out. If you can be back with them before midnight, it will mean five dollars extra for each of them and ten dollars extra for yourself. Bring plenty of gasoline for the launches, and provisions for two days for yourselves."

"I can get the men and boats all right," Captain Brown said, doubtfully, "but they will want ten dollars apiece per day, and not knowing you, they will want some money down."

Charley reached down into his pocket and pulled out the roll of bills at which the man gazed in amazement.

"Here's the first day's pay for each in advance," he said, counting out fifty dollars, "and remember there is five dollars extra apiece in the job if they are all at the Roberts dock ready to start at midnight."

. . "We'll all be ready in two hours," Captain Brown declared. "Here we are at the dock. I won't stop. Just jump out and give me a shove off. Time is worth money now," he grinned.

The three jumped out on the little pier, shoved the launch off, and it was quickly lost in the darkness.

Charley grinned as he stood for a moment listening to the rapid popping of the engine's exhaust.

"He's got that engine turning up as fast as it will go," he commented. "He means to get that

extra ten dollars, all right. Gee! but I've been using my nerve, spending money that belongs as much
to the rest of you as it does to me."

"That's all right," approved Captain Westfield.
"You are planning out this thing. Spend the last
penny if you want to. I believe in letting one at a
time run a thing. Others butting in only gum
things up—a ship don't work well under more than
one captain."

The light was still burning in the Roberts boys'
cabin and a tap at the door brought forth an invitation to come in.

When the three stepped into the lighted room
they were greeted with exclamations of amazed
pleasure.

"It's good to see you all are safe again," cried
the husky Bill, as he shook hands with a heartiness
that made them wince. "We were mourning you
as drowned. We did not believe your launch could
have lasted out that gale."

"She didn't," Captain Westfield said. "She
went to pieces on shore a good many miles down the
coast."

"Tough luck," said the big fisherman, sympathetically. "You fellows do seem to hit it rough.
It's too blamed bad, that's what it is."

"I believe our luck is due to change pretty soon,"
Charley said, with a smile. "How are things coming with you now?"

"Couldn't be much worse," Bill stated, briefly. "Goodness only knows what's become of all the fish. We haven't wet a net since the gale. What we lack of being stone-broke isn't much. We have only got about a hundred dollars in cash left but you are welcome to half of that. I guess you are worse off than we are."

The three chums' hearts warmed with gratitude at the big fellow's generous offer.

"We'll take the whole hundred, if you please," Charley said, calmly, "but not as a loan. We want you three as partners for a couple of days and the hundred will go to pay expenses. Can you give us a cup of coffee? We haven't had a bite to eat since noon."

While the big fisherman rustled around fixing a lunch and making the coffee, Charley told of their discovery.

"Whew, it sounds like finding money," Bill commented, when he had finished. "But we don't deserve any half share for just going with you and helping you out. Just pay us the same as you do the other fishermen."

"No," Charley said, and his two chums nodded vigorous approval of his words. "It isn't what you are going to do but what you have already done that counts with us. You helped us out when we were friendless, and it is only just that you should share in our good fortune if we have any. But we must not count our chickens before they are hatched. The fish may be all dead by the time we get there, or someone else may have found them— they were making noise enough to be heard a mile.

"Oh, we are making you no gift," he said, as Bill still protested against an equal division. "We may need your help and we need your money to pay off the launch men in case the trip is fruitless. It will take more cash than we've got. Besides, there may be some fighting."

"Too bad we have got to have anyone in this but ourselves," Bill observed.

"We have got to have help," Charley declared, "and, really, I do not fear any trouble from those who go with us. They are taking no nets with them, (I figured your three nets would be all we could use to advantage in such a small place). They have no idea as to our destination or what we are after. When they get there they will realize that it is too far away for them to come back, get their nets and return and do anything all tired out as they will be from the trip. Besides, I planned to offer them a bonus in money after we get there, provided they work good and hard."

"You've got a long head on you," Bill said, admiringly. "You've evidently got it all planned out."

"I tried to plan so far as I could," Charley said,

modestly. " Where I fear trouble is when the fish begin to come into Clearwater.   There will be a stampede of the other fishermen on us then.   Put all your guns and ammunition in the launch.   We may need them."

While the three were eating, the Roberts packed up groceries and rolled up blankets for the trip. These, and the rifles, they carried down to the launch while the chums were finishing their coffee.

They were ready none too soon, for as the chums drained their cups, they caught the mingled popping of the coming launches.

It still lacked twenty minutes to midnight when the last launch came churning up to the end of the little dock.

Charley counted out five dollars and handed it to each of the launch captains. " This is for being ahead of the time set.   You'll each get your ten dollars apiece at the close of each day.   Now, if you are all ready, we'll be off."

" Where are we going, Boss? " questioned one of the captains.

" I do not know the name of the place," the lad replied, thoughtfully. " Just follow our launch. We will lead the way."

In a few minutes the things were all stowed aboard and Bill started up the engine.   The launch leaped ahead and, with bow headed down the coast, sped away in the darkness closely followed by the other boats containing four contented, but thoroughly mystified, captains.

As soon as they were fairly under way, our three chums stretched out on the launch's cushioned seats for a nap. They were completely worn out by the eventful day and night.

At sunrise Charley was awakened by Bill.

"We've been running without a hitch all night," the big fisherman informed him. "We must be getting near to your creek by now. We passed Tampa over an hour ago."

Charley stood up and surveyed the shore-line. "I took a landmark before I left," he said. "There's a great, dead, pine tree standing up amongst a clump of palmettoes just to the south of the creek. I believe I can see it ahead there a couple of miles."

At the end of ten minutes, he could make out the big, dead pine plainly.

He awakened his chums and the three sat tense and impatient waiting to see if all their hopes and trouble had been in vain.

When within a few hundred yards of the creek, Charley could stand the suspense no longer.

"Stop the engine," he requested, in a fever of impatience.

Bill threw off the battery switch. The four wondering captains trailing behind followed his example and the throbbing of the engines ceased.

The lad stood up and listened intently.   His quick ear could just distinguish a faint, peculiar noise, like the soft smacking of thousands of lips.

He sank back into his seat with a sigh of relief. .

" It's all right," he exclaimed, delightedly.   " I can hear them.   Run in close to shore and anchor."

CHAPTER XXXII.

ABOUT MANY THINGS.

As soon as the anchors were dropped all scrambled into the skiffs, eager to be ashore.

They landed close to the sand spit that barred the creek's entrance, and a few steps brought them to where they could look in on the little inland lake. All stood silent for a moment, gazing at the thousands on thousands of little, open, gasping mouths.

" I expected to see some fish from what you told us but I didn't expect anything like this," said Bill, drawing a deep breath. " Boy, there's a pot of money waiting for us in that little pond."

The other fishermen's faces were expressive of amazement and envy.

" You might have let us in on this," one of them grumbled.

" Would any of you have done it for us if you had found them?" Charley demanded.

" I wouldn't," the man admitted. " But, all the same, ten dollars a day looks mighty small with all this money in sight."

" We need every dollar we can make off of this thing," the lad said, " but we want to be as generous as we can afford to be. We are going to do better by you than we bargained to do. If you all do your best to help us put these fish into Clearwater, we will give you ten per cent on what we make in addition to the ten dollars a day we promised you."

"That's more than fair," declared Captain Brown. "We will do our best. All hands had better get to work at once. Those fish are about all in. I doubt if they will live thirty-six hours longer."

Charley had planned everything on the way down the coast and he had already arranged each man's part so that the work might be done with system and despatch. The Roberts and himself were to do the work with the nets. The fishermen were to do the loading, with the captain to help them. All of them were to work on one launch at a time and as soon as it was loaded it was to start for Clearwater while the next one received its cargo.

To Chris was assigned the job of cooking for all hands, so that no time would be lost in the preparation of meals.

Charley and the Roberts had taken on themselves the hardest part of the work, but the four went at their nasty, disagreeable task with vigor and cheerfulness.

Taking an end of the joined nets, they waded across one end of the shallow lagoon stringing it out behind them. As soon as they had gotten the end to the opposite shore, two got to each end and pulled lustily.

They had been careful to cut off only a small portion of the lagoon, but even so, they found that the fish between the net and shore were almost more than they could handle. They had to pull with all their might to drag in the ladened net, and as they pulled, they feared each minute that the fine twine would give way under the tremendous pressure.

But at last they got the net ashore, its meshes full of struggling, silvery mullet.

Then began the tiring work of getting the fish out of the fine, tangling twine. As fast as they were taken out they tossed them into a large box, and as soon as the box was filled, a fisherman carried it to the waiting skiffs and dumped the load, returning for another.

In two hours the first launch was loaded, and started back for Clearwater.

Walter, his ankle done up in splints and bandages, and using a cane for a crutch, limped into the fish house, the day following his accident, and sought a seat on a pile of old nets in a corner where he was not likely to be seen by Mr. Daniels. He had not sought the kindly fish boss yet to tell him of the loss of the launch. He was deferring the unpleasant task in hopes that his chums would be successful when the telling would be easier. Besides, he was not feeling equal to the task of explaining. His foot pained him intensely. He was also depressed by the doctor's statement that he had suffered a compound fracture of the ankle and must not try to use his foot for many days to come. He had but little money in his pocket and had not dared spend any of it for board and lodging. Instead he had slept miserably in a skiff pulled up on shore and had breakfasted off of cheese and crackers. Taking it all in all he did not feel equal to the unpleasant task of breaking bad news. He had been drawn to the fish house, however, knowing that there he would be likely to hear the first news of his absent chums. He was hoping Mr. Daniels would not spy him in his secluded corner.

But Mr. Daniels was having troubles of his own. A dull season is hard on the fishermen but harder still on the fish boss. On the desk before him was a heap of letters and telegrams from customers demanding fish. If he could not supply them at once, they would of course buy elsewhere. Building up a trade is slow work, and if you cannot supply its wants, it is soon lost. He was worrying through the mass of mail when the telephone bell rang. He lifted the receiver off the hook.

" Hello! who's this?" he demanded, curtly.

" It's Captain Brown, Cap," answered a tired voice. " I'm at the dock. Send down for some fish, will you?"

"How many have you got, twenty pounds?" demanded Mr. Daniels, sarcastically.

"Call it twenty pounds if you like," drawled the tired voice. "I calculate, though, that they will come nearer tipping the scales at ten thousand pounds."

"Good boy," exclaimed the fish boss in delight. "They will help me out a lot. Where did you catch them."

"I didn't catch them," said the weary tones. "Credit them to the account of those new guys, 'West, Hazard and so forth.' Good-by, I've got to go back for another load."

Walter in his secluded corner caught enough of the conversation to tell him that his chums had succeeded. He forgot his pain and discouragement. Things took on a rosy tinge. He suddenly remembered the dime's worth of cheese and crackers, for breakfast, had only put an edge on his appetite. He stole out of the fish house and hobbled down the street to a little restaurant where he was soon seated behind a big, juicy steak and mashed potatoes.

As soon as his hunger was appeased, he hobbled back to the fish house.

There he remained all the balance of the day and far into the night for the fish house was the scene of great excitement. One after the other the launches arrived with their finny cargoes. When the last one was unloaded the first to arrive was back again with another load. The house's regular force was unable to handle the deluge. Men, boys, and even women were hired at fancy prices to assist. Packing in barrels became impossible. As many as could be were packed that way but the most were hustled, unpacked, into a car and heavily iced down.

"For goodness' sake, how many more are coming?" Mr. Daniels demanded of a midnight arrival.

"Not many," answered the launch captain. "They were making their last haul when I left. Some of the fishermen followed the first launch back and are trying to butt into the snap."

"The rascally scoundrels," exclaimed Mr. Daniels, indignantly.

The man grinned wearily. "You needn't worry," he said. "When I left, Bill Roberts was standing off the gang with a rifle, while the other fellows got out the fish."

"They must be about tired out by this time," commented the fish boss.

"Tired!" exclaimed the launch captain. "I am pretty well worn out myself and we launch men have the easiest part of the job. Those fellows who are handling the nets are earning every dollar they will make. Their fingers are worn through both skins handling that fine, wet twine.

Their hands are just bleeding raw, and you know how salt water and fish slimes smart the smallest cut. They have bent over the nets so long that they can't straighten up without bringing the tears to their eyes. I'd like to have the money they will make, but hanged if I would work that hard for it."

The launch captain had not overstated the case. The little party on the beach below were very near the limit of human endurance when the last fish was taken out of the nets. The launch captain had to assist them to the skiffs and into the launches. Once aboard the motor boats, they stretched out on the seats and slept the sleep of utter exhaustion.

Another day had dawned when the fish captain awoke them at Clearwater.

Walter, radiant of countenance, was waiting on the dock to welcome them.

It took Charley several minutes to regain his sleep-scattered wits.

" How much did they weigh?" he asked eagerly, as he wrung his chum's hand in congratulation.

" Just an even hundred and fifty thousand pounds," Walter said.

" Good! at two cents a pound, that's three thousand dollars."

" Better than that," beamed his chum. " Owing to the scarcity of fish, the market has gone up a cent a pound."

"Four thousand five hundred dollars," cried Charley, in delight. "Over two thousand dollars to be divided up amongst us four. It's almost too good to be true."

"And that's not all," added Walter, eagerly. "We are not going to lose much on the launch, after all. Mr. Daniels says she was insured for nearly her full value."

"All's well that ends well," Charley commented. "We have not come out of our fishing venture so badly after all."

"I am afraid we haven't reached the end just yet," said Walter, his countenance sobering. "I've got something pretty serious to tell you as soon as we are all alone."

"If it's nothing real pressing, save it a while," said Charley, hastily. "I want to get some money from Mr. Daniels and pay off the launch captains. Then, I want a good long sleep with nothing to worry me. The Roberts have insisted on our staying with them a couple of days until we get straightened out. We will go over to their camp as soon as I get the fishermen paid off."

It took but a short time to get the money and pay off the sleepy launch captains. They were all well-pleased with their share of the venture. Besides the ten dollars a day, they received four hundred and fifty dollars to be divided among them.

This business attended to, our little party joined the Roberts in their launch and the run to camp was quickly made. As soon as it was reached, the workers turned in for a good, long sleep, and Walter was left alone with his secret.

CHAPTER XXXIII.

THE SMUGGLERS AGAIN.

WHILE his chums were making up the sleep they had lost, Walter took the Roberts launch and ran over to Palm Island.   Brief as had been their stay on the little isle, he had grown quite fond of it and his anger rose as he viewed the work of the wreckers.   The vandals had done their work well. Not a stick remained standing of the former cozy, little cabin.   The wharf, too, was gone, even its posts had been hacked short off at the surface of the water.

Leaving the scene of the ruin, Walter hobbled slowly over the little island looking all about with thoughtful interest.   At last, he made his way back to the launch and returned to the Roberts camp.

His companions were awake and stirring about. Chris was busily engaged in cooking dinner, while the rest were applying salve and bandages to their sore hands.

Charley greeted his chum with an affectionate smile.   " How's the foot? " he inquired.

" Coming on all right," said Walter, cheerfully. " How about you, feeling better? "

"Feeling fine and dandy," declared the other, "and I am as hungry as a wolf. I remember you had some bad news to tell me. Let's hear it. I feel able to face all kinds of trouble now."

"I don't know as it is exactly bad news for us," said his chum. "In a way it doesn't concern us at all, unless we want to make it our business."

"You are getting my curiosity aroused," Charley laughed. Let's hear this news of yours."

"The night you all left me in Clearwater, I did not go to a boarding house to stop. It had cost quite a bit to have my ankle fixed up and I did not have much money left and I was afraid to spend what little I had, for I knew, if you fellows were not successful in your trip, there was going to be mighty hard times ahead. I went out on the dock and looked around but I didn't quite fancy sleeping there so I went back uptown and hung around until the stores closed. I was getting pretty sleepy by this time, so I went down again to the bay and looked around until I found what I wanted, a skiff pulled up high and dry on the sand. There were some old nets in the bottom and I crawled in, stretched out on one of the nets, and pulled the other one over me, getting my head under a seat to keep out the dew. I went to sleep as cozy as a bug in a rug. I don't know how long I had slept when I woke up to the sound of voices. Four men were sitting on the edge of my skiff talking together. It was too dark to see their faces but I knew one of the voices. It was Hunter's and you can bet your life I laid mighty still and listened.

"They were talking about us at first and it made my blood boil to hear them chuckling over the harm they had done us, but there was nothing I could do but lay quiet and stand it. They talked about the cache and wondered where we had hidden the liquor. At last they came to what, I guess, was the real object of their meeting where no one could hear them. Having disposed of us, as they thought, they have arranged to bring in another large lot of aguardiente."

"When?" Charley demanded, eagerly.

"To-night. They expect the schooner at the island at about midnight. They talked it over and arranged all the details of the job before they separated."

"To-night at midnight," Charley mused. "We had better go right over and tell the sheriff."

"That was the first thing I thought of," Walter said. "I was up at his house by sunrise the next morning but it was no use. His wife told me he was very ill and could not be seen."

"Queer, he is never around when that smuggling is going on," observed Charley, suspiciously. "I wonder if it can be that he is standing in with the smugglers for a share of the profits."

"Not Sheriff Daley," spoke up Bill Roberts,

warmly. "He is as square a man as ever lived. Queer, though," he added, slowly, "I saw him just the day before and he looked the picture of health, but then, it may be appendicitis or some such sudden illness that's struck him."

"It's too bad," said Captain Westfield. "It leaves those rascals free to carry out their devilment. Of course, it's none of our business, but it seems wrong to have such things going on."

"No, of course it is none of our business," Charley agreed, hesitatingly. "How many of them are there in it, Walt? Did you hear?"

"Only the four that met," his chum replied. "They were discussing getting a couple more men to help, but Hunter objected as it would mean more division of the profits. He said the schooner's crew could help land the stuff."

"Did he say how many were on the schooner?" Bill Roberts inquired.

"Four men and a boy," replied Walter.

"Well, as you have all said, I reckon it is none of our business," Bill observed.

They sat in thoughtful silence for a few minutes.

"It would be hard on Hunter's wife, if he was caught," Charley said, finally.

"It would be the best thing that could happen for her," Bill declared. "She is a good woman. She works like a slave to support them both.

Hunter blows in all the money he makes and lives on her earnings. He beats her like a dog, too."

" The brute! " Walter exclaimed, hotly.

" Dar's five hundred dollars to be gib to de one what catches de booze sellers, ain't dey? " Chris inquired. " 'Pears like hit would be a powerful good thing for some one to cotch him an' send all dat money to dat poor woman."

Captain Westfield looked from one to the other with a sheepish grin. " Thar isn't any use of our saying it's none of our business," he said. " Down deep in his heart each one of us knows it is his business. It's always a *man's* business to stop wrong-doing."

" Right you are," agreed Bill Roberts, with gruff heartiness. " I know we are all thinking about the the same things. It isn't so much that this man and his gang are breaking the law that counts, it's the misery and suffering which he causes that calls for action. There have been ten men killed in the fish camps here the past year, and what caused the killing? Rum, rum brought in and sold by Hunter. And that isn't all the misery he's caused. Think of the beaten wives and neglected children. It's time there was a stop put to it."

" Yes," Captain Westfield agreed. " We are as much our brother's keeper as in the days of Cain."

" I guess we are all pretty well agreed," smiled the practical Charley. " The question is, how are we going to take them. There are nine of them and only seven of us. Of course one of them is only a boy, but then, Walt is pretty well crippled up."

"I'll be right there when the fun begins," his chum said, determinedly. "What if they are two more in number. We will be well armed, and surely a surprise counts for something. I went over the island while you were all sleeping and planned it all out. There is only one piece of the beach where a boat can land safely. There is a group of palmettoes close to it. Now what I planned is this. We had better start out in the launch early and run straight out of the pass as though we were going out to the reef. Once we get behind the island, and out of sight of Clearwater, we'll skirt the shore and run around to the north end. There's a little cove there where the launch will be hidden from both the gulf and the bay. When dark comes we can hide in the clump of palmettoes and wait. When they get to work in earnest, we can slip out and take them by surprise. Then five of us can keep them quiet with the rifles, while the other two tie them up. Once we have got them secure, we can load them into the launch, carry them straight to Tampa and turn them over to the sheriff there. How does that strike all of you?"

"It sounds simple enough," Charley said, doubtfully, "too simple, in fact."

"What fault can you find with it?" Walter demanded.

"None," his chum answered, "only I have a hunch that Hunter is too clever and cunning a rascal to be caught so easily."

"Have you any better plan to suggest?" Walter asked.

But Charley had not, nor did any of the others, so, after some discussion, Walter's plan was adopted.

As soon as dinner was over, some lunch was packed into a basket, and storing it and the loading rifles in the launch, they steered boldly out of the inlet. As soon as the island was between them and Clearwater, however, they shifted helm, and hugging its shore, ran down to its northern end.

Here they found the little cove Walter had mentioned. Running the launch into it, they anchored and waded ashore. They placed their launch and rifles in the clump of palmettoes, and then there was nothing to do until the coming of night, except to pass the time away as best they could. By keeping on the gulf side of the island, there was no danger of their being seen from Clearwater, and this they were careful to do. A swim in the clear, warm water and the picking up of curious shells on the beach served to while away the balance of the afternoon. As soon as dark came, they retired within the clump of palms. With the going down of the sun came the rising of the moon.' It was nearly full and its rays lit up the little island almost as brightly as day. Our little party welcomed its tropical radiance for it would allow them to see without being seen.

The hours slipped slowly away. At first some attempt was made at story-telling and conversation, but soon all lapsed into a thoughtful silence. Each realized that they were about to engage in a desperate undertaking. In fact, it was almost a foolhardy act they contemplated. The smugglers had all the advantage in point of force. They were eight, able-bodied men beside the boy, and it was more than likely that all of them would be armed. Of their own party, the three Roberts boys were really the only active men. Charley, though unusually strong for his age, was only a boy, while the captain, vigorous though he still was, was getting well along in years. Walter was practically helpless with his broken ankle, while Chris was too small to be of much help where strength was required. But for the advantage that would lie in taking the smugglers by surprise, they were more likely to be the captured than the captors.

These reflections and the long, expectant waiting were beginning to tell on their nerves, when they heard the welcome put-put of a distant launch.

"They are coming, at last," said Charley, with a sigh of relief. "I can recognize that exhaust.

The Hunters launch is the only one that sounds just like that."

"The schooner must be somewhere near but I don't see her lights," Walter observed.

"Why, thar she is," exclaimed the captain, "sneaking inshore like a thief in the night."

CHAPTER XXXIV.

THE SURPRISE.

So silently that they had been unaware of her approach, the strange craft had stolen in like a phantom ship to within two hundred yards of where they lay concealed. She now lay directly in the moon's path and its rays so bright set out every rope and sail in dark relief. Not a light shone aboard. Her captain had evidently been made wary by his former alarm and was taking all possible chances against drawing the attention of others.

As silent as a ghost ship the graceful craft crept in to within a cable's length of the beach. Then, with a faint creak of traveling blocks she rounded gracefully up into the wind and a muffled splash told that her anchor had been dropped.

She made a beautiful sight laying, swan-like, full in the glowing pathway of the moon, her great white sails quivering in the gentle breeze.

"The bird is ready to flit away at the first alarm," whispered the captain. "See, he has got his anchor hove short and has taken in none of his sails but the jib.   He could get under way again in half a minute.   He's wary all right."

" We had better not talk any more," cautioned Charley in a whisper.   " Sound carries a long ways over the water and the launch is nearly here."

With nerves at highest tension the little party waited.

The loud throbbing of the launch's engine suddenly ceased.   There came a splash from a dropped anchor, and more splashing as its crew waded ashore.   Then came a murmuring of voices and the sound of footsteps, and the watchers drew further back into their hiding place as four figures came into view.   They passed so close to the bunch of palms that their features were plain to the hiders.   One was Hunter, himself, the other three they recognized as members of his gang.

The four hurried down to the water's edge.

" Ahoy," Hunter hailed the schooner.   " It's all right.   Come ashore."

" Are you sure no one else is around? " cautiously inquired a voice from the schooner.

The response had been in perfect English but something in the tones and the faint foreign accent made the chums stare at each other as though they had heard a voice from the grave.

" No, there's no one here but ourselves," Hunter replied, impatiently.   " Do you think I would be here if everything wasn't all right?   Come, get a

move on you, and hustle that stuff ashore. There's
a lot to do, and it ain't many hours till daylight."

Those on the schooner fell to work with feverish
haste. A small dingy carried on deck was launched
over the side. Two figures leaped into it and received the cases, two others brought up from the
hold.

As soon as the dingy was loaded, the two on deck
scrambled aboard and one sculled her into shore.

The moment she grounded, the captain leaped
ashore. "Here is part of our goods," he said
smoothly. "We can bring it all in in three more
trips."

"Good," Hunter growled. "Come, unload it.
What are you waiting for?"

"Only for our money, kind sir," said the
schooner's captain, in smooth, suave tones which
stirred in the chums old, cruel memories. "I think
it would be best for each boat-load to be paid for
as it is brought in."

"Don't be a fool, man," said Hunter, roughly.
"We can settle up when the job is done. We have
got no time to waste, now."

"Pay before unloading," insisted the captain of
the schooner, politely. "Gentlemen in our business cannot be too careful. Of course I know
you are the soul of honesty, but you are forgetful,
my good friend. You have never remembered to
pay me for that last lot I brought you."

" How many cases? " Hunter demanded, with an oath, as he pulled out a greasy roll of bills.

" Twenty cases, one hundred dollars," said the stranger.

Hunter counted out the bills, and the schooner captain recounted them carefully and thrust them into his pocket.

" You are still forgetting that little bank account of a hundred dollars," he remarked, pleasantly. " Surely, now is a splendid time to settle it."

Hunter's face grew livid with anger, but he controlled his temper with an effort. He was quick to realize that he could only lose by a display of anger. The man already had a hundred dollars of his money, and still remained in possession of the liquor.

The chums in their concealment chuckled inwardly at his plight. At last the rascally fisherman had met his equal in cunning.

Grudgingly, he counted out another hundred dollars which the smuggler pocketed with a mocking bow of thanks.

" It's a pleasure to do business with a spot-cash gentleman like you," he declared. " Now, you may have your liquor, and there's three more boat-loads, just as good, at a hundred dollars a load."

" You'll have to help us carry it up to the cache," Hunter growled. " There's too much of it for us four to get out of the way before daylight."

"Always glad to oblige such a pleasant gentle-man," said the smuggler, swinging a case up on his shoulder. "Many hands make light work." His companions silently followed his example, each shouldering a case and the fishermen similarly loaded fell in behind them.

Hunter and one of his gang brought up the rear. As they came alongside the clump of palmettoes, Hunter nudged the man ahead.

"Drop behind a bit," he said, softly.

The man slowed his walk.

"That fellow's got too much of our money to get away with it," he declared in tones too low to reach those ahead.

The man nodded. "We've got to take it from him," he agreed.

"We'd better wait until all the stuff is landed," planned Hunter. "We'll jump him just as he gets ready to leave and make him shell out. He can't make any trouble about it. He dasn't make any kick to the authorities. Tell the rest of the boys when you get a chance."

The whispered conference had taken less than a minute but the alert smuggler glanced suspiciously back at the two plotters and they quickened their steps.

"Our work is half done for us if they are going to fight amongst themselves," exulted Charley, as the procession passed out of hearing. "We had better wait till the trouble starts and then come down on them."

"Did you notice that smuggler captain's voice?" asked Captain Westfield, eagerly.

Walter's eyes were gleaming. "It's Manuel George, the Greek interpreter," he exclaimed, softly. "The rascal that caused us so much misery and stole our schooner from us."

"And that's our dear old 'Beauty' lying out there," declared Charley, a thrill in his voice. "We have got to take her, if we risk our lives doing it. But here they come back again."

The smugglers were losing no time but working with all possible rapidity. The first dingy load was quickly transferred to its hiding place and a second load brought ashore, the smuggler captain insisting on his pay before a case was unloaded, a third load quickly followed the second, and just as the morning star began to show in the east, the fourth and last load was brought ashore.

To the hidden watchers it seemed a century of waiting. With the coming of the last load, the tension became almost unbearable. A few minutes now would decide whether or not they were to recover their dearly loved ship which they had long since given up as lost, to them, forever.

The fisherman and smuggler captain seemed to be in excellent spirits as the work progressed. They laughed and joked with each other, but it seemed to

Charley, keenly observant, that their gaiety was forced. He imagined a sinister note under their high spirits and the watchful, alert smuggler captain, for all his affected friendliness, seemed to be watching every movement of the fishermen. All were working at top speed now to complete the unloading before day, and the pile of cases in the dingy rapidly diminished.

As the carriers passed back and forth to and from the new cache they were making, there would be a few minutes each trip when they were far enough away from the concealed ones for the little party to hold low, whispered conversation.

"We want to act all together," Charley said, during one of these intervals. "When I say, 'Now', we will cover them with our rifles and step out upon them. I am going to wait till the last minute to give the word. If they have a mix-up and get to fighting among themselves, it will make our job doubly easy."

As the procession passed by on its last trip, the lad chuckled softly.

"That Hunter is certainly one clever rascal," he whispered. "Did you notice he and his men head the procession this trip for the first time?"

"I don't see the advantage in that," Walter remarked.

"Don't you? Why, they will be the first to unload and consequently the first to turn back. That will put them between the Greeks and the dingy. Something is going to happen pretty quick. Be ready. Here they come back."

Empty-handed, the eight were returning to the beach chatting gaily together. As Charley had prophesied, Hunter and his three companions were well in the lead. At the dingy bow, the four turned and gathered close together.

The Greek captain was quick to notice the move. A few words in Greek brought his men crowding around him. If he felt any fear, however, it did not show in his face or manner.

"Our agreeable business is pleasantly ended, gentlemen," he said, smoothly. "When will you want more of the liquor, Mr. Hunter?"

"Won't want any more," Hunter growled, surlily. "The game's too risky. There's too many getting on to it. It's time to quit."

"Very well," said the smuggler, coolly. "Now, we must bid you good-by, gentlemen, and be on our way."

"You Greek fool," Hunter snarled. "Do you think you are going to leave here with all that money? Hand it over, quick!"

"Out of the way!" cried the Greek captain, as he leaped forward, followed by his men.

In a second smugglers and fishermen were mingled together in a fierce struggle.

"Now," called Charley, clearly, and his companions stepped forth with leveled rifles.

"Hands up—all of you," he shouted.

The fighting instantly ceased and the surprised combatants turned to face the new enemy.

Then came an interruption that struck both parties with fear and dismay.

From the gulf rose a huge, bat-like thing which swept down upon them with a whirling, sucking mumble.

"De haunts," shrieked Chris, and fled as fast as his shaking legs would carry him.

CHAPTER XXXV.

AND THE LAST.

THE others were hardly less frightened than the little darkey. The Greeks fell to their knees and mumbled prayers, while the fishermen stood white-faced and panic-stricken. Even the party with the rifles in their hands felt a thrill of fear as the gruesome object swept down on them. Suddenly the whirling sound ceased and the creature of the night glided down to the ground before them.

" A hydroplane," cried Walter, with a sigh of relief, fervently echoed by his companions.

From the air-ship stepped out three men, two of whom they recognized with a thrill of joy. They were Sheriff Daley and his deputy. The third man was a stranger to them.

The three approached the panic-stricken group of smugglers with drawn revolvers.

" I arrest you all in the name of the United States of America," announced the stranger, throwing back his coat and showing a marshal's star. " Put the handcuffs on them, Sheriff Daley."

The sheriff stepped back to the hydroplane and

brought out a bunch of jangling handcuffs which he proceeded to lock on the cowering captives who offered no resistance.

"Take them down to their launch and run them over to Clearwater, Sheriff," the stranger directed, as soon as the job was done. "Keep them guarded close till evening, then we will take them on to the Federal prison in Atlanta. I will follow you in the hydroplane in a little while. I have a few words to say to our friends here before I leave."

As soon as the sheriff was gone with his prisoners, the stranger turned to our friends with a smile.

"There is considerable explaining to be done, gentlemen," he said, pleasantly. "Let's go out aboard the schooner where we will be more comfortable."

Chris was called down from the top of a tall palmetto where he had taken refuge and the bewildered party followed the stranger aboard the dingy and were soon standing on the deck of their well-beloved "Beauty." The boys felt a lump in their throats as they looked upon the familiar, beautiful ship. The captain was here and there and everywhere over her deck. Examining everything like a parent with a long lost child.

"They haven't harmed her at all," he declared, with joy. "Only painted her over a different color and altered the rigging to disguise her. No wonder we thought she looked familiar to us."

It was with reluctance that the delighted old sailor obeyed the marshal's summons down into the cabin.

" My friends, you have unknowingly made me a lot of trouble and pretty nearly caused me a failure," the stranger said, when they were all seated around the cabin table.

" We will have to ask you to explain," Charley said. " We are all thoroughly bewildered."

" I suppose things do seem rather mixed up to you," smiled the stranger. "Well, I will try to make everything plain. For some time the government has been receiving complaints of liquor being smuggled into various places along the West coast, and at last, I was assigned to trace up the smugglers and this seemed to me to be as likely a place as any to start my investigations. Well, it didn't take long to determine who disposed of the liquor here, but it was quite another thing to discover the identity of the smugglers. I had a pretty full description of the schooner from several parties who had seen her hanging around at different places along the coast. One man had even seen the crew and he described them to me pretty accurately. But when I tried to find out who were the schooner's owners and what port she hailed from I ran against a snag. No ship answering her description was registered in either America or Cuba. Quite by chance, when in Tarpon Springs, I heard of your lost ship, and the description of her and the Greeks on her, tallied so exactly with the schooner and the smugglers that I was convinced that they were one and the same. Having got a clue to the smugglers and the receivers, the next thing was to catch them in the act. I took up my residence in Tarpon Springs with a friend who happened to be an enthusiastic air man, and went to work. I spent most of my nights on the island going there after dark in my friend's hydroplane. I was getting along very nicely when you took up residence on the island and upset my plans. I was quite out of patience that first night when you were the means of frightening the schooner away. And then when you found the cache of liquor, I almost gave up hope. I was afraid you would ring in the local authorities and that they would mess up things without the evidence necessary to convict the offenders. To discourage them at the start, if they should take any action, I removed the liquor from the cache. In fact, I was almost as anxious as Hunter to have your party leave the island. However, all's well that ends well, and I have got the rascals at last, where they cannot escape long jail sentences. I was posted on to-night's doing through having easy access to Hunter's mail when it passed through the post-office. An accident to the hydroplane's engine came near making me too late to take the rascals in charge. As it is, I will have to have the testimony of your party taken down in writing to-morrow, for I did not see the actual handling of the smuggled goods myself.   And now, I guess that is the whole story.   It will doubtless explain many things which have puzzled you."

"Then it must have been you whom Chris took for a ghost?" Walter said.

"And you are the one who brought us the liquor and the doctor when Walter was so ill," Charley exclaimed.

"I plead guilty to both charges," said the marshal, with a smile.   "One other thing I would mention that is important to you," he added.   "In smuggling cases, the government usually seizes the vessel, but in this case, you, the real owners, are so entirely innocent of wrong-doing, that I am going to assume the responsibility of leaving you in uninterrupted possession of your vessel.   And now, I am thoroughly tired out and so I'll wish you good night, or rather good morning.   Meet me in Clearwater this afternoon and we will finish up our business together."

When the marshal was gone and the Roberts boys had departed for their camp, the four chums sat in happy content in the "Beauty's" cozy cabin.

"Pinch me that I may make sure I am not dreaming," Walter sighed, blissfully.   "All this seems too good to be true."

"If you are dreaming, I am, too, and do not want to be wakened," Charley said.   "Gee! a few weeks ago we had nothing but the clothes on our backs. Now we have over two thousand dollars in cash and a ship that we can easily sell for three thousand dollars more, and best, of all, we have been able to assist the Roberts, who were so friendly to us when we sorely needed friends, to a share in a part of our good fortune."

" It's the good Lord's kindness," said Captain Westfield, reverently. " Let's thank him for the blessings he has showered upon us."

All were silent for a time after the heartfelt prayer was ended. At last Walter said, practically:

" What shall we do now? No use to start fishing again, it's only a few days till closed season."

" I can tell you what we had better do, next," Charley said, rising.

" What? " his chum demanded.

" Turn in and get a good sleep," Charley responded, yawning.

And safe in their bunks, dreaming blissfully of the future, we must for the present leave our four friends.

What the future held in store for them our readers can discover in the next volume of their adventures: " The Boy Chums Conquering The Wilderness; or, Charley and Walter Amongst the Seminole Indians."

THE END.

THE BRONCHO RIDER BOYS SERIES

By FRANK FOWLER

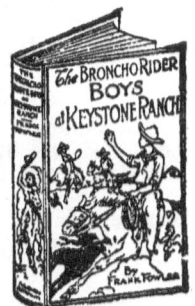

A Series of Stirring Stories for Boys, that not only contain considerable information concerning cowboy life, but at the same time seem to breathe the adventurous spirit that lives in the clear air of the wide plains, and lofty mountain ranges of the Wild West. These tales are written in a vein calculated to delight the heart of every lad who loves to read of pleasing adventure in the open: yet at the same time the most careful parent need not hesitate to place them in the hands of his boy.

HANDSOME CLOTH BINDINGS.

PRICE, 60 CENTS PER VOLUME.

THE BRONCHO RIDER BOYS AT KEYSTONE RANCH; or, Three Chums of the Saddle and Lariat.

In this story the reader makes the acquaintance of the devoted chums, Adrian Sherwood, Donald McKay, and William Stonewall Jackson Winkle, a fat, auburn-haired Southern lad, who is known at various times among his comrades as "We Willie Winkle," "Broncho Billie," and "Little Billie." The book begins in rapid action, and there is surely "something doing" up to the very time you lay it down, possibly with a sigh of regret because you have reached the end; yet thankful to know that a second volume is within reach. Besides the adventure, there is more or less rollicking humor, of the type all boys like to read about.

THE BRONCHO RIDER BOYS DOWN IN ARIZONA; or, A Struggle for the Great Copper Lode.

The scene shifts in this story, from the free life of the cattle range, and the wide expanse of the boundless prairie, to that rugged mountainous section of Arizona, where many fabulous fortunes have been won through the discovery of rich ore. The Broncho Rider Boys find themselves impelled, by a stern sense of duty, to make a brave fight against heavy odds, in order to retain possession of a valuable mine that is claimed by some of their relatives. That they meet with numerous strange and thrilling perils while enlisted in this service, can be readily understood; and every wideawake boy will be pleased to learn how finally Adrian and his chums managed to outwit their enemies in the fight for the copper lode.

THE BRONCHO RIDER BOYS ALONG THE BORDER; or, The Hidden Treasure of the Zuni Medicine Man.

Once more the tried and true comrades of camp and trail are in the saddle, bent on seeing with their own eyes some of the wonderful sights to be found in that section of the Far Southwest, where the singular cave homes of the ancient Cliff Dwellers dot the walls of the Great Canyon of the Colorado. In the strangest possible way they are drawn into a series of happenings among the Zuni Indians, while trying to assist a newly made friend; all of which makes interesting reading. If there could be any choice, this book would surely be voted the best of the entire series, and certainly no lad will lay it down, save with regret.

THE BRONCHO RIDER BOYS ON THE WYOMING TRAIL; or, A Mystery of the Prairie Stampede.

As the title will indicate to readers of the previous stories in this Series, the three prairie pards finally find a chance to visit the Wyoming ranch belonging to Adrian, but which has been managed for him by a relative, whom he has reason to suspect might be running things more for his own benefit than that of the young owner. Of course they become entangled in a maze of adventurous doings while in the Northern cattle country. How the Broncho Rider Boys carried themselves through this nerve-testing period makes intensely interesting reading. No boy will ever regret the money spent in securing this splendid volume.

For sale by all booksellers, or sent postpaid on receipt of price by the publishers, A. L. BURT COMPANY, 114-120 East 23d Street, New York

THE BIG FIVE MOTORCYCLE BOYS SERIES

By RALPH MARLOW

A Series of Splendid Stories, in which are contained the Strange Happenings that befell a bunch of five lively boys, who were fortunate enough to come into possession of up-to-date motorcycles.

HANDSOME CLOTH BINDINGS.

PRICE, 6C CENTS PER VOLUME

THE BIG FIVE MOTORCYCLE BOYS' SWIFT ROAD CHASE; or, Surprising the Bank Robbers.

It is doubtful whether a more entertaining lot of boys ever before appeared in a story than the "Big Five," who figure in the pages of this volume—Rod Bradley; "Hanky Panky" Jucklin; Josh Whitcomb; Elmer Overton; and last, but far from least, "Rooster" Boggs. From cover to cover the reader will be thrilled and delighted with the accounts of how luckily they came by their motorcycles; and what a splendid use they made of the machines in recovering the funds of the robbed Garland bank.

THE BIG FIVE MOTORCYCLE BOYS IN TENNESSEE WILDS; or, The Secret of Walnut Ridge.

In this story the boys with the "flying wheels" take a trip through Kentucky, and into Dixie Land. The wonderful adventures, and amusing ones as well, that were their portion on this glorious spin, have been set down by the author in a way that will be most pleasing to the boy reader who delights in tales of action. There is not a single dry chapter in the book; and when the end is finally reached, the happy possessor will count himself lucky to have it handy in his library, where, later on, he may read it over and over again.

THE BIG FIVE MOTORCYCLE BOYS THROUGH BY WIRELESS; or, A Strange Message from the Air.

Even in a quiet Ohio town remarkable things may sometimes happen calculated to create the most intense excitement. The five motorcycle boys were put in touch with just such an event through a message that came to their wireless station while many miles away from home. What that "voice from the air" told them, and how gallantly they responded to the call for action, you will be delighted to learn in the third volume of this intensely interesting series.

THE BIG FIVE MOTORCYLE BOYS ON FLORIDA TRAILS; or, Adventures Among the Saw Palmetto Crackers.

Once more a kind fortune allows Rod Bradley and his four "happy-go-lucky" comrades a chance to visit new fields. Down in the Land of Sunshine and Oranges the Motorcycle Boys experience some of the most remarkable perils and adventures of their whole career. The writer spent many years along the far-famed Indian River, and he has drawn upon his vast knowledge of the country in describing what befell the chums there. If there could be any choice, then this book is certainly the best of the whole series; and you will put it down with regret, only hoping to meet these favorite characters again in new fields.

For sale by all booksellers, or sent postpaid on receipt of price by the publishers, A. L. BURT COMPANY, 114-120 East 23d Street, New York

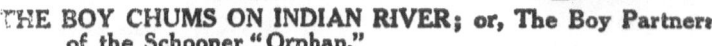

The Boy Spies Series

These stories are based on important historical events, scenes wherein boys are prominent characters being selected. They are the romance of history, vigorously told, with careful fidelity to picturing the home life, and accurate in every particular.

HANDSOME CLOTH BINDINGS

PRICE, 60 CENTS PER VOLUME

THE BOY SPIES AT THE BATTLE OF NEW ORLEANS.
A story of the part they took in its defence.
By William P. Chipman.

THE BOY SPIES AT THE DEFENCE OF FORT HENRY.
A boy's story of Wheeling Creek n 1777.
By James Otis.

THE BOY SPIES AT THE BATTLE OF BUNKER HILL.
A story of two boys at the siege of Boston.
By James Otis.

THE BOY SPIES AT THE SIEGE OF DETROIT.
A story of two Ohio boys in the War of 1812.
By James Otis.

THE BOY SPIES WITH LAFAYETTE.
The story of how two boys joined the Continental Army.
By James Otis.

THE BOY SPIES ON CHESAPEAKE BAY.
The story of two young spies under Commodore Barney.
By James Otis.

THE BOY SPIES WITH THE REGULATORS.
The story of how the boys assisted the Carolina Patriots to drive the British from that State.
By James Otis.

THE BOY SPIES WITH THE SWAMP FOX.
The story of General Marion and his young spies.
By James Otis.

THE BOY SPIES AT YORKTOWN.
The story of how the spies helped General Lafayette in the Siege of Yorktown.
By James Otis.

THE BOY SPIES OF PHILADELPHIA.
The story of how the young spies helped the Continental Army at Valley Forge.
By James Otis.

THE BOY SPIES OF FORT GRISWOLD.
The story of the part they took in its brave defence.
By William P. Chipman.

THE BOY SPIES OF OLD NEW YORK.
The story of how the young spies prevented the capture of General Washington.
By James Otis.

For sale by all booksellers, or sent postpaid on receipt of price by the publishers, A. L. BURT COMPANY, 114-120 East 23d Street, New York

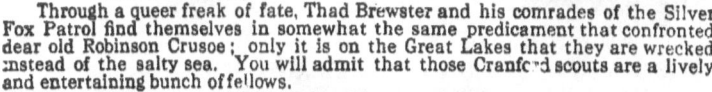

The Navy Boys Series

A series of excellent stories of adventure on sea and land, selected from the works of popular writers; each volume designed for boys' reading.

HANDSOME CLOTH BINDINGS

PRICE, 60 CENTS PER VOLUME

THE NAVY BOYS IN DEFENCE OF LIBERTY.
A story of the burning of the British schooner Gaspee in 1772.
By William P. Chipman.

THE NAVY BOYS ON LONG ISLAND SOUND.
A story of the Whale Boat Navy of 1776.
By James Otis.

THE NAVY BOYS AT THE SIEGE OF HAVANA.
Being the experience of three boys serving under Israel Putnam in 1772.
By James Otis.

THE NAVY BOYS WITH GRANT AT VICKSBURG.
A boy's story of the siege of Vicksburg.
By James Otis.

THE NAVY BOYS' CRUISE WITH PAUL JONES.
A boy's story of a cruise with the Great Commodore in 1776.
By James Otis.

THE NAVY BOYS ON LAKE ONTARIO.
The story of two boys and their adventures in the War of 1812.
By James Otis.

THE NAVY BOYS' CRUISE ON THE PICKERING.
A boy's story of privateering in 1780.
By James Otis.

THE NAVY BOYS IN NEW YORK BAY.
A story of three boys who took command of the schooner "The Laughing Mary," the first vessel of the American Navy.
By James Otis.

THE NAVY BOYS IN THE TRACK OF THE ENEMY.
The story of a remarkable cruise with the Sloop of War "Providence" and the Frigate "Alfred."
By William P. Chipman.

THE NAVY BOYS' DARING CAPTURE.
The story of how the navy boys helped to capture the British Cutter "Margaretta," in 1775.
By William P. Chipman.

THE NAVY BOYS' CRUISE TO THE BAHAMAS.
The adventures of two Yankee Middies with the first cruise of an American Squadron in 1775.
By William P. Chipman.

THE NAVY BOYS' CRUISE WITH COLUMBUS.
The adventures of two boys who sailed with the great Admiral in his discovery of America.
By Frederick A. Ober.

The Jack Lorimer Series

5 Volumes By WINN STANDISH

Handsomely Bound in Cloth
Full Library Size — Price
40 cents per Volume, postpaid

CAPTAIN JACK LORIMER; or, The Young Athlete of Millvale High.

Jack Lorimer is a fine example of the all-around American high-school boy. His fondness for clean, honest sport of all kinds will strike a chord of sympathy among athletic youths.

JACK LORIMER'S CHAMPIONS; or, Sports on Land and Lake.

There is a lively story woven in with the athletic achievements, which are all right, since the book has been O.K'd by Chadwick, the Nestor of American sporting journalism.

JACK LORIMER'S HOLIDAYS; or, Millvale High in Camp.

It would be well not to put this book into a boy's hands until the chores are finished, otherwise they might be neglected.

JACK LORIMER'S SUBSTITUTE; or, The Acting Captain of the Team.

On the sporting side, the book takes up football, wrestling, tobogganing. There is a good deal of fun in this book and plenty of action.

JACK LORIMER, FRESHMAN; or, From Millvale High to Exmouth.

Jack and some friends he makes crowd innumerable happenings into an exciting freshman year at one of the leading Eastern colleges. The book is typical of the American college boy's life, and there is a lively story, interwoven with feats on the gridiron, hockey, basketball and other clean, honest sports for which Jack Lorimer stands.

For sale by all booksellers, or sent postpaid on receipt of price by the publishers

A. L. BURT COMPANY, 114-120 East 23d Street, New York.

THE CAMP FIRE GIRLS SERIES

By HILDEGARD G. FREY. The only series of stories for Camp Fire Girls endorsed by the officials of the Camp Fire Girls Organization. PRICE, 40 CENTS PER VOLUME

THE CAMP FIRE GIRLS IN THE MAINE WOODS; or, The Winnebagos go Camping.

This lively Camp Fire group and their Guardian go back to Nature in a camp in the wilds of Maine and pile up more adventures in one summer than they have had in all their previous vacations put together. Before the summer is over they have transformed Gladys, the frivolous boarding school girl, into a genuine Winnebago.

THE CAMP FIRE GIRLS AT SCHOOL; or, The Wohelo Weavers.

It is the custom of the Winnebagos to weave the events of their lives into symbolic bead bands, instead of keeping a diary. All commendatory doings are worked out in bright colors, but every time the Law of of the Camp Fire is broken it must be recorded in black. How these seven live wire girls strive to infuse into their school life the spirit of Work, Health and Love and yet manage to get into more than their share of mischief, is told in this story.

THE CAMP FIRE GIRLS AT ONOWAY HOUSE; or, The Magic Garden.

Migwan is determined to go to college, and not being strong enough to work indoors earns the money by raising fruits and vegetables. The Winnebagos all turn a hand to help the cause along and the "goings-on" at Onoway House that summer make the foundations shake with laughter.

THE CAMP FIRE GIRLS GO MOTORING; or, Along the Road That Leads the Way.

The Winnebagos take a thousand mile auto trip. The "pinching" of Nyoda, the fire in the country inn, the runaway girl and the dead-earnest hare and hound chase combine to make these three weeks the most exciting the Winnebagos have ever experienced.

For sale by all booksellers, or sent postpaid on receipt of price by the publishers
A. L. BURT COMPANY, 114-120 East 23d Street, New York.

THE BLUE GRASS SEMINARY GIRLS SERIES

By CAROLYN JUDSON BURNETT

Handsome Cloth Binding   Price, 40c. per Volume

*Splendid Stories of the Adventures
of a Group of Charming Girls*

THE BLUE GRASS SEMINARY GIRLS' VACATION ADVENTURES; or, Shirley Willing to the Rescue.

THE BLUE GRASS SEMINARY GIRLS' CHRISTMAS HOLIDAYS; or, A Four Weeks' Tour with the Glee Club.

THE BLUE GRASS SEMINARY GIRLS IN THE MOUNTAINS; or, Shirley Willing on a Mission of Peace.

THE BLUE GRASS SEMINARY GIRLS ON THE WATER; or, Exciting Adventures on a Summer's Cruise Through the Panama Canal.

THE MILDRED SERIES

By MARTHA FINLEY

Handsome Cloth Binding   Price, 40c. per Volume

*A Companion Series to the Famous
"Elsie" Books by the Same Author*

MILDRED KEITH	MILDRED'S MARRIED LIFE
MILDRED AT ROSELANDS	MILDRED AT HOME
MILDRED AND ELSIE	MILDRED'S BOYS AND GIRLS
MILDRED'S NEW DAUGHTER	

For sale by all booksellers, or sent postpaid on receipt of price by the publishers
A. L. BURT COMPANY, 114-120 East 23d Street, New York.

The AMY E. BLANCHARD Series

MISS BLANCHARD has won an enviable reputation as a writer of short stories for girls. Her books are thoroughly wholesome in every way and her style is full of charm. The titles described below will be splendid additions to every girl's library. **Handsomely bound in cloth, full library size. Illustrated by L. J. Bridgman. Price, 60 cents per volume, postpaid.**

THE GLAD LADY. A spirited account of a remarkably pleasant vacation spent in an unfrequented part of northern Spain. This summer, which promised at the outset to be very quiet, proved to be exactly the opposite. Event follows event in rapid succession and the story ends with the culmination of at least two happy romances. The story throughout is interwoven with vivid descriptions of real places and people of which the general public knows very little. These add greatly to the reader's interest.

WIT'S END. Instilled with life, color and individuality, this story of true love cannot fail to attract and hold to its happy end the reader's eager attention. The word pictures are masterly; while the poise of narrative and description is marvellously preserved.

A JOURNEY OF JOY. A charming story of the travels and adventures of two young American girls, and an elderly companion in Europe. It is not only well told, but the amount of information contained will make it a very valuable addition to the library of any girl who anticipates making a similar trip. Their many pleasant experiences end in the culmination of two happy romances, all told in the happiest vein.

TALBOT'S ANGLES. A charming romance of Southern life. Talbot's Angles is a beautiful old estate located on the Eastern Shore of Maryland. The death of the owner and the ensuing legal troubles render it necessary for our heroine, the present owner, to leave the place which has been in her family for hundreds of years and endeavor to earn her own living. Another claimant for the property appearing on the scene complicates matters still more. The untangling of this mixed-up condition of affairs makes an extremely interesting story.

For sale by all booksellers, or sent prepaid on receipt of price by the publishers

A. L. BURT COMPANY, 114-120 East 23d Street, New York

The Girl Comrade's Series

ALL AMERICAN AUTHORS
ALL COPYRIGHT STORIES

A carefully selected series of books for girls, written by popular authors. These are charming stories for young girls, well told and full of interest. Their simplicity, tenderness, healthy, interesting motives, vigorous action, and character painting will please all girl readers.

HANDSOME CLOTH BINDING.
PRICE, 60 CENTS.

A BACHELOR MAID AND HER BROTHER. By I. T. Thurston.

ALL ABOARD. A Story For Girls. By Fanny E. Newberry.

ALMOST A GENIUS. A Story For Girls. By Adelaide L. Rouse.

ANNICE WYNKOOP, Artist. Story of a Country Girl. By Adelaide L. Rouse.

BUBBLES. A Girl's Story. By Fannie E. Newberry.

COMRADES. By Fannie E. Newberry.

DEANE GIRLS, THE. A Home Story. By Adelaide L. Rouse.

HELEN BEATON, COLLEGE WOMAN. By Adelaide L. Rouse.

JOYCE'S INVESTMENTS. A Story For Girls. By Fannie E. Newberry.

MELLICENT RAYMOND. A Story For Girls. By Fannie E. Newberry.

MISS ASHTON'S NEW PUPIL. A School Girl's Story. By Mrs. S. S. Robbins.

NOT FOR PROFIT. A Story For Girls. By Fannie E. Newberry.

ODD ONE, THE. A Story For Girls. By Fannie E. Newberry.

SARA, A PRINCESS. A Story For Girls. By Fannie E. Newberry.

The Girl Chum's Series

BENHURST, CLUB, THE. By Howe Benning.

BERTHA'S SUMMER BOARDERS. By Linnie S. Harris.

BILLOW PRAIRIE. A Story of Life in the Great West. By Joy Allison.

DUXBERRY DOINGS. A New England Story. By Caroline B. Le Row.

FUSSBUDGET'S FOLKS. A Story For Young Girls. By Anna F. Burnham.

HAPPY DISCIPLINE, A. By Elizabeth Cummings.

JOLLY TEN, THE; and Their Year of Stories. By Agnes Carr Sage.

KATIE ROBERTSON. A Girl's Story of Factory Life. By M. E. Winslow.

LONELY HILL. A Story For Girls. By M. L. Thornton-Wilder.

MAJORIBANKS. A Girl's Story. By Elvirton Wright.

MISS CHARITY'S HOUSE. By Howe Benning.

MISS ELLIOT'S GIRLS. A Story For Young Girls. By Mary Spring Corning.

MISS MALCOLM'S TEN. A Story For Girls. By Margaret E. Winslow.

ONE GIRL'S WAY OUT. By Howe Benning.

PEN'S VENTURE. By Elvirton Wright.

RUTH PRENTICE. A Story For Girls. By Marion Thorne.

THREE YEARS AT GLENWOOD. A Story of School Life. By M. E. Winslow.